She's traded everything for her job. He's turned his back on the world. Can two stranded souls open themselves up to love?

Tabitha has her sights set on the top of the corporate ladder. She has all the plans in the world to make more time for her family after locking down her Wall Street promotion. But when her stubborn father needs convincing about heart surgery, she jumps in her car and speeds toward home... straight into a snowbank...

Arnie doesn't ask for much. All the widower war vet wants is his farmland and his privacy. But when a fast-talking city slicker crashes her car near his house during a blizzard, he's forced to take her in. After Tabitha pries into a past he'd rather forget, he wonders if he'd be better off in the storm...

As the snow piles higher and Christmas approaches, Tabitha and Arnie begin to warm up to each other. Is Arnie willing to open himself up to a better future? When the snow melts, will Tabitha make a sacrifice for what her heart truly desires?

SNOWSTORM

Jennette Green

DIAMOND PRESS

Snowstorm

A Diamond Press book / published in arrangement with the author

ISBN: 978-1-62964-025-9

Library of Congress Control Number: 2017917940
Library of Congress Subject Headings:
Man-woman relationships—Fiction
Love stories
Inspirational fiction
Christian fiction
Christmas stories
Christmas —Fiction

Diamond Press
3400 Pegasus Drive
P.O. Box 80043
Bakersfield CA 93380-0043
www.diamondpresspublishing.com

Published in the United States of America.

May the God of hope

fill you with all joy and peace

as you trust in him,

so that you may overflow with hope

by the power of the Holy Spirit.

Romans 15:13

Also by Jennette Green

Romance novels

The Commander's Desire
Her Reluctant Bodyguard
Ice Baron
The Pirate's Desire
Snowstorm

(Kaavl Chronicles Quadrilogy)
Kaavl Conspiracy
Kaavl Quest
Kaavl Calamity
Kaavl Conqueror

(Christian Apocalyptic)
Beyond the Rapture

Castaways
(a novelette)

Shorter Works

Toot of Fruit
(a children's story)

Murder by Nightmare
(a novelette)

Chapter One

*"Come to me, all you who are weary and burdened,
and I will give you rest."*
Matthew 11:28

Tabitha McCroy peered out the windshield into the pitch black night. Fat white flakes drifted down, as they had been for the past hour, slowing her progress on the rural highway. Heat blasted her charcoal gray pantsuit and her slim, well-manicured hands, but she still felt cold inside. The Christmas song, "Let it Snow," crooned from the rental car's satellite radio. Unfortunately, it was an appropriate song for her current adventure.

She glanced at her speedometer. Thirty-five miles per hour. Snowflakes smothered the road in white. Tabitha hadn't seen another car for a half hour—ever since she'd turned onto this lonely strip of road.

Her unease grew. Trying to ignore it, she sang the last stanza to "Let it Snow." Luckily, she was alone in the car, so no one else had to endure her imperfect rendition. However, singing along with the radio's Christmas carols didn't cheer her up like it normally would.

Why, again, had her parents decided to move out here to western New York? She loved New York City...the noise, the lights, the energy. Any hour of the day or night she could leave her small New York apartment, buy a mint latte, wander the streets, and be with people. She loved it.

But she loved her parents, too. And once again, she felt guilty that this would be her first visit since they had moved two years ago.

Especially now.

The Christmas songs stopped. Static crackled through the speakers. She flipped it off.

The silence made her feel more uneasy.

Tabitha sang her favorite, "O Little Town of Bethlehem," but it didn't ease her fear. Or her sense of lonely isolation. She fell silent.

Snowflakes softly battered her windshield. They looked thicker than they had a few minutes ago.

She checked her odometer again. Quick subtraction told her that twenty-eight miles of her journey remained; twenty-three to Newbough, and then five more to her parents' tiny farm.

She'd make it. Nothing would stop her from getting home this Christmas. She *should* have come home two months ago, at the first sign of trouble.

Surely everything would be all right. It had to be.

Tabitha worked at Brown's Brothers on Wall Street as a financial research analyst. Last year, she'd been unable to leave New York City at Christmas. Or any time since, for that matter. At least, that's what she'd told herself. For the last seven years she'd struggled to build up her reputation as the best in her field. And she'd earned it. The stock of the companies she'd recommended had thrived, and so had their share prices on Wall Street, even during the recent bear market. Those mutual fund managers who had heeded her five star ratings had seen their funds flourish. Her own small nest egg had grown quite nicely, too, thank you very much.

Now, finally, her boss was hinting that she was a candidate for the much coveted promotion to the investment division. Only one slot per year, and finally, it might be hers.

But had her sacrifices been worth it?

The snowflakes swirled faster, hitting the windshield in explosive white bursts. Tabitha doubled the windshield wiper speed. The rental car's black blades barely kept up with the fat, heavy flakes.

Only twenty mph registered on the speedometer now. At this rate, it would take her an hour and a half to reach her parent's home.

If she made it.

Her hands ached from clenching the steering wheel like a drowning woman clinging to a life preserver. She *would* make it home. And she'd make her father listen to reason, too.

The doctor said his heart was a ticking time bomb. He needed a quadruple bypass, but refused to submit to the operation. The stubborn man.

Tabitha had inherited that stubborn streak from him. Maybe it wasn't the best quality—especially when it ended up hurting the people they loved most.

The headlights cut a scant thirty feet through the relentless curtain of falling white now. Tall snow ridges lined the road; snow plowed aside from an earlier winter storm.

Those ridges were her only road markers now. The thick white stuff blanketed the highway, and she steered for the middle in order to try to avoid accidentally driving into a ditch.

If only another set of headlights would appear—any sign she wasn't alone. A snow plow would be even better. But she was in the middle of nowhere, and probably too few people lived out here to warrant an emergency plow. In fact, the last farm house she'd passed had been miles back. Of course, she had been watching the road, and not looking for signs of civilization, so maybe she'd passed more farms.

The car inexplicably slowed down.

"Not good." She jammed her high-heeled boot onto the gas pedal. The car leaped forward. Just as abruptly, however, it slowed. The back tires spun, and the car quit moving.

She clenched the steering wheel, fighting back her fear.

Maybe if she steered right, the tires would gain purchase in the thick snow.

Tabitha edged the wheel right and stomped on the gas. The car bolted forward, startling her, and rocketed toward a snow ridge. With a gasp, she jerked the wheel left, but it was too late. The car careened sideways into an invisible ditch, and the passenger side door slammed into a wall of snow. Only her seatbelt prevented her from flying across the car.

Heart racing, she took several gasping breaths.

Now what?

Her cell phone. 911. Or the car's emergency OnStar button. She pushed it. Interminable moments crept by. Finally, static crackled.

"OnStar, how....help..." The woman's voice cut out.

"Hello!" Tabitha called out, anxious that the woman hear her. "I'm stuck. I need a tow truck. Or a snow plow. Right away, please."

"Where...you?"

Tabitha relayed her location down to the precise mile click.

"...can't. Storm too...sit tight....find shelter."

Nothing but static.

Great. Now what?

Her cell phone. Maybe she could call her parents for help. She flipped it open. No bars, thanks to the storm.

Tabitha bit her lip. No more options. OnStar knew where she was, but couldn't help because of the storm. How long would it take for a snow plow to make out here, in middle of the boondocks? She could freeze to death in her car, waiting for help to arrive.

She swallowed back panic, and struggled for calm. Everything would be fine. She'd figure something out.

Her headlights cut a swath of light into the inky black night. The windshield wipers continued to fight their fruitless battle with the cold, deadly snowflakes. Except for the engine's muffled purr, it was as silent as a tomb.

Stories of people freezing to death in their cars on rural highways besieged her mind.

Why, oh *why* had her parents moved out here, to such a God forsaken spot?

"Stop it," she whispered. Nowhere was God forsaken. In fact, perhaps she should pray. Surely snowstorms didn't short-circuit prayers to the Almighty.

It had been a long time since Tabitha had prayed. "Ah..." she cleared her throat. "Lord...if you're listening, I'm in a pickle. I don't want to die. Help me. Please."

She opened her eyes. Still the snow fell in thick, silent, swirling sheets. Tabitha twisted around in her seat and peered into the pitch blackness behind her. No cars. No snow plows of salvation. But she did smell something acrid.

Exhaust.

Quickly, she switched off the car. Heat stopped blowing onto her chilly hands.

How much poisonous exhaust had seeped inside? Carbon monoxide could kill her. Should she open the door?

At least she'd placed her long woolen winter coat in the back seat. Maybe it was more fashionable than weather-wise, but it kept her warm enough when she scurried from building to building in New York City.

Was she becoming light-headed, or was that only her imagination?

Tabitha unbuckled her seat belt and pulled the black woolen coat from the back seat. After struggling into it and buttoning it down to her knees, she opened the driver's door a crack. Arctic air and snowflakes swirled in. She shuddered. She couldn't stay in the car for long. The OnStar lady was right. She needed to find shelter.

Tabitha thought about the few farm houses she had passed. Warm, welcoming yellow lights had gleamed from the windows. *Please God,* she prayed. *Let one be close by.*

She collected together her purse and laptop, which she always carried with her, no matter the circumstance, and shoved the door open. Since the car was parked at a crazy angle, it wanted to swing back and shut on her.

Giving it a mighty heave, Tabitha shoved it open wide enough to struggle out. Her knees felt wobbly when she stood up. Reaction, probably, from driving into a snow bank. It certainly couldn't be because she was scared to death.

Everything will be fine.

Hands trembling despite her self-lecture, she grabbed the keys from the ignition, and then slammed the door and pressed the lock button on the key pad. Obligingly, the headlights flashed and the vehicle gave a friendly chirp. Then it fell silent—as silent and dark as the thick snow flurrying around her.

Tabitha had heard the term "pitch dark" before. And alone. Both took on entirely new meanings now. She stood still, heart thumping against her ribs. Bright and busy New York City seemed a galaxy away. With the headlights off, she felt half blind, and saw only the flakes swirling closest to her face. Gradually, her eyes adjusted and she differentiated the dark gray snow from the black sky.

No lights glowed across the road, or in any other direction, for that matter.

She struggled to ignore her rising sense of panic.

Maybe she should climb on top of the snow ridge the car had just rammed into. It would give her a higher vantage point from which to survey the vast barrenness surrounding her.

Her pointed, heeled black boots slipped on the first step up the snow ridge. Arms flailing, Tabitha barely managed to catch her balance. Taking a breath, she paused and then kicked her boot into the snowy mound. As she'd hoped, beneath the three inches of new snow, the old snow felt firm beneath her boot. Her city girl, pointed boots might come in handy after all.

She stabbed one toe into the drift. With a satisfying crunch, she found a toehold purchase. Another kick found purchase for the other toe, as well. Carefully, she clambered to the top.

Soft, cold snowflakes brushed her cheeks and clung to her eyelashes. She scanned the horizon while turning slowly in a circle. Nothing. Nothing but dark, billowing flakes. Fear threatened to choke her.

Try again. Don't give up.

More slowly, she searched the horizon once more, trying to discern the slightest hint of light. When she turned east again, backtracking the way she had come, she saw it.

A small, warm light shone in the darkness.

Hope lifted her spirits. The feeble glow shone from a location set back from the road a bit, and across the field from the snow ridge where she now stood. She squinted, wondering if her mind might be playing tricks on her. Did one see mirages of light in a snow storm? Certainly not a fact she would know. City girls like her knew nothing about surviving in the wilds.

The light remained, shining faintly but steadily through the falling snow. A miracle! Her Christmas miracle.

"Thank you," she breathed heavenward, and headed straight for it. The back side of the snow ridge sloped abruptly downward, merging a foot below into a sheet of pure, untouched snow. Tabitha stepped forward, expecting a solid surface, but her foot plummeted into thigh deep, soft snow. Thrown off balance, she pitched forward, arms flailing.

Her laptop, purse, and face went headfirst into the snow. Soft, cold snow shot up her nose, pressed freezing cold flakes against her eyes, and the crisp, metallic bite of snow filled her mouth. Terror billowed as she floundered, and crazy thoughts of drowning in snow screamed through her mind. She struggled to her knees and stood.

Snow filled her boots now, and iced her legs up inside her linen pants, all the way to her knees. Not only that, but snow had jammed up into the wide sleeves of her coat, too, and a clump slid inside the neckline of her silk blouse and dripped down her chest.

What a dumb move.

Tabitha wanted to cry. Of course the field wasn't plowed like the road was. She needed to stick to the main highway. A city girl she may be, but she knew she had to find shelter, and fast, or she would freeze to death.

Shaking uncontrollably with cold now, she struggled back up the ridge, and then slipped down the other side, landing on her fanny. Only the soft snow prevented her leather cased laptop from serious injury. The same couldn't be said for her backside. It felt as if she'd landed on a sharp stone. A tear slipped down her cheek.

Under normal circumstances, Tabitha rarely cried. It ruined her mascara, but even worse, for hours afterward she suffered from puffed pink eyelids and a bright red nose. Crying made her look like a cartoon character. But right now it didn't matter. Who would see her?

She shook harder with cold, and struggled to her feet. *Get back on the road,* she told herself. *Walk. Look for a lane to the house.*

She could barely see the highway through the thickly falling snow. Only its level surface gave a clue to its location. In fact, now she couldn't see the warm beacon of light, either. Fear tightened its hold on her heart. Had the friendly glow only been a figment of her imagination?

Stop it. It's there.

It had to be.

Look for a driveway, she counseled herself.

More cold snow trickled inside her boots with each step. A cutting breeze froze into her exposed face and hands. It must be thirty degrees. Or twenty-five. How long had she been walking? Two minutes? Ten? Time seemed to stand still as she struggled through the deepening snow.

She tried to focus on numbers rather than on how cold and frightened she felt. Numbers were comfortable and safe. In ten minutes she could assess a company's balance sheet, cash flow sheet and income statement, and determine the stability of that company—even estimate, if the numbers were shaky, how long before the company went under.

Tabitha liked facts, and she liked people who spoke their minds. She liked to know exactly where she stood at all times. She liked hot cocoa. And bubble baths. And warm fires. And the cheerful voices of lots of friends around her.

She did not like being alone in the pitch black, heading toward a phantom light.

Was that a break in the snow to the left? Maybe a driveway? She hesitated, straining to catch a glimpse of the warm, glowing light again. But the thick, swirling flakes obscured her vision.

Should she take a chance and step off the main road? What if she got lost, and wandered in a field until she collapsed from hypothermia?

Or what if she didn't try, and instead froze to death yards from safety? How smart would that be?

She carefully stepped forward, remembering her earlier disaster. Thankfully, she didn't sink down into a ditch, or into a deep field of snow, either. It must be a driveway of some sort. The snow grew deeper, but only eight inches or so.

And still her eyes strained for a glimmer of light. Nothing.

Tabitha's fingers felt like ice, and she had long since lost the feeling in her toes. Her teeth clattered uncontrollably.

After long moments of walking, with only her quiet puffs of air for company, a faint light glowed through the curtain of snow. Barely daring to hope, she walked faster. The light—actually two lights, close together—grew steadily brighter. *Thank God. Bless the people who live here, whoever they might be.*

As a child, she had often wondered who lived in small farmhouses like this, nestled off the beaten path. Perhaps an older couple. Or a nice big family, with lots of children and a dog. She liked dogs. One that would lay its great head on her feet and warm them.

Or maybe a hermit with a shotgun.

At last, the outline of a medium-sized, one-story house loomed out of the darkness. Brick columns supported the small front porch. She climbed the steps, noting the porch swing to her right, and the welcome, hollow sound of wood beneath her feet. Bright windows flanked the solid wooden front door.

A porch swing was good, right? Surely no homicidal maniac would own a porch swing.

Was her mind beginning to slip? She raised her fist and pounded on the door before old horror movie commercials could gallop through her mind. Of course, she'd seen none of those movies. She didn't like to be scared. She didn't want to be scared right now.

No response.

Surely someone was inside. The lights were on. Tabitha pounded harder. "Hello?" she called out. "Help! Please."

A chain rattled, and then a deadbolt clicked.

The door swung open. Tabitha gazed up at a very large man. She swallowed.

Now here was a man she would not want to meet in a dark alley in New York City.

CHAPTER TWO

THE FEARSOME STRANGER towered over her. He was at least six foot two, but more than that, he was either well-muscled or solidly built. In a glance, she took in his red and black flannel shirt which encased his broad shoulders, and blue jeans that hugged lean hips. Thick gray socks encased his feet.

Her gaze jerked back up to the man's deeply tanned face. He wore his brown hair in a buzz cut. Dark eyes of an indeterminate color assessed her beneath straight brows. His jaw was square cut, and he watched her without speaking.

Tabitha's teeth clacked together as she stared at this formidable creature. She had half a mind to turn tail and run back to her cold car. But surely this man wasn't alone. Surely he had a wife...or mother...or a dog....someone, here with him. She forced her frozen jaw to move.

"I...My...I'm stuck. My car's stuck, I mean. In the snow. Down there." She pointed. A mighty shudder swept through her. "I...I'm going to freeze if you don't let me in."

The man moved aside, and she took this as her welcome into his home. Intimidating though he may be, Tabitha needed no second invitation. She stepped inside and then stood there, dripping snow onto a rag rug just inside the door. A quick glance took in the main part of his house.

It appeared to be an older home, if the wood paneled walls in the kitchen, to her left, were any indication. The paint in the living room, to her right, however, looked new, and so did the flooring. The dark, hardwood floors led from the open kitchen to the living room, which was furnished with couches upholstered in dark brown. Some sort of a white, fluffy rug lay on the floor before a blazing fire.

Knickknacks decorated a few spare surfaces; a trio of framed photos on the mantel, a vase of dusty, dried flowers, and several ceramic Christmas figurines, faintly yellowed with age on a side table. A scraggly Christmas tree, decorated with white lights, stood in a corner beside a worn corduroy recliner, and it was flanked by another window.

Surely this man couldn't be too scary if he had a Christmas tree, her cold brain reasoned. To her left, Tabitha noticed that the kitchen had tile counters, black appliances, and a wooden table with four chairs. Four chairs. Another good sign. He didn't live alone.

The man's gaze fell to the purse and laptop in her hands, and then he regarded her face again. A faint frown creased his brow.

A man of few words, Tabitha decided. She felt colder by the minute. "Do...do you mind if I take off my coat?" Her teeth clicked uncontrollably.

"No." Finally, the big man moved. He pulled her purse and laptop from her frozen hands and put them on the table. Tabitha struggled with the buttons of her long coat. Her fingers wouldn't cooperate. Numbly, they grasped and slid over the buttons, feeling weak and unable to clutch a button with any strength.

The man watched her frustrated attempts for a full minute before stepping forward—reluctantly, it appeared. She was pretty good at reading people, and she'd quickly perceived that the man did not want her in his house. In fact, under any other circumstance, she got the distinct feeling he would speedily send her on her way.

"I can do it," she said quickly. "And you might..." her teeth clattered in a sudden, seizing fit, "w...w...want to move my purse and computer to the counter. They're wet, and will ruin your table."

He frowned at her again, as if she spoke a language he did not understand. He made no move to do as she suggested.

Tabitha felt quick, nonsensical tears form and looked down, struggling to concentrate on the large charcoal buttons of her coat. She felt more uncomfortable by the moment. Using the side of her thumb and the heels of her hands, she struggled to push one through the slotted hole.

An impatient sigh came from the man and then warm, large hands brushed hers aside. In short order, he unbuttoned her coat. Tabitha felt like a child, having him perform such a simple service for her. He stepped back the instant the job was done, as if she possessed some fatal virus he might catch.

Tabitha shrugged out of the coat. Not sure what to do with it, she stood still, clutching it in her arms. Its cold, wet fabric seeped into her already wet pantsuit.

Silently, the man extended a hand, and she handed him the coat. He hung it on a rack beside the door.

Tabitha felt increasingly awkward, standing there so silently. Why didn't he speak? At home, a stranger would have peppered her with a thousand questions by now.

The fire's licking orange flames beckoned to her. "Do mind if I...I..." More teeth clacking interrupted her words. She pointed.

He nodded, and she hurried over to the fire. He followed, which disturbed her. She sat gingerly on the couch and looked up at him.

"Your clothes are wet." His voice was quiet and deep.

"Yes. I...I...fell in a snow drift." She shuddered.

He disappeared down a hallway directly opposite the front door. It neatly bisected the living room and kitchen and led toward the back of the house.

Tabitha edged closer to the fire. Her dark hair straggled from its French twist in wisps down her cheeks. She longed to pull off her boots, but her fingers still felt too numb and clumsy. She wouldn't be able to work the boots' zippers. With a sigh, she knelt on the soft, fuzzy rug near the iron grate.

The stranger reappeared with clothes heaped in his arms. He carried a dark green corduroy robe—his, no doubt—a black and white checked flannel shirt, and sweat pants. Gray socks adorned the top of the pile.

He said, "You need dry clothes."

Tabitha did not want to remove her clothes in this stranger's house. The potential vulnerability of the situation made her shudder still more. "Thank you, but I'm fine." She held her hands closer to the fire.

The man stared at her, but said nothing more.

Her clothes would dry soon enough by the fire. She heard him move away, and then the sound of running water came from the kitchen. He filled a kettle with water. Coffee or tea would be nice.

"Do you live alone?" She wished she'd bitten her tongue instead of asking the question. Foolish as it might be, she'd rather believe that his wife might appear at any moment

Except she doubted if he had a wife. If she were to draw conclusions from the past few minutes, she'd have to say the taciturn man exhibited hermit qualities. She didn't know what to make of him. Not at all.

"Yes." His quiet word interrupted her scattered thoughts.

Tabitha forgot what she had asked. "Yes, what? ...Oh. You live alone. But you're out in the middle of nowhere. Don't you feel lonely?"

His frown didn't abate. "I like to be alone." He growled this softly, between his teeth. "No one bothers me."

Clearly, he did not want her here. Although she felt increasingly uncomfortable, she strove to hide it. "I don't want to be a bother to you. As soon as the storm passes, I'll be on my way."

His mouth curled down in apparent displeasure. "Why would you drive in weather like this?"

Was he judging her? Tabitha tried not to take offense. He appeared to be blunt, and a man of few words. And he probably said what he meant without a bunch of fluff. In these parts, any woman with half a brain wouldn't drive in such horrible conditions.

He was a very different sort of man than any she'd met before. Men in New York City were polished, fast-paced, quick to speak, and slow to hear. She didn't know what to make of this one. He was very difficult to read. Little expression registered on his face, except for that frown.

"I'm trying to get home. My parents live twenty-eight miles from here. Just past Newbough." He said nothing. She wondered if her parents knew him. "Do you go into town often?"

He frowned harder. "Only when I need to."

Oh, goodness. She *had* stumbled across a dyed in the wool hermit. Living alone. Rarely going into town... Surely he wasn't dangerous. So far he had exhibited a grudging solicitation by helping her take off her coat and bringing her dry clothes. Now he was making her a hot drink. But she felt more than a little uncomfortable. So far, he'd spoken so little that it was difficult to know what was going on inside his head.

Tabitha wrapped her arms around her knees and leaned closer to the blazing fire. Her face felt nice and toasty by now, but her back and wet appendages felt like ice. She couldn't seem to stop shivering.

She glanced over her shoulder at her host, who had returned his attention to making hot drinks. One large hand opened a cupboard and pulled out a box. Tea? He moved slowly, as if time held no meaning for him. Another concept that was completely foreign to her. In New York City, her life ran headlong at a frantic pace all day long, seven days a week. Even on Sundays she read financial papers and business magazines so she could keep her competitive edge over the others in her field.

What did this man do, she wondered. Besides farm, of course. Did he hibernate in this house until spring, when he started planting whatever it was he planted? Like a bear. The description fit him. Big, and a little scary.

"Will the snow stop soon, do you think?"

He faced her. His frown had eased, but he still didn't look particularly happy. "It'll let up tomorrow. But a stronger storm is chasing it."

"What does that mean?"

"Best case scenario, a snow plow will make it out here tomorrow."

"And worst case?"

"A blizzard will hit tomorrow afternoon."

"A blizzard!" She had to get home before the blizzard hit. Only two vacation days remained to see her father. She'd been lucky to get those few days, too, with her department drowning in end of the year deadlines. Her boss had decided in October—when Tabitha had first learned that her father had a heart problem—that this year all reports must be finished by December 31, instead of by the end of the fiscal year, in May.

She had been unable to come up for air during the last twelve weeks. But she had done it. Only two reports remained for her to do. And her boss was pleased. He expected her back on Wednesday for an important meeting. He'd hinted that they would discuss her future. Hopefully, that long awaited promotion.

It was already Saturday night. Little enough time to spend with her parents already, and it was a visit two years overdue. She *had* to get home quickly. Surely she could find a way.

A thought came to mind, and she attempted to spring to her feet. It came to pass in a slow stumble. Her feet felt numb, and her legs uncoordinated. A quick, steadying hand on the mantle saved her from falling.

Embarrassment warmed her cheeks. "Do you have a phone? My parents will be worried about me. And my cell phone doesn't work."

The man watched her, his gaze measuring. As Tabitha waited, half-baked images of him holding her prisoner until spring scrambled through her mind. Ridiculous. She'd seen too many grisly news reports. This man didn't want her here. He'd made that clear enough. Right?

CHAPTER THREE

AN INTERMINABLE MOMENT ticked by, and then the stranger's gaze cut to an olive green phone on the wall.

"Great! Thanks." Tabitha hurried over. Since her cell phone address book wasn't immediately at hand, she was grateful that she'd memorized her parents' number the first time she'd seen it.

With a faint frown, he turned toward the whistling kettle.

The phone buzzed in her ear as it rang at the other end. Surely her parents would be home. She needed to let them know that she was alive, and at this stranger's house.

Relief eased through her when her mother answered.

"Mom, it's Tabitha."

"Tabitha! Where are you? Are you all right?"

"I'm fine. But the car is in a snow bank, I'm not going to make it home tonight."

"A snow bank?" Nancy McCroy sounded horrified. "Tabitha, tell me where you are this instant."

"Just a sec." She put her hand over the mouthpiece and asked her unwilling host, "Excuse me, but where am I, exactly?"

Her host growled his address, which she relayed to her mother. Nancy McCroy was not satisfied with this, however. "Whose house is that? There are some strange types out that way."

Tabitha slid a glance at the big man dipping tea bags into mugs. "Um...just a minute, Mom." Again, she put her hand over the receiver. "Excuse me. What's your name?"

"Reginald Arnold," he said shortly.

Tabitha repeated it to her mother.

"Arnie!" Nancy exhaled. "Thank goodness. You can trust Arnie. He'll keep you safe. I feel so much better now."

Tabitha glanced at her host. Arnie. "How do you know him, Mom?"

"From church, honey. He puts together hayrides for the children. He builds sets. Whatever we need, Arnie does."

"Mmhm." From intimidating bear to near saint, according to her mother. "I'll call as soon as the snow plow arrives. I'm hoping I'll be able to drive home tomorrow."

"Not likely, honey. This storm has lots of kick, as your father likes to say. It might snow through tomorrow morning. The weatherman is predicting a blizzard by tomorrow afternoon. He says it's likely to stall here for several days."

Tabitha drew a dismayed breath. "But Christmas is the day after tomorrow. I want to be with you and Daddy. Not stuck here."

"As long as you're okay, that's all that matters to us. We can celebrate whenever you arrive."

"But I have to go back to work on Wednesday."

Silence came from the other end of the phone.

Guilt grew. What was wrong with her? She had come all this way. Surely her boss could postpone the meeting until Thursday. And certainly she could wait an extra day to see if she had secured the promotion that she'd longed and labored toward for the last seven years. As far as her unfinished reports were concerned, she could easily finish them by the 31st, as long as Robert didn't transfer more work to her in-box in her absence.

"I'll e-mail my boss. I'll do my best to stay an extra day," Tabitha promised.

"Good." The word sounded sharp. "You haven't taken a day off in two years, Tabitha. And you haven't had weekends off, either, for the last three months. You need a break." Her voice softened, "You know your father is looking forward to seeing you. So are your brothers. Steven has a job off campus, and has to leave on Wednesday. Jake is leaving Thursday. We miss you, honey. We need to be a family again, at least for a little while."

"I want that too," she said softly. "How is Daddy's heart?"

"No better. You have to convince him, Tabitha. You're so logical, just like he is. He needs you." A sob choked her mother's voice. "We all need you."

"I'll be there," she whispered. "Don't worry. Tell Daddy I'll see him soon."

"Good." Her mother sounded in control again. "The phones may go out. They often do. Don't worry. As soon as the snow stops, we'll send a snow plow your way."

"Bye, Mom. See you soon."

Slowly, she hung up the receiver. Dread squeezed her heart. Her father was worse. Her mother hadn't said it, but Tabitha knew it by that barely stifled sob. And her entire family was counting on her to change his mind about the bypass. Yes, of course she would e-mail her boss. Somehow, she would get more days off.

❀ ❀ ❀ ❀ ❀

Arnie cast a frowning glance at the dark-haired woman hanging up the phone. Alarm bells had gone off in his head the instant he'd opened the door. She was breathtakingly beautiful. A high maintenance female, if he'd ever seen one. Painful experience had taught him to be wary of the type. They meant nothing but trouble. Thankfully, he'd finally wised up during college and discovered Theresa, right under his nose since junior high. No one would ever replace her, or match her.

The old, deep pain ripped through his heart, as fresh as if it had happened yesterday, instead of eleven years ago.

The city woman—Tabitha was her name—hobbled to the fire again. Arnie had her type nailed down, all right. Sharp suit, perfectly done up hair, make-up so precise her face looked like a plastic mannequin. Her sharp blue eyes seemed to look right through him.

Arnie hated pretense, and every sort of air city women donned like a second skin. He had never fit into that world. He had never wanted to. Inside, he was a down-to-earth, homespun kind of a guy. He liked his solitary life. He had a few good, lifelong friends. What more could a man want?

Since he couldn't have Theresa, he had long ago decided to settle for peace and quiet. Not something Tabitha would provide, he suspected with a sinking feeling in the pit of his stomach. If only the snow would break soon.

If necessary, he'd haul out his four wheel drive and escort her to her parents' house himself. In fact, the sooner, the better.

❀ ❀ ❀ ❀ ❀

Tabitha glanced at her obviously unwilling host, now dipping tea bags in the mismatched mugs. It seemed too dainty of a task for such a large man to perform. Clearly, he wished she would disappear. It made her feel uncomfortable. Back in New York City, people liked her. Everywhere she went, she made new friends. His silence and subtle hostility disturbed her. Especially since her mother claimed he was some sort of a saint. Did he dislike *her* for some reason?

But how could that be? He didn't even know her.

Tabitha sat in front of the fire, rubbing her hands together. Cold still ached through her bones. She should count her blessings. For one, she was indoors, near a warm fire. She wouldn't freeze to death. And while Arnie wasn't the friendliest man, according to her mother he wasn't a chainsaw murderer, either. Of course, her mother tended to look at life through rose colored glasses. The fact that Arnie helped kids would win her over.

Then again, he attended church. That had to be positive.

Tabitha shuddered. The fire felt nice on her face, but her wet pants clung like ice to her legs. She was so cold. Her teeth chattered nonstop.

She sensed her host's presence behind her. He offered her a steaming white mug, which was nearly dwarfed by his deeply tanned hand. With longing, her gaze riveted upon the mug, but she shook her head, not certain if she could hold it without sloshing it.

He frowned.

"Th...thank you," she chattered. "I don't...don't think I can hold it right now."

He placed the mugs on the coffee table, and then pulled the fire screen away from the fire and draped the robe, socks, and other clothes over it. The clothing hung on the side facing the living room, protected from the sparks. With one gray socked foot, he shoved it a bit closer to the fire. He retreated to the couch.

Tabitha eyed the clothes, imagining them growing warm and toasty from the fire. She imagined the heat of them against her cold, goose pimply skin.

He silently sipped tea. Tabitha endeavored to ignore him, and also the discomfort she felt in the quiet house. At home, she never lived in silence for long; only at night, while she slept. At other times she habitually turned on either the television or her favorite soft rock radio station. During the day, of course, she lived in the fast-paced world of Brown's Brothers. She had few quiet moments to herself.

Silence appeared to be all she had here. And time. And she was all alone, except for Arnie.

Her fingers stung and smarted as they warmed. Sensation slowly returned to them. Her feet, however, remained unbearably cold, and worse, numb. They must be swimming in ice water. She had to get the boots off.

Tabitha fumbled with a boot zipper. Her fingers were able to grasp it now, but with little strength. They felt sluggish and clumsy. The feeble tugs moved the zipper exactly nowhere. For long minutes, she struggled to grip the zipper and tug it down. Frustration built with each failed attempt.

A shadow blocked the light, and Arnie sat down beside her with his back to the fire. Silently, he extended his hands a few inches.

He'd help her, if she let him. Silently, she put one booted heel into his hands.

In short order, he unzipped and tugged both boots from her feet. Water sloshed onto the fireplace. Her sodden nylons clung to her calves and feet. Tabitha hooked a thumb in each, pulled them off her purple feet, and thrust her cold appendages toward the fire.

"No," he said in a low voice. "Give them to me."

"Why?"

"They're almost frostbitten. You need slow warmth."

Cautiously, Tabitha extended her feet, and he pulled them both onto his thickly muscled thigh. No hint of softness or flab lived there. She felt pressure as he gently held one foot between his hands. Slowly, his big hands moved from her toe to her heel, warming them.

Tabitha leaned back on her hands, supporting her weight, and glanced into the fire. She felt embarrassed to have this stranger perform such an intimate task for her. The fire couldn't explain the warmth in her cheeks, however. She felt his hands move up her calves, just a little way, where they were red with cold. His palms felt warm and calloused. Pleasantly so. All of the men she knew had soft hands. Soft handshakes. Instinctively, she knew his would be neither.

Further warmth suffused her, and she cast a wary glance at his face to evaluate if he might be coming on to her. For the first time, she met his gaze at close range, and she drew a quick, involuntary breath. His eyes were a clear, dark amber; a warm color, with tiny gold flecks. And keenly intelligent. In them she saw his calm confidence in himself and his place in the world...his world.

"Thank you."

He broke eye contact and nodded curtly. He transferred his attention to her other foot.

Soon her feet began to hurt, and Tabitha bit her lip against the pain. It felt as if knives pierced her skin. "That's enough." She attempted to pull them free.

"It hurts?"

"Yes."

"A few more minutes, then."

Tabitha endured the agony, and gradually the pain settled into sharp tingles. He lowered her feet to the floor and stood.

Harshly, he said, "Put aside your pride and put on warm clothes."

Tabitha drew a sharp breath. "Excuse me? I appreciate everything you've done. But you don't have to be rude."

His lips pressed together, and he strode back into the kitchen.

CHAPTER FOUR

THE UNFRIENDLY MAN had opened up his home to her. He had given her warm clothes to wear and saved her feet from frostbite. Tabitha reminded herself of this as she plucked the clothes from the fire screen and headed down the hall. The first door to her left opened into a large room with a wide, king-sized bed covered in a dark blue comforter. A blue rug lay on the hardwood floor.

On her right, she passed two smaller bedrooms. The first contained a double bed covered in a quilt, and the other small room had been made into an office, complete with a wooden desk and computer. The bathroom was at the end of the hall.

She flipped on the light and locked herself inside. The walls had been painted lime green long ago. White towels hung over the shower door rack, and a fluffy, dark green rug covered the linoleum floor. Other than that, the room looked sterile. Just a white sink, toilet, and shiny mirror. Over the toilet, someone had hung a framed picture of a dried white rose, pressed onto lavender paper.

Not a decorator's heaven, she thought, quickly changing into the huge, warm, black and white checked shirt. But that wasn't a surprise. It appeared he was a bachelor. The men she knew hired decorators to furnish their apartments. From the little she knew about Arnie, he probably preferred to spend his days in the great outdoors.

Again, she wondered what he did in the winter months, when snow on the ground prevented most farm work.

The shirt hung down to her knees, and she quickly pulled on the warm socks. Ahh. She sighed with delight. Warm. Toasty and yummy. She didn't even attempt to pull on the sweat bottoms. She knew they'd fall off. But she did pull on the heavy green robe. It dwarfed her frame and hung past the tops of her gray socks. She belted it securely, and then gathered up her soaked suit and blouse and returned to the living room to drape them over the fire screen. Hopefully they'd be dry by morning.

Morning. For the first time, Tabitha realized that she'd spend the night in this house.

Arnie moved slowly about the kitchen. A sizzling sound drew her attention, and her stomach gurgled. A glance at her watch said it was seven o'clock. She edged closer. Frying onions. And bacon.

"May I help?"

"No. Thanks." The words were curt. Clearly, he'd prefer that she leave him alone.

Suddenly, she'd had enough of his unfriendly attitude. "What is wrong?"

His muscular shoulders stilled. A long moment passed, and she wondered if he intended to answer.

"I'm not used to company." The words sounded stiff.

"I understand. But I feel as if you dislike me in particular. Why?"

He growled, "I like peace and quiet."

"And I've disturbed you. I'm sorry I ran into a ditch on your property."

He did not respond, but set to chopping potatoes a little faster. Tabitha huffed out a small, frustrated breath. "I find it disconcerting that you'll barely look at me and you clearly don't want to talk to me. I wish I could leave, but I can't."

His gaze finally settled on hers. "You're welcome to stay as long as you need to." Although he frowned as he said it, the words sounded sincere.

"Thank you. If it's all right, I'd like to set the table."

He gestured toward a cupboard, and moved his hip away from a drawer, which was presumably where the silverware lived. Tabitha felt reluctant to approach him, but did so anyway. She set the table, and then peered in the refrigerator for drinks. It was well stocked with food and beverages. At least they wouldn't starve anytime soon.

Apple juice appealed, and she poured a half glass for herself, and after asking her host his preference, she poured a full glass of milk for him.

Next, she searched for napkins, but wasn't surprised when she found none. Instead, she ripped off paper towels and folded them into little birds. She took great pleasure in creating these works of art, and smiled as she set the last one into place.

Arnie threw a hot pad onto the table, and set the skillet on top. Potatoes, eggs, onion and bacon were mashed together, and topped with cheddar cheese. It smelled heavenly. Tabitha's stomach gurgled in anticipation, and she reached for the serving spoon.

"I'll say grace," he rumbled, and her hand faltered. She lay it back on her lap.

"Of course," she said, and bowed her head. How long had it been since she'd prayed over a meal? Or since she'd thanked God for anything? Tabitha whispered her thankful "amen" after her host's. As she eagerly dug in, Arnie reached for his napkin, but paused. An inscrutable expression crossed his face as his hand hovered over the preening bird.

Tabitha grinned. "Do you like it?"

He said nothing, as if not sure what to think.

"It's a peace offering," she said. "A dove. For Christmas."

The tiniest smile softened his mouth. But his eyes still looked wary—perhaps even alarmed. A strange reaction.

Tabitha continued to smile, and decided to ignore her host's unfathomable behaviorisms. It might take a while for him to warm up to her. But he would. She hoped.

❊ ❊ ❊ ❊ ❊

Arnie didn't know what to make of Tabitha. Fiery, feisty. Sugar and spice all mixed into one. Why would she be so friendly to him when he'd been so rude to her? He felt guilty for his behavior, but something inside him balked at the idea of letting down his guard. He couldn't trust her. Not yet.

He flicked a glance at the fire screen. She worked in a man's world. That barracuda suit gave her away. Logic and experience warned him that she probably chewed up men like him and spit them out for breakfast.

His gut warned him to be careful.

Her sweet smile and beauty were a lethal combination. He'd be an inconsequential notch in her belt if he succumbed to her charm. Not that he would, of course. And certainly not in a romantic way.

Now where had that thought come from? He frowned, disturbed. In any case, it was impossible. His heart was dead and buried with Theresa. Long ago, he'd accepted that he would live the rest of his life alone. He liked it that way.

"Tell me about your farm," Tabitha said, interrupting his thoughts. The interest in her eyes looked genuine, which only served to make him feel more uneasy.

Shortly, he said, "I grow corn and alfalfa."

"Has the farm been in your family for a long time, or did you buy it?"

The question seemed guileless, but again he frowned, feeling uncomfortable. To him, the question seemed too personal. As if she was pushing hard to become quick friends. Why?

"It belonged to my parents."

She remained silent, waiting for more.

With reluctance, he elaborated, "They died almost five years ago."

She drew a sharp breath. "I'm so sorry. What happened? An accident?"

He frowned harder. "My mother died of cancer. My father died right after her." Of a broken heart. But Tabitha didn't need to know that. An Arnold family trait, to love once, and love well. He was living proof. Only he'd been too young when Theresa had died, so he couldn't die of a broken heart. Instead, he'd live with one for the rest of his life.

To his relief, Tabitha fell silent. A faint frown pulled at her delicate brows. Had he discouraged conversation? He felt even more guilty for his rudeness, but also relieved that she'd at last quit speaking to him.

❄ ❄ ❄ ❄ ❄

Tabitha contemplated her host, who ate silently across from her. What was wrong? He was so closed and unfriendly. And yet he had treated her kindly by warming her feet, and by making her tea and dinner.

He didn't want to let anyone get close to him. That came through loud and clear. And he didn't want to speak to her.

However, she didn't want to stay silent for the rest of the meal. But what could she say to help him relax a little? "My mother knows you," she offered.

His eyes widened slightly. Surprise?

"Who are your parents?" His question came slowly, as if reluctantly asked.

"Nancy and Daniel McCroy. You attend the same church, I gather. Mom says you give hayrides to the kids and perform other good deeds."

Arnie frowned a little. "I do what I can."

He didn't like praise or flattery. Tabitha filed this tidbit away. "I'm sure they appreciate it." She forked up a delicious bite of potato.

"Please stop."

Tabitha's gaze flew to his. "What?"

"Don't pretend that you're my friend."

Taken aback, Tabitha stared at him, her mouth slightly agape. "I'm trying to be civil."

He didn't answer.

"Have I done something to offend you?"

Arnie laid down his fork. Placing his large hands deliberately on the table, he said, "Let's make things easy on both of us."

Tabitha felt certain she would not like his next words.

He said, "We'll be stuck together tonight. Follow three ground rules and we'll get along just fine."

"Ground rules?"

"Number one. I don't play games."

It was clear he didn't mean board games. She hissed in a breath of outrage, but he continued before she could speak. "Number two. Ten minute showers—period. Number three. We'll get along best if you leave me alone."

Trembling with indignation, Tabitha vaulted to her feet. What had she done to warrant this tirade? "First of all," she said in a shaking voice, "I don't play *games*. I've been trying to have a normal conversation with you. Clearly, however, that is impossible, because you are a complete boor!"

She crumpled the paper bird in her fist, barely aware of what she was doing. "In addition, I would sooner die than touch one drop of your precious hot water."

She flung the paper wad onto the table. "Good night!" she gritted. On swift feet, she entered the spare bedroom and shut it firmly behind her. It had a flimsy lock, but she pushed it. Not that he'd try to open it. Clearly, he wanted to keep her at the end of a ten foot pole. And he had succeeded.

Trembling with anger, she flung herself on the bed. The quilt felt cold against her cheek. In fact, the entire room felt like an ice box.

Tabitha slipped under the meager covers. Only a sheet and the quilt covered the bed. She shivered harder, feeling miserable. The flimsy coverings would not keep her warm.

What if she folded the quilt in half and draped it over her? Long moments later, she realized that didn't help, either. She needed more blankets.

A sliding closet occupied the far end of the room, and she swung her feet to the icy floor and hurried to investigate. No blankets. Only cardboard boxes piled high to the empty, horizontal clothes pole.

She padded to the bedroom door and opened it again. Warmth spilled down the hallway from the living room.

Tabitha ignored it. Exiting, she searched for a hall closet. None. Next, she entered the dimly lit office and slipped over to the closet. She slid one side open.

The overhead light blazed on.

Tabitha blinked and spun around to face her unwilling host.

She glared. "I'm not stealing your valuables, if that's what you're worried about." Turning her back on him, she scanned the closet. Nothing but boxes of old games were stacked on one side, and more packing boxes were piled on the other. Amazing how much easier it was to see with the light on.

Crossing her arms, and shivering hard, she faced Arnie again. He hadn't moved from the doorway. She walked purposefully toward him, certain he'd move aside, eager to avoid her. He didn't.

"Excuse me," she said pointedly.

"What do you need?" he said in a low voice.

"Blankets."

He turned, and she followed—until he entered his bedroom. She stopped in the doorway and watched him pull open a deep drawer in a dresser. "How many?"

"At least five. Your house is an icebox."

"I have three."

"Fine."

He pulled them out and approached her. Tabitha held out her arms, expecting him to drop them into her hands. He didn't.

What now? With a frown, she looked up.

"I'm sorry for how I've behaved," he said quietly.

Surprised, she quickly searched his brown eyes. He meant it. Why, then, did she sense reluctance undergirding his words? "You are?"

"Yes. I've been a complete jerk. Please forgive me."

The man was a complete enigma. He bewildered her. She didn't know what to say for a minute. "I'm sorry, too," she said at last. "I didn't mean to push you. I just wanted to talk."

A faint smile softened his mouth. "I'm sorry. I'm used to being alone, Tabitha. I like it that way."

She liked the surprisingly gentle way he said her name. "You said that before. Isn't it awfully lonely?"

He looked away for a moment. "I'll live with solitude for the rest of my life. I've made friends with it."

He'd just opened up, just the tiniest crack. "I'd think you'd have a dog, at least."

"I did. A golden retriever." Pain flickered, and Tabitha saw the door to his heart shut again. "She died last year."

"I'm sorry," she said softly. "And thank you for the blankets."

He glanced at the fuzzy blankets, as if surprised to find them still in his arms. He handed them to her. "The heater is temperamental. The repair man is scheduled to come out tomorrow. Hopefully he'll make it. Goodnight."

She hugged the cozy blankets close. "Goodnight."

Tabitha didn't lock her door this time, and quickly piled the three blankets on her bed and curled up underneath them. Slowly, the shivers left her.

A freezing house. A cold, lonely man. His parents were dead. His dog had passed away. What else had happened? Why would he want to spend the rest of his days alone? And why had he been pushing her away from the moment she'd first arrived?

It was none of her business. But now that the ice had finally cracked between them, Tabitha couldn't help but wonder more about her host. Who was he, really? Although from the first he'd adopted a crusty, stand-offish demeanor, his actions suggested a warmer man might live inside. That would be good news, especially if the blizzard swooped down tomorrow, trapping her here. To coexist, she'd need to find a way to become friends with him.

But hopefully she would be able to get home in time for Christmas. She must speak to her father, face to face, about his bypass surgery before it was too late.

CHAPTER FIVE

THE NEXT MORNING, when Tabitha ventured out of her room, Arnie was nowhere to be seen. But sunshine blazed through the living room windows. Outdoors, a soft sea of snow sparkled like a thousand diamonds. Hopefully, she peered outside.

Ominous black clouds bunched on the western horizon. The blizzard would be here before long. She wondered if the snow plow would make it here before the storm hit.

Outside, Arnie shoveled the driveway. He wore a black cap and a dark blue coat, which stretched and rippled over his wide shoulders as he heaved up great mounds of snow and sent them flying to the side. No doubt he was praying for the plow's quick appearance, too. The house had been freezing last night. She didn't want to think how cold it might become if the heater repairman couldn't get out here before the storm hit.

In any event, the sunshine brightened Tabitha's spirits, and she decided to hope for the best.

The living room felt surprisingly warm this morning, although the burnt logs in the fireplace looked dark and cold. Then she saw the pellet stove in the corner and realized that it was radiating the cozy warmth.

She gathered her dry clothes from the fire screen and retreated to the frigid bathroom. The shower was hot, but she was careful to get out in five minutes. The bathroom floor felt icy after the warm tub, and after pulling on her rumpled clothes, she decided to pull on the gray socks again.

Tabitha needed her suitcase. She couldn't wear the same clothes two days in a row. After breakfast, she'd hike to the car.

Out in the kitchen again, Tabitha now noticed her purse and laptop lying on the counter. Carting them to her room, she set her cell phone to recharge and then returned to the kitchen. Her stomach gurgled, and she perused the cupboards. A coffee cup rested in the sink, but she saw no sign of breakfast dishes.

Smiling to herself, she found pancake mix and bacon and set to work. It was step one of her plan to make friends with Arnie. Hopefully, though, this would be a celebration breakfast. Perhaps the snow plow would arrive soon, and she'd merrily speed on her way home. She spied a radio on the counter and tuned it to a station that broadcast Christmas carols.

Singing softly to herself, Tabitha placed the last of the golden brown pancakes in the oven to keep warm. The front door opened, letting in a blast of cold. Arnie came in, stamping his feet, and peeled off his cap. His ears looked red and cold. He spotted her in the kitchen and stopped moving. He stared.

"Good morning!" Tabitha offered a smile. The man certainly needed sunshine in his life. She wondered if she'd been presumptuous by taking over his kitchen. "I hope you don't mind. I was hungry, so I started breakfast."

He shook his head, shrugged off his heavy jacket, and hung it beside hers on a hook on the wall.

When he disappeared down the hall, Tabitha placed the platter of food on the table and helped herself to several pancakes.

A few moments later, Arnie slowly sat down across from her. "Thank you."

"It's the least I could do. Count it as payment for the five minutes of hot water I used." She smiled, to let him know she was joking.

After a second, he returned her smile. "The hot water runs out in ten minutes. I'm sorry about how I said it last night."

"Oh." Now it made sense. What had come across as dictatorial and rude had actually been a warning. And he'd apologized again. Could this be the start of a beautiful friendship? Tabitha suppressed a smile at that improbable thought.

❄ ❄ ❄ ❄ ❄

Arnie forked up a bite of pancakes. Sweet maple syrup dripped as he lifted the warm cakes to his lips. Light and delicious. He couldn't help but sigh with contentment.

Minutes earlier, when he'd come inside and smelled the warm, welcoming aroma of pancakes and bacon, he'd felt disoriented and lost in time. As if he was a boy again, and his mother had prepared his favorite breakfast. She'd always kept the pancakes in the oven, piping hot and ready for after he'd played outside in the snow.

Tabitha had smiled at him, too, and welcomed him inside.

Arnie swallowed a lump of pancake. It had felt good, just for that second, to imagine that someone was waiting for him inside his home. Someone who loved him.

Of course Tabitha didn't love him. Arnie forked up another bite and chewed a little faster. But the illusion...the sharp longing had twisted through his gut.

He couldn't want love, or companionship. He was happy alone, wasn't he?

Feeling disturbed, Arnie cast Tabitha a quick glance. Today she wore her dark hair down around her shoulders. It was longer than he had suspected. She wore no makeup, but was still beautiful. Her beauty was softer, and he liked it.

Could he have misjudged her? She smiled at him now, and its unexpected sweetness kicked him in the gut. It confused him, and so he looked down, not sure what to think.

Arnie did know that he'd hurt Tabitha last night with his rude words, and he deeply regretted them all over again. Underneath the polished, high gloss surface she'd projected last night, her feelings were vulnerable. She may not be the stereotypical big city woman he'd tried to convince himself of last night.

This realization unsettled him still more. He had acted like a jerk. But this morning she'd gone the extra mile and made breakfast for him. What had he done to deserve that?

Exactly nothing.

Arnie glanced at her, and for the first time gave her an honest survey, ignoring his prejudiced preconceptions that he'd hastily formed last night. Yes, Tabitha was beautiful, and undoubtedly sophisticated, too. But she also appeared to be a sweet, genuine woman as well.

Discomfort knotted his stomach. Instinctively, he knew a nice Tabitha would be far more dangerous to his peace of mind than the cold, plastic woman he'd believed her to be in the first place.

He would need to be very careful. He'd be friendly and courteous to her, yes. It was the least she deserved. But he wouldn't allow the ice to melt around his heart. Not for her. Not for anyone, ever again.

❄ ❄ ❄ ❄ ❄

Tabitha watched Arnie silently eat across from her. He ate with apparent enjoyment and approval of her cooking skills. At least he approved of something about her.

"You're a good cook," he said, after razing through his first stack of pancakes. Tabitha was glad she'd made plenty.

"Thank you." She felt pleased by his obviously sincere compliment.

"Want some coffee?" he said, surprising her. "I can brew more." Unexpected warmth lurked in his eyes. Another crack in the ice?

"I'd love some. Thank you."

Moving at an unhurried pace, he dumped out the old coffee and set the new on to percolate. He helped himself to more hotcakes.

"When will the snow plow get here?" she asked, forking up a bite of pancake drenched in butter and syrup.

"It won't."

She stilled. "What do you mean, it won't? How do you know?"

He flicked a glance out the window. "The storm will be here in two hours."

"You mean they won't send a plow at all?" She felt horrified. She needed to get home to her parents. Her father needed her.

She jumped up and headed for the phone.

"What are you doing?"

"Where's your phone book?"

"Who do you want to call?"

"The snow plow department."

Arnie chuckled and wiped his mouth with a napkin. Tabitha's eyes narrowed. "What's so funny?"

"Snow plow department?" He rose to his great height and plucked a paper from a small, crowded paper holder on the counter. He handed her the rumpled bit of paper. "Call Scully. Be my guest."

"Scully? He runs the snow plows?"

"He runs one plow. It's all we have." Arnie still regarded her with amusement, which Tabitha did not like at all. She turned her back on him and punched the numbers into the phone.

The phone rang and rang.

Finally, she hung up. Arnie had cleared the table and now ran water in the sink. Soap bubbles clouded up his muscular, tanned forearms. He glanced at her. A faint smile twitched his lips. "Scully there?"

Tabitha forgot her intention to make friends with this ornery man. "No. Hopefully he's out working. Otherwise your repairman won't be able to to get here to fix your heater. You'll freeze in the blizzard."

"I've survived worse." He did not sound too concerned.

Anxiety tightened like a fist around her heart. Tabitha moved to the kitchen window. She had a good view down the road to the right, toward Newbough.

Unfortunately, she saw nothing but sparkling white and a few brave black birds soaring across the darkening sky. Where was her rental car, by the way? If he was right, she'd better get her suitcase out before the next storm hit.

Tabitha moved to the fireplace, where her boots remained from last night, and tugged them on. Then she headed for the door and pulled on her long charcoal coat. Her car keys jangled in the pocket.

The sound of water sloshing at the sink stopped. "Where are you going?"

"I'm hiking to Newbough, can't you tell?" She flung open the front door and marched outside.

CHAPTER SIX

COLD INSTANTLY BIT into Tabitha's face and hands. She longed for the mittens she'd packed in her suitcase. Well, she'd get them.

At least Arnie had cleared a path to the road. Striding purposefully, she headed down the uneven track toward the rural highway.

Footsteps crunched behind her. She walked a little faster. "I don't need rescuing," she announced. "Your assistance is not required."

A firm hand caught her arm, stopping her.

A white cloud of indignation puffed from her mouth, and she glared at him. He'd only donned his jacket. No cap, no gloves. And he was frowning again, surprise of surprises.

She twitched her arm free. "Don't trouble yourself, Mr. Arnold. I don't need your help."

Striding as swiftly as she could—although not nearly as fast as she could walk on the smooth sidewalks of New York City—she soon reached the rural highway. Pure white, untouched snow glittered in the sunlight, stretching as far as she could see. Beautiful. She drew in a soft breath of appreciation, and regretted that she would mar that beauty. Still, what other choice did she have? She needed her clothes.

Tabitha headed toward her car. Her feet sank deep into the soft snow.

Arnie tramped beside her, walking remarkably fast, compared to the slow way he'd ambled since the first moment she'd met him. "You're not foolish enough to try to walk to Newbough, are you?"

Tabitha rolled her eyes. "Please, Mr. Arnold."

He was silent for a moment. "Don't call me Mr. Arnold."

"Why not? You want us to stay strangers. That's clear. You can call me Ms. McCroy."

"Ms." Disapproval was clear in his voice.

"Do you live in a time warp, here in the middle of nowhere, Mr. Arnold? Women don't need to be identified as married or unmarried, you know. Most of us survive just fine without any man. Hence..." she sketched a cold hand toward his house, "you can go home."

"What are you doing out here?" he growled.

She plowed ahead as fast as she could. At last, she spied a lump on the side of the road. "My car!" she exclaimed with relief.

She fished the keys from her pocket and pressed the 'unlock' button. Obligingly, it chirped. Next, she found the button to pop the trunk. Unfortunately, when she pressed it, the snow shivered a little, but the lid didn't pop up like it should have.

The snow was probably too heavy.

Using her elbows, Tabitha swiped at the snow covering the trunk lid, trying to keep her hands dry. Last night's numb fingers and toes were fresh in her memory.

Arnie edged by her, sinking deeper into the ditch. "I'll clear this side and you clear that side."

Tabitha tried to ignore her feelings of vexation, and focused on clearing her half of the car. Finally, Arnie shoved his fingers under the lip of the trunk and heaved it open.

Her suitcase and bag of presents lay inside. Relieved, she pulled them out. Arnie shoved the trunk closed again. It clicked. Good. Tabitha locked the car, and it gave another friendly chirp. She felt reluctant to leave it in its snowy, frozen cocoon. Although only a rental, it felt comfortable, familiar and safe. The last thing she wanted was to return to this annoying man's house.

Although he *had* helped her. She should be grateful.

"Thank you," she managed, and quickly unzipped her suitcase and pulled out her hot pink mittens. Then she grabbed her heavy suitcase in one hand and the plastic bag of gifts in the other. She hadn't seen any sense in leaving the latter in the car.

Tabitha headed back toward Arnie's house, and he walked silently beside her.

❄ ❄ ❄ ❄ ❄

Maddening woman.

Arnie flicked a glance at Tabitha. She walked fast—no doubt used to rushing about in the city.

Maddening and prickly and fiercely independent. Again, nothing like his quiet and sweet Theresa.

Tabitha marched as quick as she could, her shoulders stiff and straight beneath that thin, useless coat. She was steamed at him.

He smiled a little, surprising himself. True, he had been obnoxious. Maybe he should apologize.

Unfortunately, he had enjoyed talking to Tabitha far too much at breakfast. Knowing they'd be stuck together for the next few days hadn't helped. He'd wanted to push her away, which had unfortunately inspired his behavior in the kitchen, and now outdoors, too.

Temper stained Tabitha's cheeks a faint rose color. She was even prettier when she was riled up.

Theresa had rarely flared with temper at him. True, sometimes her lips had thinned, but far more often, she'd pouted prettily to get her own way. Tabitha and his perfect Theresa were like night and day.

The thought should have encouraged him. It didn't.

Arnie decided it was time to make up for his comments.

"Give me your suitcase." He'd noticed that the huge bag sagged closer to the ground with every step she took. No doubt it was filled with all sorts of appliances Tabitha believed she needed in order to stay beautiful. Hair dryer, curlers, lotions, potions... Who knew what else? He wouldn't tell her that she didn't need them. Bad enough that he was paying closer attention to her than he'd like. No need for her to know that.

Tabitha frowned at him. Then, for some unknown reason her scowl intensified into a glare. "Why are you smiling?"

Arnie didn't bother to stop. "You look fit to be tied. Like a child in a tantrum."

Tabitha drew a quick, gasping breath.

Now, why did I say that, Arnie wondered. So much for his planned apology. Did he actually enjoy seeing her bent out of shape?

It was a side to his calm nature that he hadn't seen in a long while. Unfortunately, he couldn't seem to stop himself, now that he'd started. His smile edged higher, and he met Tabitha's gaze with a steady one of his own.

❋ ❋ ❋ ❋ ❋

Tabitha eyed Arnie with a frown. What sort of a look was he giving her? "Do I amuse you?" She handed over the suitcase. It was the least he could do if he insisted on laughing at her.

Slowly, he allowed, "You do."

"Would you like to carry my other bag, too?"

"The price for peace?" he said, more quickly than she'd expected.

Tabitha smiled. "Yes."

He silently held out a hand, but Tabitha felt a pang of guilt.

"No. Thanks for taking that one." She hitched the bag to her shoulder and trudged on, trying to step in the footprints she'd already made.

Tabitha felt him watching her. "What?"

"You're a hard woman to figure out."

"And you're a cakewalk?"

He lifted a brow, as if surprised by the idea.

Tabitha had reached the drive now. For the first time in the daylight, she took in his white paneled house, trimmed with brick, and the various buildings behind it, including a large gray shed and a big brown barn further back.

An imp drove her to call out, "Race you!" Although she ran on the treadmill at home, that didn't prepare her for the uneven patches of snow in the driveway, nor the bite of cold air stinging her lungs.

She ran alone. Arnie hadn't taken the challenge.

Reaching the house, Tabitha tossed her bag down and faced him, chest heaving. Did he think she'd acted like a child? Something about the country did make her feel younger and more carefree than she'd felt in years. It felt good, and she wouldn't apologize for it—not to herself, nor to anyone else.

A faint smile tugged at his lips as he passed by. Tabitha wasn't quite sure what made her do it. But when he put one booted foot on the porch step, she scooped up a handful of snow, squeezed it, and hurled it.

Snow spattered between his broad shoulders.

She giggled. She couldn't help it. Slowly, Arnie turned. Surprise warmed his eyes, and he placed the suitcase on the porch. Scooping up a bunch of snow with his bare fingers, he scrunched it and tossed it at her.

Tabitha squealed and flipped sideways to evade it, but it hit her squarely on the shoulder.

"You'll pay now," she warned, retreated a few steps in order to put a good distance between them. She patted together another ball of white stuff between her pink mittens.

He grabbed up another handful of cold snow and circled toward her, his mouth lifted in a half smile.

Without warning, Tabitha let hers fly, and the battle began. Snowballs flew fast and furious. She quickly realized that she was getting the worst of it. Arnie was a terrific shot, and threw with unerring accuracy. White covered her coat, and one even tipped over her collar, sending a shower of ice down her neck.

"Now you've done it!" she cried, and aimed for his head. He warded it off with an upraised hand and lobbed another at her, underhanded. It hit her in the stomach.

Tabitha stopped making snow balls. She just threw snow she'd crunched once in her fist. To her satisfaction, one slid down his jean clad leg, and another smacked into his torso.

He laughed out loud, and the transformation made her stare. Why, Arnie was actually handsome when he smiled! Her transfixion didn't last for long, however. He continued to throw lightly compacted snow balls at her.

She noticed that he was coming closer.

"What are you doing?" she demanded breathlessly. "You're getting on my turf. Back off!"

"The loser eats snow," he informed her.

"No!" Alarmed, she threw more white stuff, but he just lifted his arm and twisted his hips, evading most. All the while, one last snow ball remained in his hand.

Although she knew it was a lost cause, she scooped up one last, fluffy ball. "Don't you dare," she warned. "You'll regret it." A bit of fear accelerated her pulse when he stopped a spare foot away. What did he mean to do?

He lifted his snow ball and gently brushed it across her lips. She smashed snow into his jaw.

His head turned slightly from the force of the impact. "Now that wasn't fair," he told her mildly.

Tabitha felt foolish. "I thought...I thought you were going to smash that in my face."

He smiled. "No."

"I'm sorry," she offered weakly.

His red fingers brushed the snow from his cheek. "I think you won after all."

"Your hands must be freezing. How about I make you some hot tea, or cocoa. For a peace offering?"

He continued to regard her with a faint smile, even as melting snow dripped down his neck. His dark amber gaze looked serious, though. Steady and measuring, he looked into her eyes, as if trying to see into her soul. "I'd like that."

Tabitha nodded, and escaped into the house. She draped her gloves over the fire screen to dry as Arnie carried her luggage to her room.

She remembered how he'd gently brushed the snow against her lips, and wondered what that had been about. She knew him well enough to know he hadn't made a move on her; at least, not intentionally. But still, she'd felt something pass between them, just for a second.

Chapter Seven

ARNIE HAD APPARENTLY turned the radio off, so she turned it back on to Christmas carols, and prepared two mugs of hot cocoa for them both.

When he reappeared from the back of the house, he took his cup and retreated to the recliner near the Christmas tree. Ignoring her, he flipped open a magazine.

Good, Tabitha thought, sipping the hot, sweet chocolate. Perfect. All appeared to be well. Her gaze drifted to the Christmas tree, and for the first time, she noticed that the floor beneath it was bare.

"Don't you have any gifts?"

Arnie glanced at the tree. "No." He turned a page. "I already gave presents to my friends, and they gave theirs to me."

"You didn't keep any for Christmas Day? Not even one?" The thought both dismayed and saddened her. How did he intend to celebrate Christmas? "Do you normally spend Christmas alone?"

"I'd planned to go to the church's Christmas program." He glanced outside, where the sky had turned a pewter gray. "Now I won't."

Tabitha had never heard of anything so sorry in her life. True, she'd spent last Christmas on her own, too, but she'd been invited to three parties. She hadn't had a moment to feel lonely. But Arnie... Suddenly, she had to know the truth. "How do you usually spend Christmas?"

He shrugged. "I bake a ham, and maybe potatoes. I read the second chapter of Luke."

"The Christmas story." Amazing she remembered that, as she hadn't read her Bible in years. She glanced outside at the lowering gray sky. The blizzard would arrive soon.

The chance of the snow plow arriving appeared miniscule. Her spirits sank at the creeping realization that she would not be able to go home for Christmas. She'd wait a little longer just to be sure, and then call her parents with the news.

Tabitha glanced back at Arnie and a little of her customary optimism returned. The snow fight had invigorated her. "I guess now you'll be stuck with me." On impulse, she said, "Let's make it fun."

She figured that if she had to stay in this house, she might as well try to make it a bright Christmas for both of them. After all, she didn't want to sit and stare at the walls all day long.

He gave her his full attention. "What do you mean?" He sounded wary now; very different from the laughing man of a few minutes ago. His walls were back up.

"I could bake cookies, or a pie."

"I like pie," he said slowly.

"Good. What ingredients do you have?" Tabitha retreated to the refrigerator to look inside.

"I have apples in the shed."

"Apple pie," she approved, shutting the refrigerator door. "And I'll make sugar cookies, too. We'll decorate them together."

He stared at her, but said nothing.

"Am I being presumptuous?" she asked, hands on her hips. "I know it's your house and everything..."

"No! No, be my guest." He waved a hand toward the kitchen. "Bake all you want. I don't mind."

"Okay, then. So you'll decorate sugar cookies with me?"

His delayed response indicated this was not first on his list of preferred activities. She waited patiently, not sure why garnering his participation was so vital to her. Maybe because she'd enjoyed their snow ball fight so much. She'd liked seeing him smile.

Besides, it could be step two of building a tentative friendship. They'd need it if the snow plow abandoned them alone together for an unknown number of days. Besides, how could anyone not have fun decorating cookies?

"Okay," he said at last. "Since you're making that apple pie."

"Good." With a smile, Tabitha retreated to the kitchen to search for the necessary ingredients. Satisfied with what she found, she carried her laptop to the kitchen and pulled up her favorite recipe files. In New York she usually ate dinner out, but in truth, she liked to bake. In fact, she liked to cook, period—a fact that would shock all of her brainy analyst friends.

Humming along with the carols on the radio, she first mixed up the cookies, and then rolled them out and searched for cookie cutters in the drawers. She found an old metal Santa shape, a bell, and a candy cane. She cut them into shapes. Then, while they baked in batches, she set about the longer task of making the pie.

Arnie lugged in a sack of apples for her, and so she decided to make two pies. It wasn't that much extra work, after all.

Soon, delicious apple and cinnamon smells filled the kitchen. Tabitha realized she'd skipped lunch, and instead snacked on cookies. Only the misshapen ones, of course. Arnie built a sandwich and stood near her for a moment, eyeing the cookies. "Soon," she told him. "After we decorate them, you can eat them."

At last, she pulled the last sheet of cookies from the oven and popped the two pies in to bake. Now for the icing. She'd found an old box of food coloring in one cupboard; probably his mother's, so it must be really old. But she guessed food coloring didn't go bad. And she only needed several drops each of red and green.

"Okay," she said. "Time to show me your artistic side."

He slowly approached the table. "Don't expect a masterpiece."

"I only expect to have fun. Now, choose your weapon and go for it." Tabitha waved at the Ziploc bags she'd filled with different colored icings. She'd snipped off a tiny corner of each one.

She sat down, grabbed the bag of red, and squirted stripes on a candy cane. After a moment, Arnie lowered himself into the chair and outlined a bell in green. Tabitha grinned. "That's the spirit! It looks great."

Arnie's eyebrow raised fractionally.

Tabitha said, "When you were a child, did you ever decorate cookies with your mother?"

"Yes. A few times." His large hand reached for the white frosting bag, and with a fist, he gently squeezed white onto Santa's beard. Silently, he worked.

As Tabitha watched him, she wondered more about the silent depths living inside this man. If she were a betting woman, rather than one who carefully evaluated risks, she would wager that Arnie hid a deep well of pain behind that quiet exterior. She wondered what had hurt him so badly. "Do you have any brothers or sisters?"

"No. Do you?"

"Twin little brothers, Jake and Steven. They're at Syracuse University."

"I went there," Arnie offered, surprising her.

"You did?"

"You don't think farm boys go to college?"

"I'd never thought about it, honestly." Tabitha gathered her thoughts. "What did you study?"

"Business. My dad wanted to make me a partner in the farm. He never went to college, so he wanted me to learn everything he didn't know."

"He must have been very proud of you."

"He was," Arnie said shortly.

Tabitha eyed her host. The porcupine quills were bristling again, so she decided not to pursue the matter. She grabbed one of the cookies he'd frosted.

"Time for inspection, Mr. Arnold." She pretended to look at the bell from every angle. "Excellent. But now for the true test." She bit off a corner, and closed her eyes, pretending bliss. "Yum! You pass."

When she opened her eyes again, Arnie regarded her with a steady, if somewhat unsettling look. A slow smile tugged at his lips. "I'm glad you approve, Miss McCroy."

"Now don't start that again. And why don't you like to be called Mr. Arnold?"

"It reminds me of my dad."

"Oh. I'm sorry."

"You didn't know."

"No. But you asked me to stop. Sometimes I don't listen very well." Tabitha looked away. That had been the case in early November, when her mother had asked her to come home and talk some sense into her father about the bypass.

Tabitha and her father were alike, and Nancy believed he'd listen to logic if it stared him right in the face. Talking on the phone had done no good. He'd refused to be badgered by Tabitha long distance, and he wouldn't listen to her mother's emotional outbursts, either.

Tabitha had not gone home. In truth, she hadn't wanted to believe that matters were as bad as they truly were. And with her workload doubled at Browns Brothers, she'd found it difficult to consider, anyway. Now, in hindsight, she saw how foolishly short-sighted, and even selfish she had been.

Then, three weeks ago, when her mother had finally broken down in tears and confessed that Daniel's heart was a ticking time bomb—that it was just a matter of time before he had a massive coronary—Tabitha had again tried to talk to her father. It hadn't worked. And her boss wouldn't allow her to take her Christmas vacation early.

Now she wondered if she could have managed a weekend away if she had tried harder. After all, she'd managed to hang onto her scheduled Christmas vacation, even though her boss had been reluctant to let her go. To appease him, she'd brought her last two reports with her on vacation to complete.

Still, after all of that, now she was stuck twenty-eight miles from home. It might as well be eight hundred miles. She still could not speak to her father face to face. Why hadn't she tried to go home when her mother had first asked? Was she deaf to the needs of others? Only focusing on what directly concerned her?

The truth hurt. Tabitha didn't like that picture of herself, and she didn't want to be that person. And if not for this conversation, sitting here decorating cookies with Arnie, she never would have thought about it at all. How long had it been since she'd actually sat still and thought about anything besides her job?

To turn her mind away from these unsettling thoughts, she said, "Why do people call you Arnie? Isn't your first name Reginald?"

"No."

"But you said..."

"It's Arnold Reginald Arnold III. My dad was Arnold. People called me Arnie. But when teachers called me Arnold Arnold, the kids laughed. So I asked the office to drop the first Arnold for roll call."

"Kids can be cruel."

"I've told you my whole name." Arnie stroked red onto Santa's hat. "What's yours?"

"Tabitha Rae McCroy. My friends used to call me Tabby." Tabitha smiled, remembering those carefree days. "I liked to climb trees when I was a kid. One time I climbed too high and was afraid to climb down. Someone said I was like a cat. So people started calling me Tabby. It stuck."

He smiled. "Tabby. It suits you."

"Why do you say that?"

His smile widened, and in that split second, Tabitha got the distinct impression that he was beginning to enjoy teasing her. "One minute you act friendly, and the next you show your claws."

"I do not! And besides, being friendly to you is challenge, in case you're not aware. While we're talking about animal analogies, you should know you remind me of a bear."

The smile faded from his eyes.

Tabitha sighed. "See, there you go. Retreating back into your deep, dark cave."

He said nothing.

Tabitha bit her lip. "I'm sorry." She gathered up the finished cookies and piled them on a plate.

Arnie snagged a handful and retreated to his chair. On the way, he turned off the radio.

Tabitha put her hands on her hips and stared after him. Now, why had he done that? She'd been enjoying the carols. The more sensible part of her wanted to let it go. After all, it was his house. The other half of her didn't.

She walked into the living room. After a moment, he looked up. "What?"

"That's twice you've turned off the radio. Why?"

He didn't reply for a very long moment. Almost as if he was struggling with his answer. She saw the instant when he decided not to share the truth with her, because his lips tightened into a firm line. "I like it quiet in the afternoons."

"I see," she said, although personally, she couldn't think of anything more tedious than an afternoon of silence.

She retreated to the kitchen to clean up the gargantuan mess. She hoped the running water and grinding garbage disposal didn't disturb him unduly. She hummed to herself to try to regain her holiday cheer. It helped, but only a little.

The timer for the pies dinged, and she pulled them out and set them to cool on the stove top. *Mmm.* They smelled cinnamony and delicious, and helped to improve her spirits. Tabitha finished the last of the dishes and wiped her hands on a towel. Four o'clock. Now what? She didn't want to sit in that tomb of silence in the living room with that prickly man.

Small snowflakes whirled outside the window, and for the first time she heard a faint howl somewhere in the eaves. The blizzard had begun. She realized she'd never called her parents as she'd planned. Quickly, she placed the call, but no one answered. It worried her. Where could they be?

Tabitha shivered and realized she hadn't changed clothes like she'd meant to do. That soft red cashmere sweater she'd brought would be warm. And she'd brought jeans, too, and slippers. Perfect. She hurried to change, and while she did so, she put on her own socks.

Returning to the living room, she held out Arnie's borrowed gray socks. "Thank you for the loan. Where should I put these?"

To her surprise, he stood and pulled them from her fingers. His warm hand accidentally brushed hers, and a tiny shock electrified her skin.

He disappeared to dispose of them, and soon returned. His eyes ran down her new outfit. "You look nice." His tone was deep and quiet.

"Thanks." Tabitha frowned, not sure what to think. From acting almost as cold as a popsicle to delivering this warm, genuine compliment. She couldn't figure the man out.

"Are you upset?" He stopped a spare foot from her, so Tabitha had to lift her chin to look him in the eyes. His were cast in shadow. His broad frame, covered in red plaid flannel, felt very large and overpowering in the small space.

"I don't understand you," she admitted, trying to ignore her awareness of his close proximity. "One minute you're warm and friendly, and the next you're cold and...and inconsiderate."

He moved forward an imperceptible step, and then stopped. Now the light revealed the warm amber of his brown eyes. "I'm used to living alone. I didn't mean to hurt your feelings."

"Have I done something to offend you?"

"No!" He drew a deep breath. "Tabitha." Again, he said her name gently. "I'm sorry. But my behavior has nothing to do with you."

"I find that hard to believe. It feels as if you're treating me like a disease you don't want to catch."

"No. I'm sorry. I don't mean to treat you like that."

"Then why *do* you?"

Arnie scanned her features. After a long moment, he appeared to come to a decision. He turned aside to the mantel and lifted a silver framed photo. Tabitha noted the way he cradled it when he showed it to her. In a low voice, he said, "I haven't meant to hurt you. I'm truly sorry. If I'm cold, it's because my heart died eleven years ago."

Chapter Eight

Tabitha stared at the picture of a beautiful young woman with a cloud of blond hair and round, china blue eyes. A sweet, beautiful smile curved her mouth. Obviously, she was someone Arnie had loved very much.

"Who is that?"

"Theresa. She was my wife."

"Your wife?" For some reason, she was surprised.

"She was." He gently turned the picture to look at it, and pain darkened his eyes. Carefully, he placed it back on the mantel. "She was the sweetest girl who ever lived."

"She looks lovely." In fact, she looked like an angel. No wonder Arnie had loved her—and still did, by the look of it. Clearly, no woman on earth could ever match her, at least in his mind.

Gently, she asked, "What happened?"

"I'll tell you another time. I showed you her picture so you'd know..." He visibly struggled with words. "My heart is gone. If I'm rude, I don't mean to be. I don't feel much anymore."

"You mean you don't *want* to feel anymore."

His brown gaze settled on her. "No."

"Yes." Tabitha wasn't sure why she felt so certain. "You push me away because you don't want to feel." She peered up at him, struck by a surprising thought. "Are you afraid I might touch your heart?"

"No. No one will ever take Theresa's place."

"Of course not," she agreed. "But our hearts can feel all kinds of love. Friendship love, for one. And I know you love God."

He nodded.

"Caring for other people doesn't mean you're betraying Theresa's memory."

He said nothing.

"I'd like to be friends." She offered a small smile. "I'm not asking you to fall in love with me!"

His muscular shoulders relaxed. "I know."

"Then what do you say? Can we be friends?"

"You're asking me to trust you."

"I won't hurt you. At least, not on purpose."

After a moment, he said, "I'll try."

"Thank you."

A breakthrough. Perhaps this one would last.

❖ ❖ ❖ ❖ ❖

Arnie picked up his Bible and tried to read. It was difficult. His mind kept returning to Tabitha, and her plea to become friends. He did like her. A lot. At last, he admitted this truth to himself.

She was feisty, honest, and straightforward. Fun, too. And sweet and kind. She was nothing like those beautiful, highly polished females he'd dated in college. More than one of those had stamped their stiletto heels through his heart. He didn't believe Tabitha would ever purposefully hurt anyone.

Even so, his gut told him to be careful. She'd leave in a few days, after the blizzard passed. He couldn't let himself get too attached to her. But he would try harder to stop growling like the bear she thought he was. He couldn't let her get too close, though. He couldn't let her into his heart.

❖ ❖ ❖ ❖ ❖

Tabitha found an old news magazine and curled up on the couch and tried to read. Out of the corner of her eye, she noticed Arnie reading the Bible.

How long had it been since she'd read the Bible? As a child, she'd gone to church every Sunday, but she'd pretty much left God there until she went to a youth Bible camp one summer in high school. Her life had changed then.

"Which book are you reading?" she asked.

"Psalms. Do you like them, too?"

"I don't read the Bible much anymore."

"'Anymore'?"

"I was saved at youth camp when I was fifteen. I went forward and they gave me a Bible."

"What happened next?" he said quietly.

"I was excited about God for the rest of high school. Then I started college, and I guess I just...left him behind." She'd only had time for classes—and partying with her friends, of course.

He nodded. "Do you miss him?"

"Miss him?" What a strange question. "I don't know. I guess sometimes. He's been popping up in my mind a lot lately." Ever since getting stuck in the snowstorm, to be exact.

"I have an extra Bible, if you'd like to read it." He bent and fished a brown, leather bound book from a shelf built into the lamp's end table. "It's here if you ever want it." After a glance at her, he replaced it.

"Thanks. Maybe I'll read it later." She stood and wandered to look out the window. "I might have a lot of time to kill." And tomorrow was Christmas. What better time to think about God?

Outside, the snow flurried faster. The gray sky had begun to darken into night. She was glad she wasn't driving this evening. Anyone in their right mind would stay snug in their warm home tonight.

The shrill ring of the phone startled her.

Arnie moved to answer it, and Tabitha paid no attention to the conversation until he said, "Tabitha, it's for you."

Only her parents knew where she was. Worry gripped her as she took the receiver from Arnie's warm hand. "Mom?"

"Tabitha...Oh, Tabitha!"

"What is it? Where are you? I tried to call a while ago."

"It's your father. We're at Dr. Callahan's."

Tabitha glanced outside at the thick, swirling flakes. "But the roads..."

Her mother said, "The snow plows made it to our house. Thank God! Your father started having terrible pains at lunchtime. He didn't want to go!" She heaved a breath. "But I made him."

"Mom?" Tabitha's fingers clenched around the telephone receiver.

"Your father's all right. For now. Dr. Callahan thinks he had a mild cardiac event."

"Mild *cardiac event?* What does that mean? Did Daddy have a heart attack?"

"We don't know, honey. He had terrible chest pains." Her mother's voice wavered. A small silence followed, as if Nancy McCroy was trying to regain control of her emotions. "Dr. Callahan called your father's heart specialist in Buffalo. Dr. Sheahy is worried enough that we're being Medevaced to Buffalo tonight."

"Tonight?" Tabitha couldn't seem to stop repeating her mother's words. "But the blizzard! Is that safe?"

"It's not a blizzard yet. The pilot said we'll be okay." Her mother sounded flustered. "Honey, I have to go. Dr. Callahan is motioning to me. I'll call you when we get to Buffalo. It'll probably be tomorrow morning, after they've evaluated your father."

"But Mom..." The phone clicked dead in her ear. Tabitha stared blankly at the receiver, not sure what to do with it. After a moment, she hung it up.

Arnie stood nearby, frowning.

"My dad..." Tabitha swayed, and reached for the wall to steady herself. "I think he just had a heart attack." Tears blurred her eyes.

"He's alive?"

"Yes. But they're worried. They're going to Medevac him to Buffalo tonight." She needed to sit down.

Tabitha moved toward the couch, but her knees felt like jello. A tinny ring echoed in her ears. She felt cold, and black spots danced before her eyes.

CHAPTER NINE

FROM NOWHERE, Arnie's strong arms caught her. He pulled her close against his chest, steadying her. He felt solid and secure. In fact, in some distant part of Tabitha's brain, she realized that everything about him felt secure and steady. From his wide, powerful shoulders to the solid body beneath the red plaid flannel shirt, to his sturdy jeans with the brown leather belt secured around his waist. Her hands skimmed that now, trying to regain her balance. Instinctively, she thought better of it, and raised her palms to his chest. Slowly, her world righted.

"Are you all right?"

Tabitha lifted her head. His steady brown gaze held hers, and a bit of strength unfurled within her.

This man made her feel calm. Just holding her, he imparted some of his strength. Peace trickled into her heart, as if everything would be all right. But it was not. It was *not*. How could she forget that?

She whispered, "It's all my fault."

"How could it be your fault?"

"I should have come home sooner. I should have talked to him about the bypass more."

"Tabitha, he's a grown man..."

"I haven't been home in two years!" She fisted her hands against his chest. "Two years! All because I wanted to prove that I'm the best analyst on Wall Street." She choked on a sob. "I'm so selfish. All I care about is myself." She burst into tears.

She pressed her cheek into Arnie's soft flannel shirt, feeling as if she didn't deserve comfort, but pathetically longing for it anyway. He stroked her hair. His large, warm hand cupped the back of her head and stroked down to her neck.

Tabitha wept harder, sickened with herself. The last three month's workload could not excuse her two years of neglect. How could she have been so selfish? In New York City she'd been so caught up in her job, poring over numbers, excited about the next hot company, and chasing the dream of stock market riches. And she'd coveted that promotion. Just like her peers had.

But for what? She'd chased an elusive dream while real life slipped by. Life that mattered...loving her family, and caring about her friends.

She pressed her wet cheek harder against Arnie, overcome with despair. Now it may be too late. Her father could have another heart attack—a massive one this time— before she ever saw him again.

He could die.

"Tabitha," Arnie murmured. His calloused thumb pushed hair away from her cheek, and stroked it toward her ear.

"Oh, Arnie," she gulped, and pulled free. "I'm such a failure. No wonder you don't want to be friends with me. What kind of a friend am I? What kind of a daughter?"

Turning away, she sat on the couch and buried her face in her hands.

She felt the couch sink down beside her. Arnie's strong arm pulled her close to him. For a moment she resisted, and then crumpled against him.

He held her for a long time like that, letting her soak his shirt with her tears.

At last, she sniffled and pulled back, wiping her eyes with the heels of her hands. "Now see the drama you brought on yourself. Maybe you shouldn't have opened your door last night," she tried to joke.

"I'm not afraid of a few tears."

She gave a mighty sniff and glanced at him. He regarded her with calm compassion. He understood sorrow. And he knew pain—probably more pain than she'd ever experienced in her life.

She tried to smile, but failed. "Thank you." Self-consciously, she laced and unlaced her fingers in her lap. "I usually don't fall apart like this." Abruptly, she jumped up and ran in search of a tissue to blow her nose.

She spent a long time in the bathroom, trying to pull herself together. Never, in recent years, had she ever revealed her vulnerable side to anyone, so why had she chosen Arnie? Because he was a stranger? Because he seemed safe? She didn't know.

Tabitha splashed water on her puffy eyes. At least she hadn't put on mascara today, so no black lines striped down her face. The things she'd said to Arnie ran through her mind, and she thought about her father and her family. The truth hurt. Her career was doing very well, but she had shoved everything else out of her life. Not only had she been self-absorbed, but her life was out of balance, like a scale with a boulder on one side and tiny grains of sand on the other.

Again, she thought of the God she had forgotten for so many years. Why was she thinking about him so much lately?

She closed her eyes and whispered, "I'm sorry, Lord, for all of the selfish things I've done. Please forgive me and help me to be a better person. And please watch over Daddy."

A bit of peace crept into her soul. A peace she had long forgotten...just as she had long forgotten about God. But maybe he hadn't forgotten about her. Maybe he loved her still. And maybe she'd still get that chance to speak to her father.

At last, she left the sanctuary of the bathroom, feeling a little better. Yes, she'd made mistakes with her family. No question about that. She could do nothing to change the past. However, she could change the future.

From now on, she'd visit her parents at least twice a year. And if her mother needed her, Tabitha would go immediately, no questions asked. It was time she put her family on a higher priority than work. Since her family needed her now, she'd email her boss on Monday and request another week off; not just a few days. She'd help her mother and father get through this crisis.

Just as soon as the blizzard stopped. As soon as she found her way home.

❄ ❄ ❄ ❄ ❄

When Tabitha returned to the living area, she discovered Arnie in the kitchen at the stove with his back to her. For a moment she watched him, remembering how he had held her so gently, and with such compassion. He was a big man and, she knew, a strong one. But Arnie possessed a substance that went deeper than his physical build. He knew who he was, what he wanted, and what he believed in.

She'd never met anyone like him before. The men she knew never sat still. Each, in his own way, seemed frenetic, searching for the pot of gold at the end of the rainbow. None of them was ever sure where he might find it. And never sure if he had.

Arnie had found his treasure—his wife, who had died. And his land and his home. He was content—no, he was more than content. It was if he *knew* this was where he belonged. That this was the life God had given him.

Tabitha wanted that kind of peace. Instead, she identified with her restless co-workers. She was always searching, but never convinced she'd found the answers she was looking for.

She stepped into the kitchen. "What are you cooking?"

"Steak."

He'd set up a heavy, corrugated grill over two of the gas burners. Two steaks sizzled there. In another pan water boiled, and he poured in instant rice. She recognized the red box, which was the kind she used, too.

"Could I help? Maybe make a salad?"

"Sure."

Tabitha found lettuce and tomatoes in the crisper and set to work.

All of the food was ready at the same time, and after Arnie said grace, Tabitha tucked into her meal.

"Do you always have steak on Christmas Eve?" she asked. "Is it a family tradition?"

"No. I just like steak." After a moment, he added, "Ham and potatoes on Christmas was my family tradition."

"It still is, apparently," she gently pointed out, since he'd said earlier that he still made that meal. And then, "Do you have any aunts or uncles?"

"An uncle in Minnesota and an aunt in Florida."

No family lived close by. He truly was alone. "We eat ham on Christmas, too," she offered. "And we eat macaroni and cheese with hot dogs on Christmas Eve. It was my brothers' favorite growing up. Mine, too."

"Traditions are nice. Especially for kids."

"Yes. Mom always set up the manger scene on Christmas Eve. Each of us got to put out one of the people. We fought over baby Jesus." She smiled. "Daddy always took out his old accordion and we sang 'Rudolf' and 'Jingle Bells.' His favorite was 'White Christmas.'" Tabitha glanced out the window, and her voice caught, "He must love this one."

"When will they call you again?"

"Tomorrow morning. I wish this snow would stop. I wish I could be with him right now."

"I'm sorry." Compassion warmed his gaze.

She smiled. "Thank you. By the way, I'll clean up. Mom says cooks don't clean. Not that my dad would agree. But sometimes he helps her out."

"You have a good family."

"Do you know them well?"

"This year I worked on the Christmas set with your dad."

Tabitha smiled at that thought. Her crusty, gruff dad, working side by side with Arnie, who was calm and even-tempered. "He didn't try to order you around, did he? He has a way of taking charge of everything."

Arnie smiled, and it lit his dark amber eyes. Tabitha's breath caught, and again the crazy thought struck her. *He's awfully handsome.* With those wonderful brown eyes, his square jaw, the clean angles and planes of his face, his well-cut mouth...

He cleared his throat, thankfully interrupting her thoughts. What was wrong with her? Clearly his heart was closed, and he intended for it to remain so. That was for the best, because he was definitely the wrong man for her. A farmer and a stock analyst's worlds could never mix.

Mildly, he said, "Daniel helped *me.*"

Tabitha grinned, and eyed him with new respect. Her father would never take orders from a man he didn't admire a great deal. "Then my father paid you the highest compliment he could give."

His smile edged higher. "Really."

"Absolutely. Now, how about that apple pie?"

After clearing the dishes, Tabitha sampled the pie and sighed. The crust melted in her mouth.

"How many pies did you make?" Arnie finished his slice extraordinarily fast.

"Two."

He served himself another slice. "You're a terrific cook, Tabitha."

"One of my hidden talents." She grinned. "Who knows what you'll discover next."

Arnie eyed her, and she sensed his protective wall rising again. And then she realized why. She had just flirted with him! Mildly, yes, but still.

A flush warmed her cheeks. She raised her hand. "Don't take that the wrong way. I just meant that maybe there's more to me than just a stock analyst city girl. At least, I hope so."

She cleared the table, and did not look to see how Arnie received her comments.

❀ ❀ ❀ ❀ ❀

Arnie took Tabitha's words at face value. Clearly, she wasn't any more interested in him than he wanted to be in her.

As he forked up the last of his pie, his mind lingered on Tabitha. Vulnerability flashed through her at unexpected times, and honesty, too. He found both appealing.

And when she'd sobbed in his arms he'd felt both surprised and protective. Tabitha was a strong woman, and he bet few people had ever seen that vulnerable, broken side of her. He felt honored that she'd trusted him enough to reveal it to him.

Maybe they were already friends.

He watched Tabitha scrape plates and squirt a big dollop of blue soap in the sink. His sink.

Why did he like seeing her there?

Alarm waved an invisible red flag in his mind. *Stop it,* he told himself.

He stood abruptly and retreated to the living room to switch on the small television. Maybe the cold weather report would take his mind off of Tabitha.

❄ ❄ ❄ ❄ ❄

Tabitha went to bed early. She wished she'd brought her financial magazines or a book. She'd noticed that Arnie had a few Tom Clancy and Michael Crichton novels. Maybe tomorrow she'd try one.

In truth, she'd gone to bed because Arnie seemed to have retreated inside himself again, although he'd replied perfectly politely to the small questions she'd asked. He clearly wanted to be left alone to read his book.

On top of that, the picture on the television resembled a blizzard. After the static-filled weather report, Arnie turned it off.

Tabitha curled up under her layers of blankets, wearing warm sweats and two pairs of socks. Although the living room had been warm because of the wood pellet stove, her room was an ice box. The temperamental central heating seemed to have died for good.

Wind gusts of seventy miles per hour were predicted for tonight, and temperatures below zero. The weather system was supposed to stall over the area for three more days. Tabitha shut her eyes and hoped they would survive. And she longed to see her parents, and to see with her own eyes that her father was doing okay.

She didn't understand Arnie. His walls continued to hurt her, although she wasn't sure why. After all, she would leave in three days, and would probably never see him again.

Even though that was true, she realized she wanted to be friends, and she wanted his walls gone, too.

When Tabitha fell asleep, she dreamed that she was Humpty Dumpty sitting on a tall, stone wall, and all the king's horsemen galloped toward her at top speed, wielding swords and spears. She'd be safe inside the wall. In Arnie's castle. But he stood beneath her holding a shield of ice. Words scratched into it said, "Go home, Tabitha." The horsemen crashed into the wall. She cried out and toppled backwards. Terrified, she screamed, "Catch me, Arnie!" The ground rushed up to meet her, and a mighty explosion thundered in her head.

CHAPTER TEN

TABITHA SAT UP, gasping, and heart racing. Arctic air bit into her skin. In the dim light, her breaths puffed out in white, frosty bursts.

The shrieking wind grabbed her attention and she glanced toward the window. The blizzard.

A noise thundered again on her bedroom door. "Tabitha! Are you all right?"

Arnie. Just as she opened her mouth to speak, the door flew open and an orange rectangle of light spilled inside the room. His large frame filled her doorway.

She reflexively pulled the blankets to her chin.

"Are you all right?" he asked again, his voice deep and rough.

She noticed that he wore a heavy jacket and boots. "Where are you going?"

He moved inside the room. "You screamed. Are you hurt?"

"No. I'm fine." Tabitha felt embarrassed that she'd shrieked out loud. "Where are you going?"

"Why did you scream?" He came still closer. A frown knotted his brows.

His concern warmed her. Much as he kept up a prickly exterior, she was becoming more and more convinced that a warm heart beat inside of him. "I had a nightmare."

The warm orange light from the hall cast his face into chiseled planes. "You called out my name," he said roughly.

Tabitha's embarrassment deepened. She'd certainly never confess her dream, or that she'd wanted him to be her knight in shining armor.

"Did I?" she said weakly.

He stared back.

"Where are you going?"

He turned. "Something slammed into the house. I'm going to see what it is."

Maybe that had been the crash in her dream. And then Tabitha realized what he had just said. "You can't go out in the storm!"

He headed for the hallway. "I have to."

"Why?" She sprang out of bed and followed as he strode toward the front door. His fingers worked the bottom part of his jacket, obviously trying to start the zipper.

He meant to go out into that violent, blinding gale?

Tabitha darted in front of him and blocked his path to the door. He obviously didn't see her until he was almost upon her, because he stopped abruptly, a scant foot from her, his jacket still partially unzipped.

"Don't do it."

"Move, Tabitha."

"No. You're crazy! What if you get lost?"

"I won't." He moved to the right, in order to go around her, but she blocked him. "Tabitha," he growled, and kept coming.

She put her hands against the hard, warm wall of his chest. That stopped him. He stared down at her, as if not sure what to do with her.

"Don't do it. Please."

He said nothing for a long moment, but his warm brown eyes scanned her face. Finally, his hands settled gently around her wrists. "I'll be fine."

She bit her lip. "What about those stories of people getting lost in blizzards? They wander around until they freeze to death!" She gestured wildly at the front door. "What can you do out there anyway? It's pitch dark. You can't fix anything."

He said nothing, but just watched her, unreadable thoughts moving through his dark eyes.

"Please," she said. "I don't want you out there. I don't want anything to happen to you."

He leaned forward, and in one blinding moment she thought he might kiss her. He stopped, but his face was very close. His warm breath fanned on her lips, making them tingle. "I'll be fine. I have a rope."

She felt breathless. And then his words registered. "You have what? A rope?"

"Yes. We used to have animals in the barn. We checked on them during blizzards."

"So you've done this before?"

"Yes."

"Oh." She removed her hands from his warm flannel shirt, feeling foolish. "I didn't know."

She moved aside as he zipped his coat and pulled on his hat. He opened a small closet beside the front door and pulled out a huge coil of rope. "I'll be back soon. Go to bed."

He opened the door and stinging snow whipped inside, lashing her skin like sandpaper. And what would it do to Arnie, out there for who knew how long?

He pulled the door shut from the other side, and now Tabitha was alone in the house. Her only company was the shrieking, wailing wind. She shuddered. Not very comforting.

And if Arnie thought she'd obediently return to bed, he had severely misjudged her. Tabitha returned to her room to pull a few blankets around her shoulders, and then put water on the stove to boil. No doubt he'd be cold when he got back.

When he got back. Despite all of his logical arguments, Tabitha couldn't quite dismiss the fear in her gut. Blizzards were dangerous. Anything could happen. He'd said something had hit the house. What if another something hit him? What if the rope slipped out of his hands and...

The whistling kettle pulled her mind from her fears. She set the burner to a low simmer so the kettle would stay warm, and poured herself a cup of hot water for tea. Then she huddled with her blankets on the floor near the pellet stove. The couch was too cold, because the window behind it radiated ice.

Her drink sloshed when the front door finally flew open and Arnie came in, stamping the snow from his boots. His face looked red and cold, and so did his hands. Didn't he have gloves? Tabitha wanted to spring up and fuss over him, but refrained.

His gaze immediately zeroed in on her. Slowly, he pulled off his jacket and stepped out of his boots. He came closer. A small smile tugged at his lips. "Waiting for Santa?"

Tabitha grinned, realizing how she probably looked, huddled near the fireplace, with blankets swaddled around her. "He hasn't come yet. Of course maybe you haven't been good this year. Maybe he'll just pass you by."

His smile deepened. "Well then, maybe he'll come for you."

"I doubt if I made Santa's list, either." She nodded toward the stove. "I boiled water."

"Thanks."

He moved into the kitchen and Tabitha stood up and gathering the blankets around her. With one hand she clutched the blankets, and in the other the warm mug. "What did you find?"

"Looks like part of the barn roof flew off. It's plastered against the back wall of the house."

"Did it damage the house?"

"Nothing major. Luckily, I don't have animals on the farm anymore. When the storm stops, I'll check the house and barn more thoroughly."

She nodded and finished her tea. Moving by him, she placed the mug in the sink.

"Why did you stay up?"

Surprised, Tabitha glanced up at him. "Do you think I could sleep with you out there?"

"Why not?"

"Why *not?*" Flabbergasted, she searched for words. "What if you needed rescuing?" He chuckled, and her indignation flared. "Don't you think I could rescue you?"

"I think you can do anything you set your mind to."

"Then why are you laughing?"

"It's been a long time since anyone has worried about me."

"And that's not right." Impulsively, she blurted out the truth she felt, deep in her heart. "You're a terrific guy, Arnie. You deserve a family. And kids. Someone to love you." She raised her hand. "And don't close up on me. It's the truth. When I leave, it'll make me sad to think of you here, all alone, forever. You deserve so much more." She bit her lip, but said no more.

"Thanks, Tabitha." Again, she liked the gentle way he said her name.

"Well, it's true," she said softly.

He leaned the barest fraction closer, and Tabitha stood very still, her heart suddenly pounding as just the faintest bit of his warm breath caressed her skin.

She wanted him to kiss her. Fiercely, as she'd never wanted anything before. It shocked her. How could that be? Imperceptibly, she swayed toward him. His dark eyes slowly scanned hers. After the barest hesitation, he leaned forward and his cool lips brushed hers. Just a brief, fleeting caress, but it warmed her all the way to her toes.

Her pulse thundered in her ears.

His gaze held hers, and he said, in a deep, gruff voice, "Good night."

"Good night." Clutching her blankets tighter, she headed for her ice box of a room. The memory of his kiss lingered, and she didn't feel nearly as cold as she had earlier. And not nearly as alone, either. Arnie had lowered his shield of ice, and just for a second, she felt as if she'd finally found her way home.

❀ ❀ ❀ ❀ ❀

Arnie wondered if he'd lost his mind. He'd wanted to kiss Tabitha, and so he had. Now he regretted it.

What had he been thinking? What had he been *thinking?* He shoved a hand through his hair.

It had been a mistake. But he'd read Tabitha's eyes just before he'd kissed her. She had felt the pull, too.

A mutual moment of insanity.

He drew a deep breath. It would not happen again. If only the blizzard wasn't raging, he'd go out in the cold night air again and try to clear his head.

But the storm held him prisoner. Somehow, he'd have to find a way to deal with his feelings for Tabitha. He didn't want them. They had to go.

CHAPTER ELEVEN

TABITHA AWOKE EARLY on Christmas morning, freezing cold despite all of the blankets piled on the bed. It would be warm out in the living room, she knew, so she made herself get up and pull on her warmest clothes. Dusky light filtered through the window. The wind still howled. She wondered how her father was doing this morning. Had they made it to Buffalo last night? Hopefully they would call her early this morning.

When Tabitha ventured into the hall, Arnie's door was still closed. So, she was the first one up on Christmas morning.

A few steps later, her gaze fell upon his Christmas tree. No presents lay beneath it. That wasn't right. He deserved at least one present for Christmas.

Tabitha thought of the bag of gifts she'd brought in from her car. A whole sack full. More than her family needed, or likely wanted. Had she been trying to buy forgiveness for her neglect?

Tabitha returned to her room and dug through the bag of gifts. Her two brothers weren't as big as Arnie, but one small present would suit him perfectly.

Smiling a little to herself, she ripped off the gift tag and hurried out to the living room. She placed the gaily wrapped package under the tree.

There. Maybe it wasn't much, but at least it was something.

Tabitha toasted herself in front of the warm stove, and then scampered down the hall to take a quick shower. When she emerged at last, the pungent aroma of coffee drifted down the hall. Eagerly following her nose, she joined Arnie in the kitchen.

He stood at the stove, scrambling eggs. Today he wore a blue plaid flannel shirt tucked into blue jeans. He didn't look up when she approached him.

"Merry Christmas!" she sang out.

After a slight hesitation, he cast her a frowning glance. "Good morning."

Tabitha eyed him. So, this was the way it was going to be. Obviously, he regretted the kiss. She should have expected this sort of behavior from him. Well, she would set his mind at ease. While she had very much enjoyed his kiss, she wasn't foolish. She knew any romantic entanglement between them would only bring pain to them both. She barely had time for her family, let alone romance. Especially a romance doomed from the start.

She put her hands on her hips. "I agree, you know."

"About what?" he growled.

"That we should stick to friendship. I'm no more of a masochist than you are."

Was that relief in his eyes? Then why was he still frowning? He said nothing.

Tabitha drew an exasperated breath. "I'm saying I'll forget about the kiss, if you will. Don't you think that would be best?"

"*Yes.*" He said it with deep vehemence.

Tabitha tried not to feel offended. "Well then," she said brightly. "We're on the same page. Now, what are you cooking me for breakfast?"

At last, one corner of his mouth tugged up. "Am I cooking for you?"

"Well..." Tabitha raised an eyebrow, "Santa might change his mind about you. I see he left you a present under the tree. Maybe he'll check his list twice and find out you've been naughty, rather than nice."

Arnie glanced into the living room.

"It's small," Tabitha admitted, feeling self-conscious. "I'm not sure how good you were last year." She gave him a small smile, suddenly afraid he would reject her gift.

He wiped his hands on his jeans. Slowly, he said, "I didn't think Santa could make it here in the blizzard."

Tabitha grinned. "His elves help out when he's in a jam."

"Let's have breakfast first."

After breakfast, which Tabitha insisted on cleaning up, she followed Arnie's slow, seemingly reluctant steps into the living room.

Tabitha said nothing, but sat cross-legged near the warm pellet stove. Arnie knelt down on one knee and reached for the package.

"I don't have anything for you." His large hands cradled the gift as if it were something precious.

"Sure you do. You rescued me from frostbite. You're letting me stay in your home. What better gifts could you give me?" She added shyly, "That present isn't much. I hope you like it."

Arnie tore off the paper with one rip and pulled out black leather gloves. They were large ones, and she hoped they would fit him. "I've noticed you never wear gloves. I wasn't sure if it's because you don't have them or you don't like them."

He stroked the black leather. "Mine wore out."

"They're fleece lined. See if they fit," she said anxiously.

Arnie pulled on the black gloves and to her relief, they fit him perfectly. He checked the tag at his wrist. "Extra-large," he said with a faint smile. "Who did you buy them for?"

"Let me see that." Tabitha tugged his wrist closer so she could see. Sure enough, it read, 'extra-large.' "I thought I'd bought large." She smiled. "I guess they were meant for you. They'd be too big for my brother."

"Thanks, Tabitha."

"Don't want you to get frostbite." Crumpling the paper, she sprang to her feet and deposited it in the trash. "Merry Christmas."

"Merry Christmas," he said in a low voice. He pulled a wicked looking pocket knife from his jeans and cut the tags off.

Outside, snow whirled past the windows. She couldn't see the sky; she could only see off-white snow against a gray backdrop. Frost crystals etched the bottom corners of the panes, and Tabitha wondered how cold it was outside.

The long, empty day stretched before her. Christmas Day. Hopefully her father was all right and her mother would call soon.

"I'm going to turn on Christmas music," she said, heading for the radio. "Is that all right with you?"

A beat passed, and then Arnie said, "If you want."

Tabitha frowned, fingers hovering over the radio's 'on' button. She remembered how he'd turned off the carols yesterday, claiming that he liked peace and quiet in the afternoons. "Do you dislike Christmas music?"

"Just turn it on, Tabitha."

Clearly, that was not an answer of any sort. But equally clear, he did not want to share what might be bothering him.

Maybe Christmas music depressed him. Maybe it reminded him of Christmases past with his family and Theresa. All of whom were gone.

Her finger lingered over the radio's button, trying to decide what to do. If the carols upset him, should she turn it on?

The phone rang, startling her, so she left the radio silent and plucked up the phone receiver. "Mom?"

"You're father's fine," Nancy said. "Dr. Sheahy says he didn't have a heart attack, thank the Lord."

Tabitha drew a quick breath of relief. "Thank goodness."

"But he's a ticking time bomb. Dr. Sheahy told him so again. But your stubborn father..." Nancy sounded frustrated.

"Can I speak to him?"

"Of course, honey. Here he is."

"Angel?" Her father's voice, a shade quieter than its normal hearty tone, boomed through the receiver.

"Daddy! Are you okay?"

He laughed. It sounded uncomfortable to Tabitha's ears. "I'll be fine, soon as I get out of here. Pesky nurses keep poking and prodding me all hours of the day and night. Can't get a minute's peace."

"Daddy." Tabitha struggled for calm. "I don't want to lose you."

"You won't, sugar. You know your old man..."

"Dad!" Tabitha drew a breath and tried again. "Next time you won't be so lucky. You know it. The doctors said..."

"Pshaw on doctors," Daniel McCroy grumbled.

"I know you're scared," she said softly. "But a bypass is your only chance. Don't you want to live to see your grandchildren?" Now where had that thought come from? She didn't even have time to date!

"You got something to tell me?" Interest sparked in his voice.

"No." Uncomfortably, she turned away as Arnie moved into the kitchen. "Not yet. Dad, please. Tell me you'll consider the bypass."

Silence.

"Dad, we love you. We need you. What would Mom do without you?"

He grumbled, "Make a mess of my workshop, that's for sure."

"Dad."

"Okay. Okay! I'll schedule it. Doc'll probably want to cut me open tomorrow."

The thought frightened Tabitha, but she knew it scared him even more. "It'll be okay."

"Here's your mother," Daniel said gruffly.

Nancy McCroy's voice came, whispery soft. "Thank you, Tabitha."

"Do you really think they'll operate tomorrow?" Now that she'd finally convinced her father to have the operation, fear threatened to choke her.

"If they can, I'm sure they will. Dr. Sheahy seems to think his situation is critical."

"Call me when you know."

"I will, honey. And let me give you the number here, and his room number." After reciting the numbers, Nancy said, "I'll talk to you soon."

Slowly, Tabitha hung up the phone. Her fingers lingered for a long moment on the smooth instrument. It felt as if it was her only link to her father...to her family. Tears ached, but today she would be strong.

Arnie stopped near her, and he felt like a solid, warm presence. "He's going through with the bypass?"

"Yes. They might schedule it for tomorrow."

He said nothing, but watched her.

Tabitha turned abruptly. "When do you usually start the ham? Do you want an early afternoon dinner, or later, like at six?"

She didn't want to talk about her father. Worry and fear struggled within her, made even worse by the fact she could do nothing to help him. It was a bitter pill to swallow, because she was a doer. Maybe it was an ostrich mentality, but she had to get her mind on something else, or else she'd fret all day long.

"You don't need to cook dinner."

"I would like to do it. I really don't want to sit around all day, staring at the four walls."

He regarded her for another silent moment. "Three o'clock would be good."

"Terrific." That meant she could start preparing the meal around noon. She'd glimpsed the size of the ham when she'd pawed through the refrigerator last night.

Tears formed in her eyes for no reason whatsoever.

"Are you sure you're all right?" he said quietly.

Tabitha swallowed the lump in her throat, determined not to fall apart like she had yesterday. "I'll be fine." She glanced away from the concern in his warm brown eyes. If she accepted his comfort like she desperately wanted to do, she'd lose her composure for sure.

Tabitha licked her lips. "Thank you. But I need to stay busy." An idea came to mind. "Do you have wireless internet? I need to e-mail my boss."

From a nearby drawer, he dug out a scrap of paper with the wireless key written on it, and handed it to her.

Tabitha composed a quick e-mail, explaining about the blizzard and her father's heart condition, and requested another week off. She sent it and hoped for the best.

Placing the computer in her room again, she returned to the silent living room, feeling a little calmer now. Arnie read a sporting magazine, looking comfortable in his recliner, and backlit by the lamp on at his side.

Tabitha glanced at her watch. Ten o'clock. She was going to be bored out of her skull in short order if she didn't find something to do. And she'd fret, too. Again, she itched for her financial magazines. Or to complete one of the two reports she'd brought with her. But wasn't this Christmas? Couldn't she spend one morning without thinking about the stock market?

Feeling restless, she wandered over to the pictures displayed on the fireplace mantel. Arnie had shown her the one of Theresa. Several others were displayed nearby. With curiosity, she edged closer.

The first one was of a young Arnie in an olive drab camouflage uniform. His white teeth flashed in a grin, and his eyes looked bright and eager. The next picture showed him again, obviously older, with grimmer, black eyes. Harsh angles accentuated his gaunt face. No smile this time.

"You were in the military?" With surprise, she lifted the last picture and scrutinized it more closely. What had happened to him between the first picture and the second? Perhaps the answer would provide a clue to the puzzle of the man he was today.

"The reserves helped pay for college." He flipped a page. A faint frown drew his brows together.

Tabitha couldn't turn away from this mystery, nor his clear reluctance to speak about it. What was it about this man that made her want to melt his walls of ice? To understand all of his secrets?

He fascinated her. That was the disturbing truth.

"How long were you in the reserves?"

"Four years." Arnie's frown twitched deeper.

"Why the two pictures?"

Finally, he looked up. A muscle clenched in his jaw. "Why all the questions?"

"You look so sad in this picture. Why?"

"It's the past. Let it go."

His harsh words made her hesitate. But only for a moment. He'd shown kindness to her, and she couldn't help but care about the hurt that she sensed tightly boxed away inside of him.

"I would like to know," she softly countered, and curled up in a corner of the couch near his chair. "Will you tell me?"

An excruciatingly long moment elapsed. Finally, he flicked a finger toward the picture she held. "They took that picture when I joined Army active duty."

"You were active duty? In the Army?" Maybe that explained his buzz cut. "For how long?"

"Ten years, including reserves."

"Did you ever go to war?"

He drew a breath. "I did a tour in Afghanistan."

Tabitha gaped, but Arnie returned his attention to his magazine and said nothing more. All sorts of questions zipped through her brain, but she didn't want to be insensitive or intrusive.

After a moment, she replaced the picture on the mantel. Although she felt a bit like she was invading his privacy, she scanned the remaining photos. One was of an older couple; probably his parents. The woman was short, with curly auburn hair, and the man was tall and rawboned, with a square jaw, just like Arnie, except salt and pepper sprinkled his dark hair. They both looked happy and in love.

Her gaze moved down the mantel to a wedding photo of Arnie and Theresa. Theresa looked slender and delicate next to him, and an angelic smile lit her face. Arnie wore a black tuxedo. He appeared happy and impossibly young. And thin, like a gangly boy, but he still had the same broad shoulders. Then a boy, today a man. A man of deep hurts, if her guess was right.

She moved to the last of the framed photos. This one was a hinged set, with a picture on each side. The left picture showed Arnie in full dress uniform, standing straight and shoulders square. He'd filled out since his wedding photo. He was obviously older, too—maybe in his late twenties. A uniformed, multi-medaled man presented him with a medal with a dark colored ribbon. It was difficult to discern the exact color. The next picture showed him standing between his parents. His parents wore proud smiles. Arnie looked straight ahead, unsmiling, his dark eyes bleak, as if he'd seen too much. As if the mysteries of the world had been stripped bare before him.

"What medal did they give you?" she asked softly.

He didn't answer, so she turned to look at him. His mouth was a straight line. He did not want to answer her question, but she waited patiently, hoping he'd do so anyway. Again, she sensed that it was a link to understanding him better. To understand the hurt that had erected the wall around his heart.

He said, "Anyone ever tell you you're nosy?"

Tabitha did not take offense. She knew was pushing the boundaries of their relationship. But she wanted to help him, if it was possible that she could. "It's my job to search for the truth," she explained. "To find the real story behind a company's annual report. I'm a detective, I guess. I like to find answers to questions I don't understand."

"I'm a company you want to understand?"

"Pretty much. Yes." That wasn't the whole truth, of course. "Why?"

"You're hurting," she said quietly. "I want to understand why."

Surprise flashed, but then his face settled into uncompromising lines. "Leave it alone. You can't help me." He returned his attention to the magazine.

Tabitha eyed him, but decided to drop it for now. However, she was not one to turn away from a challenge. In fact, the tougher the challenge, the more determined she was to overcome it. That was one of the reasons why she'd become the best in her field in seven short years. But Arnie was not a company, of course. She would respect his feelings and boundaries. Her gaze returned to the photo. "Your parents look proud of you."

He said nothing, and when she looked back, found him frowning at her. She frowned back. "You're a stubborn man."

His mouth softened. "And what are you?"

"I take after my father," she admitted.

His smile edged higher. "And I take after mine."

"So you won't tell me the name of the medal you received?"

Arnie drew a breath. It sounded faintly exasperated. "I'll tell you. But only if you promise to stop asking questions."

"Okay." She grinned, ridiculously pleased.

"A Purple Heart." He returned his attention to the magazine.

She gasped. "That's not fair! How can I *not* ask another question?"

He smiled, but didn't answer. With slow deliberation, he turned the page.

Tabitha put her hands on her hips. When he glanced up, she saw the gleam in his eyes. Of course he didn't want to tell her more about his Purple Heart. But he was teasing her now, and obviously enjoying it.

"Let's play a game," she proposed.

"Truth or dare?"

How did he know? "Yes. Or maybe spin the bottle, if you'd prefer." She said this to startle him—to get back at him for tricking her.

Shock wiped all expression from his face.

Hastily, she backpedaled. "I'm joking! Okay? Puh*lease!*"

"Are you?"

Tabitha's face heated. "Of course!" She crossed her arms. "If you tell me how you got the Purple Heart, I promise to leave you alone."

His tense shoulders relaxed. "Good tactic."

"What?"

"Shock and awe. But I've seen it before."

"Come again?"

"You shock me with the spin the bottle statement. Then I'm supposed to be so relieved you didn't mean it that I'll forget your promise, and answer all of your questions."

Tabitha hadn't thought it through so clearly, but it sounded good. She smiled. "So, how *did* you get the Purple Heart?"

His smile faded, and she was suddenly sorry she'd pushed the point. She opened her mouth to tell him so, but he spoke first.

"A buddy got hit. We were in the mountains, searching caves for the enemy and for weapons stockpiles. I crawled out and saved him."

Tabitha didn't like thinking about him in danger. He could have been killed. "Did you get shot?"

"A bullet creased my shoulder."

She drew a quick breath of horror. "My goodness." A military man. A hero. It explained the self-discipline she'd sensed in him from the beginning, and his confidence in himself and in his place in the world. He'd seen the worst and survived.

And he'd served his country. By comparison, she had only served herself—and her firm's clients, who had fattened their wallets, thanks to her research and analysis. What a narrow view she'd taken of the world. All for money. Nothing for honor, and no self-sacrifice on her part, either.

Arnie regarded her steadily. "In case you want to know, my parents never saw the medal. We took that second picture before I shipped to Afghanistan. Is that all you want to know?"

No. It wasn't. She hungered to know more about this wonderfully complex man. But she'd already pushed him far enough for today. "Thank you for telling me."

"Next time I'll be asking the questions."

"My life's an open book," she returned airily.

He smiled. "Good."

Feeling suddenly uneasy, Tabitha retreated to the kitchen.

CHAPTER TWELVE

WHILE TABITHA PREPARED the ham and cheesy potatoes au gratin, she listened to Christmas carols on low volume. She hoped it didn't bother Arnie, and again wondered why it would. But she'd certainly asked him enough questions for today. His vague threat to start asking her questions had disturbed her, although she wasn't sure why.

She prepared the food all too quickly, and popped the ham into the oven to bake. The potatoes would go in later.

Then she wandered to the kitchen window. Still nothing to see but swirling snow and dark gray skies. She wondered when they would perform the heart bypass surgery on her father.

She paced back to the living room and stood near the warm stove, and then returned to the kitchen to listen to the carols. They were so soft that she couldn't hear them in the living room. At least they wouldn't bother Arnie. She leaned against the counter, arms crossed, and then, with a sigh, strode to the kitchen window again.

She wasn't accustomed to having nothing to do except worry. At home, business—and busyness—filled every minute of her day.

Tabitha felt restless. She longed to do something constructive, and wandered out to the living room to stare at the pictures on the mantel again.

"What's wrong?"

She whirled. "How can you stand being confined like this? I mean, don't you usually work outside all day?"

"Yes. Dawn to dusk, most days of the year. But rest is good, too."

"It's boring."

He lowered his magazine and leaned back in his recliner. "You don't like to sit still, do you?"

"Is that a criticism?"

"No. It's an observation."

"For your information, I'm a doer, not a sitter. I'm not good at twiddling my fingers or counting snowflakes until I fall asleep from boredom."

"Rest can be peaceful."

"Hmmph," she said. "I like noise and excitement. I'm from New York City, remember? The city that never sleeps."

"I remember," he said quietly, and snapped open the magazine again.

Tabitha frowned a little. "We live in different worlds. And I think we're both okay, just the way we are."

He sent her a measured glance. "You're awfully defensive."

"You're the one criticizing me."

"I said that you don't like to sit still. Maybe it hit a sore spot."

"I can sit," she said, plopping onto the couch. "See?"

A grin tugged at his lips. "I never said you couldn't. But for how long?"

She huffed out a breath. "Is this a dare?"

"If you want to make it one."

He did enjoy teasing her. Tabitha didn't know whether to laugh or glare.

"Fine," she said. "How long?"

"Thirty minutes?"

"You're on," she told him. "But just for half an hour. Life is too short to be wasted." She glanced at her watch. "Mark from now."

His faint smile deepened. No doubt he meant to enjoy his moments of blissful silence. He had enjoyed few enough since she had arrived.

Tabitha stared at the ceiling. No work. No T.V. She couldn't hear the radio from here. What to do? She grabbed a magazine and flipped through it. An article about Christmas at Rockefeller Center caught her eye, and she gazed at the photo of the giant Christmas tree. She'd seen it in person a week ago. In the picture the gloriously beautiful lights twinkled.

Her gaze slipped to Arnie's spindly tree in the corner. That modest one, more than the one in Rockefeller Center, reminded her of Christmases past. The anticipation. The joy. The warm time together with her family.

Now as an adult, although she'd felt horrified by Arnie's solitary celebrations, she realized she'd done little for Christmas last year in New York, either. Of course, she had attended several festive parties. She'd certainly never been alone. But Christmas wasn't the same in New York City. Not like Christmases at home...

Why hadn't she seen her family in two years?

Was she truly so shallow and self-absorbed that she cared about nothing but work? And success?

The truth hurt. But she'd already prayed for forgiveness, and she remembered enough about God to know he'd already forgiven her. Now she had to forgive herself. Maybe an important step would be to find out how to get back on the right path.

Perhaps she should read the Bible. It was Christmas, after all.

❄ ❄ ❄ ❄ ❄

Tabitha read Arnie's large brown Bible longer than she'd planned. In fact, she felt an odd sort of guilt just sitting there, enjoying herself for so long. She hadn't been able to stop with the Christmas story. As it had been when she was a teenager, she was fascinated by Jesus, and all of the things he'd said and done.

She especially liked that he wasn't afraid to speak his mind. Calling the religious leaders of the day hypocrites to their faces took guts. Tabitha liked that. And she liked his gentleness and compassion with women and children, too... And with those who had lost their way.

He reminded her a little of Arnie.

She cast a glance at her host, who was absorbed in a farming magazine. Her eyes lingered on his straight brow and the chiseled planes of his face. When she'd first met him, she hadn't noticed those handsome angles and planes as much as she did now. A faint shadow darkened his square jaw below his cheek bones. Her eyes traveled to his wonderful, warm brown ones, and she found him watching her.

Embarrassment slipped through her, but she offered a saucy grin to cover it. "I passed. See." She tapped her watch. "It's been an hour."

He smiled, and Tabitha liked how it relaxed his features, and she liked the little laugh lines at the corners of his eyes, too. In fact, she was beginning to like entirely too much about him.

"You survived."

"Whatever doesn't kill us, just makes us stronger, right?" She grinned.

"The ham smells good."

Tabitha jumped up. "I'd better put the potatoes in." She should have put them in a half an hour ago.

While the potatoes cooked, Tabitha busied herself setting the table and steaming the green beans she'd found in the crisper. Delicious smells permeated the kitchen, and her stomach rumbled loudly when they at last sat down to dinner. Arnie cast her an amused glance, but said nothing. Obviously, his mother had raised him with manners. She thought about her brothers and smiled wryly to herself. They, on the other hand, would have teased her unmercifully.

"I'll pray," she offered.

He offered her a slow smile. "Go for it."

"Thank you, Lord, for leading me to Arnie's house. Thank you for keeping us safe from the storm. And thank you for this food. Amen."

"Amen."

They ate in silence for a while, except for Arnie's compliments on her cooking.

Christmas songs caroled in the background. She'd forgotten to turn off the radio. Tabitha wondered if it bothered him, and again wondered why it would.

She chewed another bite of ham and eyed him eating silently across from her. A new song came on the radio. "White Christmas."

Her father's favorite. "This song is certainly appropriate."

After a pause, he nodded and forked more ham into his mouth. Tabitha noticed that his knuckles had gone white.

"What's wrong?"

His dark gaze looked remote again, locked behind that wall of his. An uncommonly long moment passed, and still he didn't answer.

"Is this song bothering you? I can turn it off."

"No. You're enjoying it."

"But you're not." Tabitha crossed the room and flipped off the radio. She sat again.

"That wasn't necessary."

"I have eyes, Arnie. I can see it upset you. Would you mind telling me why?" Tabitha knew she was pushing things again, but she wanted to know what was wrong.

Another long moment passed. He didn't want to answer, that much was clear. "Don't you like Christmas?"

"Sure, I do."

She waited, hoping he would say more. He didn't. "You don't like 'White Christmas'?"

"I love that song," he said in a deep, tight voice.

"Then why did you tense up when it came on?"

Another moment passed before he answered. "It was Theresa's favorite. Our song, she called it. We got married on December twenty-sixth."

"Oh." Finally, Tabitha began to understand. "I'm sorry."

"It was a long time ago."

She wasn't fooled by his attempt to dismiss the subject. Christmas brought back painful memories for him. Each one reminded him of Theresa and their wedding.

Gently, she said, "Would you mind telling me more about Theresa? When did you meet?"

To her relief, the tension relaxed out of his broad shoulders. "We became friends in junior high."

"Was it love at first sight?"

Arnie chuckled, surprising her. "No. She and my best friend, Doug, fell in love. They dated all through high school."

"So how did you two get together?"

"A year or so after high school they broke up. I was in college, and Doug stayed in Newbough to help his parents with the store. Theresa got frustrated with him because he started drinking too much. She felt he was wasting his potential, and she broke it off. She'd had enough."

Tabitha nodded.

"A few years later, during my senior year of college, I came home for Christmas. It was as if I saw Theresa for the first time. My mom had invited her family over for Christmas dinner. Theresa was here when I came home, and 'White Christmas' was playing when I came through the door. She took my breath away when she smiled at me. That's when it started."

"How romantic," she said softly. "Friends all those years and then suddenly, bam."

"Something like that."

Tabitha decided she'd asked enough questions about Theresa for now. She wanted to ask more, but was afraid they'd raise his wall again, and she didn't want that. Instead, she redirected the conversation, hoping for more information on another subject. "You said you joined the reserves in college. How did that come about?"

To her surprise, considering his prickliness on that same subject earlier this morning, he answered easily enough. "A buddy was a reservist. He told me about it, and I joined up at the end of my sophomore year. It helped pay for my master's program, too."

"Also in business?"

"Yes."

"I have an M.B.A., too," Tabitha said. "With a double bachelor's degree in Business and Finance."

"I always knew you were smart."

Obviously he was, too. She offered a grin. "That's what my boss says. It's why he pays me the big bucks. Did you ever think about going into the business world instead of coming back to the farm?"

Arnie frowned. Tension again settled over him like a mantle.

Now what had she said? The most innocuous questions seemed to send up his walls.

"Theresa wanted me to go into business," he said shortly. "But I promised my dad." He stood up fast.

Clearly, the little diversion into his past was over.

❋ ❋ ❋ ❋ ❋

Arnie had told Tabitha more than he had intended. He served himself a second helping of ham and potatoes at the counter and glanced over his shoulder. "Want more?"

She smiled. "Sure. Potatoes, please."

He dished up a small mountain of cheesy potatoes onto her plate.

A part of him wanted to open up to her.

A little couldn't hurt, he allowed. As long as he didn't let her get too close. He'd been careful all day to keep her at a safe distance. No more slips like last night, when he'd kissed her. That had been a mistake he didn't intend to repeat.

Tabitha gave him a sharp look when he sat down again. Clearly, she wanted to ask more questions. Instead, she simply said, "Thanks," when he handed her the plate.

Silence fell between them. Arnie found he wanted to ask her questions, too, but he refrained. Starting another deep, personal discussion wouldn't be smart if he wanted to keep the safe distance between them.

He scraped his plate clean. "Do you like games?"

"Games?" Her whole face lit up. "You mean like Uno, or Monopoly?"

He smiled at her enthusiasm. "Or Clue?"

"I love Clue! It's my favorite."

"Mine, too. I have a bunch of games in the closet. I've kept them from when I was a kid."

The remainder of the evening passed rapidly. Both laughed a lot and Arnie teased her when her game piece, Miss Scarlet, turned out to be the murderer over and over again.

"I didn't know you were so bloodthirsty," he said.

Tabitha pretended to show her fangs. "Watch out," she hissed. "I'm getting *hungry* again."

He chuckled, and they decided it was time for apple pie.

When he finally readied for bed in his chilly room, he thought back over the evening. He'd enjoyed himself, and had felt a lick of disappointment when Tabitha had finally, laughingly, said good night. He liked her warmth and wit. He wanted to know her better.

His hands stilled after pulling off his shirt. No, he didn't.

But he did.

As a friend, or because he was interested in her? Disturbed to be asking himself the question, Arnie shoved his arms into his sweatshirt and pulled it on.

He was not interested in Tabitha. Not in *that* way, he told himself. He'd enjoyed their evening together, so it was natural he'd feel warmly toward her, after all the laughing they'd done. His mind flashed to their kiss last night, and then he wished it hadn't. He'd liked that, too.

Stop it, he told himself. *Be careful.*

But his thoughts refused to be ruled by logic. He fell asleep still thinking about Tabitha, and of her smile that warmed a cold, lonely place inside of him.

Chapter Thirteen

TABITHA WOKE UP in the middle of the night feeling like a frozen popsicle. The wind outside shrieked louder than ever, and it was as black as pitch.

She peered out from beneath her heaped blankets. No green digital numbers shone from the bedside clock. The electricity had gone out.

Why did this knowledge make her feel even colder? She shuddered beneath her three blankets and folded quilt. Maybe she should fold the blankets in half, too, before she died of hypothermia.

She thought about the pellet stove in the living room. Arnie left it burning on low all night, she knew, because when she'd gone out yesterday morning it had been burning. It would be warm out there. What if she gathered up her blankets and pillow and slept on the floor in the living room? Or even on the couch.

The idea appealed. Arctic air froze her nose as she poked her head out from underneath her cocooning blankets. She shuddered again. Cold. Tabitha hated to be cold. Gritting her teeth, she slipped out of bed and dragged all of the blankets with her. She draped the blankets, hood fashion, over her head, and clutched the rest tightly to her body. The wooden floor felt like ice through her thin socks.

She glanced at the window, and wondered how cold it was outside. It felt like Alaska inside.

Was that a bit of gray outside, hinting that dawn was close? Clutching the blankets more tightly around her, and the pillow to her stomach, Tabitha hurried to the window and peered outside. Nothing but dark. No gray at all. No light. Frost etched the pane.

Tentatively, she pressed a finger to the lacy, crystalline structure. Coldness stuck her finger to the pane. And then she realized why, as the sharp prickliness melted beneath her warm finger and moisture dampened her skin. The lacy frost crystal had melted where her finger had touched it.

The frost was *inside* the house. She clutched her blankets tighter, and made haste for the living room. No wonder she felt so cold! Her room was a meat locker.

Only the faint light through the windows allowed her to see the shadowed shapes in the dark living room.

Shouldn't an orange glow be coming from the stove? And it felt chilly. In fact, this room felt as frosty as her own.

Tabitha quaked as cold seeped into her feet. The stove fire had gone out. Arctic air wafted through gaps in the blanket and slid icy fingers down her skin. If only she knew how to light the pellet stove, she'd start it up. But since she didn't...

She retraced her steps to Arnie's door. Although she didn't want to wake him up, she didn't want to die of exposure, either.

She knocked on the door and waited. Nothing.

So she pounded again. "Arnie!" Her teeth chattered and clacked.

She heard a swishing movement, a shuffle, and then the door swung open. His dark, shadowy body seemed large and overpowering in this small space.

"What?" He covered a yawn with his forearm.

"I'm freezing. Ice is growing inside my window."

"Don't you have enough blankets?"

"Arnie. I'm freezing. Please light the stove. I want to sleep in the living room tonight."

"Just a minute."

Tabitha retreated to the living room and perched on the sofa. "The electricity is out," she told him helpfully when he arrived.

His large body hunkered down near the stove. "I noticed."

An orange flame flared, and he carefully lit the stove and then fed pellets in through the opening. Apparently satisfied, he closed the grate again and sat back on his heels. The warm light cast his square jaw into chiseled planes.

"How can you stand it? Aren't you cold?"

"No."

Her jaw dropped. "How is that possible? Your house is ice station zebra!"

"Come over here, near the fire."

Tabitha willingly sat near him, blankets swaddled around her from head to toe. She noticed that he wore sweats of some dark, indeterminate color.

He smiled at her.

"What?"

"You look like Little Red Riding Hood."

She shoved at his muscular shoulder. It didn't move. "Don't laugh at me, you sadistic man."

"Sadistic?"

"What else do you call it when you torture your houseguests with frostbite?" She still shivered, although the stove was beginning to put out a little heat. "I know, I know. The repairman didn't make it out. But still." She shuddered mightily.

"I'm sorry your room is cold."

She muttered, "I think I've lost the feeling in my toes."

"Want me to warm them?"

Startled, Tabitha glanced at him. Warmth scorched her cheeks, and not just from the stove's growing heat, either. He regarded her, his shadowed gaze steady.

Her heart pumped a little faster and she shivered again, but not from cold this time. "What?"

He smiled a little, but his narrowed gaze was unreadable. "I'm asking if you'd like me to warm your feet."

Tabitha looked away. "They're fine," she mumbled. "Thanks."

In one fluid movement he rose, and disappeared down the hall.

Now where had he gone? Her heart still beat a little too fast for her liking. But whatever for? He'd only been solicitous. Right? Hadn't she misinterpreted his chivalrous comment? Even if Arnie actually *had* flirted with her, he hadn't done it on purpose. He'd backed off too quickly for that to be true.

He returned with a sleeping bag and knelt beside her again. "This will cushion the floor for you."

"Thank you." She moved so he could unroll the thick bag. Then she sat on top of it, blankets still cocooned around her.

He sat back on his heels. "Will you be all right?"

"Of course. I'm used to taking care of myself."

"You couldn't light the stove."

"True," she admitted.

Why was he smiling at her like that? Agitation scrambled her nerves, which made no sense at all, because his presence also made her feel secure and protected, too.

Perhaps she felt uncomfortable because she was used to taking care of herself. And yet here, in this unfamiliar environment, she needed him. She wasn't sure if she liked the vulnerable feeling of needing to trust another person to take care of her.

"Would you show me how you did that?" she said abruptly. "Start the stove, I mean."

He regarded her for a moment. "All right," he agreed. "But why? Is there a reason why that's so important to you?"

Tabitha's brows drew together, confused by his response. "Because then I won't have to wake you up again."

"True. But I don't mind."

"Well, I do."

"Why?"

Silent seconds ticked by. Finally, she said, "If you must know, I like to take care of myself. I don't need or want a man to take care of me."

"Men aren't necessary in your world?"

"You're being ridiculous. Just show me how to light the fire."

"We all need someone, Tabitha."

"Of course. But I still want to learn how to light the stove."

"I'll teach you before you leave. It's a good skill to know."

"But you won't tell me now?" She felt irked.

"I'd like to light it for you. It's one small thing I can do for you. It would make me feel happy."

"But I don't want to be a burden. Not to you. Not to anyone."

"Why not?"

She didn't know what to say for a moment, because she felt so flabbergasted. "What do you mean, *why not*? I don't want to be some pampered, petted china doll. I take pride in my work. I like to work hard and do and accomplish things. Nothing is wrong with that."

"No," he agreed. "But I'm getting the feeling you want to carry the whole load, all the time. It will break you, Tabitha."

She took a quick breath. How could he know how weary she felt sometimes? Truth to tell, most of the time. "Sometimes I feel tired," she agreed. "But I can't afford to rely on anyone else. To make it in today's world, you have to stand on your own two feet."

"You can rest while you're here."

"I can't, and I won't."

"Why not?"

Now he was pushing her outside her comfort zone, and she didn't like it. "I don't know. And why are you asking?"

"You ask me personal questions. Why doesn't it go both ways?"

She frowned. Why did he have to bring fair play into it? "Fine. If you must know, I feel guilty if I sit too long. Like I'm wasting time, or something."

"Even when you're on vacation?"

"Yes. Especially while I'm here. I feel I owe you a debt for taking me in."

"You don't owe me anything."

"But you don't even want me here!" she exclaimed. "I know I've upset your peace and quiet."

"You're wrong," he told her. "I'm glad you're here."

"You are?"

"I was getting colder every day, Tabitha. Until you came and shocked some warmth into my life, I didn't know what I was missing."

She was speechless for a moment. "Really?"

"Yes." His strong hands cupped her shoulders. "*You,* just being you, has made a difference. Not you *doing* things. Just you. Spicy, sweet, emotional, caring...everything. You need to accept that you're enough, just as you are."

What a strange conversation to be having in a dark hallway with a man she'd only known for two days.

His words warmed her. And she found them strangely difficult to accept, too. "Thank you," she said awkwardly. "But I'm not so sure that's true."

His grip tightened for a moment. "Why not?"

"I don't think my boss would agree with that assessment. Performance is how he judges my worth."

"That's only because he cares about the money you bring in. What about your parents?"

"They love me for who I am," she admitted.

"And what about you?"

"I...I don't know." She wanted to change the subject. It was all well and good if she wanted to prod him outside of his comfort zone and ask him all sorts of personal questions, but she didn't like it turned on her. Not when it made her think too deeply on issues she'd rather leave undisturbed. "It's late. I'd like to get some sleep."

After a brief hesitation, he released her. "Goodnight, Tabitha."

"You mean good morning," she tried to joke.

She settled down near the stove. The wood floor felt hard beneath the sleeping bag, but at least it was warmer here.

She closed her eyes and tried not to think about Arnie's probing questions. Although he was reticent and slow moving, deep waters stirred in that man. Why did she get the feeling he saw more in her than she did in herself? And did he like what he saw?

CHAPTER FOURTEEN

THE ELECTRICITY WAS STILL OFF when Tabitha woke up. More than ever, she felt cut off from civilization, and marooned in a sea of white. No electricity, so no stove, hot water or lights. No phone, either, because Arnie's phone only worked by using electricity.

And her cell phone still got no reception. She'd checked. So there was no way to hear word from her parents regarding her father's looming surgery, either. And she could not turn on her computer, do her reports, or check for the e-mail she was expecting from her boss. Not that she could make it to work if he'd denied her request, of course.

What could she do with all of this time on her hands? Even worse, she uneasily wondered if electricity could be restored in a raging blizzard. This state of affairs could last for a long time.

After a breakfast of cold cereal and juice, she curled up on the couch with the latest Michael Crichton paperback in hand. The moan of the wind continually distracted her from the dimly lit pages.

She wished she had a copy of the *Wall Street Journal* or *Barron's*—anything normal to engage her mind. ...While she was at it, maybe she should wish for a mint latte and spring thaw, too.

Snow drifted in piles on the windowsill outside. The porch was covered in snow.

How much longer would the storm rage?

With the complete silence and dim lighting, the whole situation felt surreal. As if it wasn't the twenty-first century, but instead the eighteenth, and she and Arnie were trapped alone on the farm; maybe for weeks or months.

Her mind slipped deeper into the game of make-believe—something she hadn't done since she was a child, which was the last time when she'd had long stretches of time to dream and imagine.

She slid a glance at Arnie. He held his magazine tilted at an angle so the dim light could hit it. If the two of them were stuck here for months on end, they'd certainly get closer. Closer than he wanted, that was for sure. Eventually, his wall would crumble.

Why did she want that to happen? Why did she wish it would happen during the remaining few days she'd be trapped here?

As if sensing her scrutiny, his steady brown gaze met hers. He said, "You're not reading."

"I'm thinking."

"What about?"

"About how primitive our conditions are."

"We still have running water."

"It's dark and we're trapped," she pointed out. "Like in the olden days. You'd probably fit in just fine back then."

He relaxed more in his chair. "You think I belong in the old days?"

"You could," she agreed. "But not me. I'm not so good with boredom."

"Back then you'd wash clothes by hand, and dip candles. And you'd have a passel of young'uns to keep you busy."

Tabitha's face warmed as the quick, vivid thought of being the mistress of Arnie's house and caring for half a dozen of his children flashed through her mind. "As I said, I wouldn't fit in," she said, averting her face, pretending to look outside.

A long beat passed, and then he said, "You don't want children?"

"Of course. But a passel... Hardly. Two or three centuries ago, a home was all a woman had. I have a life. A job that means everything to me. When the time comes, I won't have more than two kids. I wouldn't be able to give more the attention they deserve."

Something flickered in his gaze.

She raised her brow. "Are you one of those men who think a woman's place is in the home?"

"No. But I think children should be given a higher priority than a career."

"You mean for a woman. Not for a man."

"No. I think family should be a man's first priority, too."

"You mean above your whole farm?" She found this hard to believe.

"Yes. If I was married and had kids, my wife and family would come first with me. Work never ends, and more people can be hired. A family can never be replaced."

Tabitha let his words sink in. They made her feel warm and secure...and faintly jealous. "Someday, if you ever let down that wall, you'll make a lucky woman very happy."

His lips tightened. "That won't happen for me."

How could he make such a blanket statement? "What a waste."

"You know nothing about me, Tabitha."

"I know more than you think. You loved your wife deeply. You're a war hero..." His jaw tensed, so she stopped. "I could go on. But I don't understand why you hole yourself up here on the farm, away from the world."

"I'm not a hermit." His dark eyes flashed.

"I know. You go to church and you have friends. But you're basically alone. You come home every night to an empty house. Why?"

"Drop it, Tabitha."

"Why are you choosing this life?"

He frowned and lifted his magazine again.

She frowned with frustration at the stubborn man beside her. Okay, so she'd pushed him again. Unfortunately, his wall seemed higher and thicker than ever before.

Her gaze scanned the room and fell upon the pictures on the mantel again. The clue to this man must lie there. Something in his past had made him close up. Was it something to do with his marriage to Theresa, his military career, or his parents?

Then she mentally put on the brakes. Why *was* she pushing him so hard? More importantly, why did she care so much? It was none of her business. They were virtual strangers. In a few days she'd leave and would probably never see him again.

Melancholy slid through her at the thought, and she realized that she cared about him, although they'd only just met. And she cared that he was suffering from deep hurt from his past. Her gaze returned to the photos again. Should she ask more questions, or should she back off?

❀ ❀ ❀ ❀ ❀

Tabitha had hit a sore spot. Arnie liked being alone. Again, he reassured himself of this fact. In any case, long ago he'd made his bed, and now he would lie in it, as his father used to say.

Tabitha turned to him now with a bright smile. Caution raised a yellow flag in his mind. Clearly, she'd just plotted a new way to extract information from him.

Why did she care? Or maybe, like she'd said before, she had a curious mind. She liked to ferret out the answers to puzzles, and clearly she was bored.

Maybe he should suggest a game. The more mind intensive, the better. Before she could speak, he said, "Want to play chess?"

She blinked. "Well, sure. I love chess."

"Great." He retrieved the game and quickly assembled the pieces on the board. He chose dark wood pieces for his army, and she chose light. Maybe the colors were symbolic of their lives.

The melancholy thought surprised him. But then again, maybe it shouldn't. Before Tabitha had arrived he'd been content, but she'd brought such warmth and sunshine into his home that it would seem empty when she left.

His life would feel empty.

He frowned.

❀ ❀ ❀ ❀ ❀

"Ladies first."

"I know what you're trying to do." Tabitha moved her first chess piece.

"What do you mean?"

"You want to distract me, so I'll stop asking questions."

"Yes."

They played silently for a while.

"I'm sorry," she said. "I don't mean to be nosy. I just want to understand you better."

"Why?"

"I care. And I really like you, Arnie. I want you to be happy."

"I'm happy right now, playing this game with you."

She smiled, and when he smiled back, her heart somersaulted. "All right," she said softly. "No more questions. For now."

The morning passed quietly as they played three games of chess. Tabitha won only one of them. Then they played Uno until lunchtime. Tabitha won most of these games, until she noticed that Arnie kept losing with high scoring cards in his hands—the cruel ones, which would make her draw lots of cards.

She pulled his latest failed hand from the table and scanned it. She frowned. "What are you doing?"

He said nothing.

"You have to be *mean* to win this game, Arnie. I'm not holding back. I just made you draw eight cards!"

"I had other cards to play."

Tabitha gaped. "It doesn't work that way. Not if you want to win."

He smiled, but said nothing.

She crossed her arms. "Come on, now. This has got to be fifty-fifty."

"I need to be cruel to you?"

"You have to come out with both guns blazing. Don't let me win!"

"I'm not *letting* you win, Tabitha. You don't appreciate kindness?"

She stared at him. "This is a card game. Not real life."

"You want me to be ruthless and cutthroat?"

"Yes. Bring it on." Eagerly, she dealt the cards again. He gave her a smile, but puzzlement lurked in his eyes. She tacked on, "Don't tell me you play this way with your friends."

"Of course not." He gathered up his cards in one big hand and flicked a glance at them.

"Then why with me?" She slapped down her first card.

"Sometimes women have...delicate feelings."

"Oh, pooh," she said. "I don't need to be mollycoddled, and neither do any women I know." Arnie threw down a draw four card, and she grinned. "*Now* we've got a game."

They played more cards, and Tabitha's hand grew unwieldy and thick with cards.

Arnie was good. He definitely had the killer instinct. Maybe even sharper than her own. He won that game easily, and the next two, as well.

Tabitha stacked the cards. "I can see how a thin-skinned person could get rattled," she admitted. "Thanks for toning it down so I could win a few rounds."

"It's nice to play with someone who doesn't get upset."

"Who gets upset?"

He said nothing for a moment, as if reluctant to answer. Finally, he said, "Theresa. She said that my winning all the time was a power trip. If I loved her, I'd treat her with kindness."

Tabitha didn't know what to think about that. It wasn't in her nature to want to win because someone lobbed her fat, slow balls. She'd rather take her victories where she'd earned them. But maybe Theresa had been a gentler, more sensitive personality. Likely.

A frown creased Arnie's brow, as if he was sorry he'd said anything remotely negative about his dead wife.

Quickly, Tabitha said, "Losing all the time would get old, I'm sure."

The tension in his shoulders relaxed a little, and he stood. "How about lunch?"

❊ ❊ ❊ ❊ ❊

After lunch, the light seemed dimmer outside, and therefore darker inside. Tabitha prowled about the kitchen and living room. Anxiety grew for her father. She'd done her best to set aside her worry this morning. The games had helped. But now she couldn't ignore it any longer.

When would his surgery be? Today?

Although she knew the phone was dead, she lifted the receiver yet again to check. Nothing. Frustration climbed higher within her. This unpleasant feeling mixed with the eerie howl of the wind outside. How she hated that sound. How she wished this interminable storm would end! How much longer would she be trapped here?

If she knew what was happening with her father, she'd feel so much better.

Arnie moved into the kitchen and filled a glass with water. He left the faucet dripping a little to prevent the pipes from freezing. By tactic agreement, they'd elected to keep the refrigerator door shut as much as possible to prevent the cold air from escaping. Although Tabitha supposed they could throw the food into the storm to keep cool. One good thing about this miserable blizzard was that at least the perishables wouldn't go bad.

On his way back to the living room Arnie paused beside her. He felt like a strong, warm presence. "Anything wrong?"

Tabitha flapped her hand toward the window. "That *storm!* I want to get out. I feel trapped. I wish I knew what was happening with my dad."

"I have a cell phone," he said quietly. "You can use it, if you'd like."

"Thank you." She remembered her own cell phone, and that she'd been unable to get any bars of reception this morning. "Do you think you can get a signal?"

"I'll try." He moved to the end corner of the counter, where Tabitha noticed a pile of keys, a black wallet and a silver cell phone. He moved it through the air. After a moment, he shook his head. "Only one bar."

But he had received a little signal. An idea sprang to mind, and she darted for her room and retrieved her own cell phone. Maybe she couldn't get a strong enough signal to talk, but maybe, just maybe, she could download her voice mail. At least she'd recharged the phone when she'd first arrived. Perhaps that would help it pick up signals. Or maybe she was just thinking wishfully.

Phone turned on, she wandered through the icy back part of the house, holding her cell phone up and out in different directions, trying to get a signal. Probably the higher, the better, she assumed. And maybe pointing to the west would be best, because it would be closer to Buffalo, the nearest city. At least that was her reasoning. She had no idea, really, where the nearest cell tower might be. The western rooms of the house were the kitchen or Arnie's bedroom.

She was hesitant to pursue the latter idea, and returned to the relative warmth of the kitchen. She picked up a tiny signal where Arnie had stood at the counter.

A new idea came to mind. The other night, when Arnie had gathered up blankets for her, she'd noticed a window in his room that faced west. Perhaps that would be her best hope for success. And the higher she stood, the better.

Arnie watched from his chair. "Any luck?"

"No. Do you mind if I try in your room?"

"Of course not."

"Thanks." Tabitha grabbed a kitchen chair and hefted it up in her arms. It was heavier than she'd expected, because it was made of all solid, polished wood.

Arnie rose surprisingly fast. "Let me help you." He pulled it from her arms.

"I'm not a pip squeak, you know."

He looked down at her with quiet amusement, all broad strength. "A man can be helpful sometimes."

She knew he referred to their discussion last night, when she'd said she didn't need a man's help. Maybe he was right. Maybe she should enjoy a man's help while she had it. Not that she *needed* it, of course.

Unable to help herself, she smiled and affected a southern accent. "Well, aren't you the manly man?... Ah do declare, how *did* I get along without you all my life?"

His white teeth flashed in a grin, and for a dizzying moment, Tabitha realized how very handsome he was. Heart beating quicker, she wiggled her fingers toward the hall. "In your room, if you please."

"Yes, ma'am."

Inside the room, Tabitha dropped the ridiculous accent. "Near the window, if you don't mind."

Ahead of her, he deposited the chair where she asked, still looking faintly amused. Eager to test her theory, Tabitha hurried the remaining distance and vaulted upon it.

She misjudged her forward momentum and the slipperiness of her socks. Her feet skidded, and her arms flailed for one agonizing, heart stopping moment.

She was going to fall. She was about to break her head open.

CHAPTER FIFTEEN

FEAR SHOT THROUGH TABITHA'S mind as her feet skated out from under her. And then Arnie's big hands gripped her waist, steadying her.

She clutched his arm for support. "Thanks," she squeaked, trembling. "You must think I'm silly."

His concerned frown eased into another smile. "I'm not sure what to think of you, Tabitha. But silly is not at the top of the list."

Her heart skidded to slower pace. "I hope you have good adjectives for me, too," she said. "Not just stubborn and bullheaded, silly and nosy."

He smiled even more, and laugh lines crinkled from the corners of his wonderful, warm brown eyes. "I have great ones. But I don't want to add 'big head' to the list, so I won't tell you."

Tabitha's mouth opened in pretend outrage, but then she couldn't suppress her smile. She liked it when he teased her.

His warm hands released her, and that reminded her why she was in this position in the first place. She tilted her phone toward the window and the reception bars doubled.

"Yes!" The bars flickered as another gust of wind buffeted the house. "Come on," she murmured. "Come back to me."

The bars strengthened again. Maybe the reception wasn't good enough to complete a call, but perhaps it was enough to check her voice mail. She'd seen in that one flicker that she had two messages.

Pressing speaker phone, so she could still hear the phone while holding it aloft, she waited for another strong bar and then scrolled through the list. One was from a friend, and could wait. The other was from her mother's cell. Tabitha pressed to listen.

"...bitha," the message broke up, "surgery...two this afternoon. Soonest avail...call later. 'Bye."

"This afternoon?" Tabitha replayed the message. It wasn't much better, but the gist remained clear. "Two o'clock today?"

"It's two now."

Now? Tabitha felt suddenly shaky. Her father was going under the knife right now. He could die any minute, right on the operating table.

Of course, she knew the doctors were skilled, and every precaution would be taken, but still... Today he could live. Or die. Tabitha stood still, shivering, and hugged her arms to herself.

"Come down, Tabby," Arnie said gently.

Blindly, she accepted his hand and stepped down from the chair.

Moving without thinking, she returned to the warm kitchen, where Arnie pushed the chair under the table.

Tabitha pulled out another chair and sat. She felt shaky, and pressed her hands to face and swallowed back the growing ache in her throat. Now was the time to pray, but what should she say? It had been so long. Would God even listen to her?

Don't let him die. Please don't let him die!

Her prayers felt weighted by lead, as if they went no higher than the ceiling. Was God close? Did he hear her? She felt frozen by fear.

Arnie silently took the chair opposite her. Tabitha wiped her face. She whispered, "I'm scared."

His big hands covered hers. "Want me to pray?"

She nodded.

He spoke in a quiet, low voice, "Father, please protect Daniel and guide the surgeon's hands. We pray for good health for him, and for a complete and quick recovery."

"Amen." Tabitha looked up. "Thank you."

His grip tightened, and his dark gaze held hers, steadying her still more. "I'll keep praying this afternoon."

She nodded, "Thank you." After a moment he released her, and Tabitha immediately missed his secure warmth. She wished she possessed his strong faith.

Her father had to live. She loved him so much. Why hadn't she come in November when her mother had asked her? If her father died, she'd never forgive herself.

❄ ❄ ❄ ❄ ❄

Tabitha curled up on the couch with a thriller novel in hand, but she couldn't concentrate. Worry ached like a tight lump in her throat. She prayed again, and hoped God was listening. Logically, she knew he was.

Maybe now would be a good time to read Arnie's Bible again. Maybe something in it would speak to her heart.

Quietly slipping it from the shelf, she glanced at Arnie, but he didn't seem to be paying any attention. He was reading a sports magazine.

Tabitha pulled the heavy, soft, leather-bound book into her hands and opened it. She didn't know where to start, so she decided to begin where it fell open. The Psalms.

She read David's poems as he cried out to God from the pit of despair. God always answered him. She especially liked Psalm 42:5.

"You okay?" Arnie asked. Concern warmed his brown eyes.

Tabitha flipped the Bible closed. "I'm trying. But I feel so worried. I hate it when I can't do anything."

"I know what you mean." He seemed to withdraw, as if looking into his past.

More silence passed, and then Arnie surprised her by saying, "Want to play a game to pass the time?"

"Thank you, but I couldn't." Tabitha stood and paced. Her steps took her to the fireplace and his pictures, and the mysteries behind each one. She fingered the one in which he looked grim—when he'd joined active duty.

What had caused the pain in his eyes? And why did he still suffer? For she knew he did. Something had happened when he'd joined active duty that had changed him forever.

"What happened to you?" she said softly. "Will you tell me?"

Arnie regarded her for a long moment. Unknown emotions battled across his features. "I'll tell you a little," he said at last, as if the words were wrenched from him at great cost.

Tabitha felt honored that he would trust her. Wanting to be closer to him, she perched on the couch beside his chair and met his gaze soberly.

He drew a deep breath. "Theresa died the weekend I finished school for my M.B.A."

She gasped.

He looked away. "I came home that night and my parents told me there'd been a terrible crash. Theresa was dead. I couldn't believe it." He drew a ragged breath. "I didn't want to believe it. It was Theresa's birthday. I was late...I was going to join her at her party, and then..."

He took another unsteady breath. "It all passed in a blur. It didn't seem real. The funeral. People saying they were sorry. I had a hole inside of me the size of a combine. I went through the motions for a week, maybe two. I'd planned to move back to Newbough, but suddenly I couldn't. All the memories of us growing up together... Everywhere I went I saw her. But she wasn't there."

Grief etched into his features, and compassion filled Tabitha's heart. She wished she could take away his pain. And she wished she hadn't asked the question and made him live through this agony again.

Arnie swallowed. "I couldn't stay," he said in a low voice.

"So you joined active duty?" It seemed the logical conclusion.

"Yeah," he said roughly. "Made my C.O. happy. He'd been trying to convince me to do it. That day."

"The day Theresa died?"

He didn't answer, but he didn't need to. The tension humming through his body said it all.

"I'm so sorry." She closed her hand around his. His fingers tightened on hers.

"It was a mistake," he said quietly.

"What was?"

"Joining active. I wasn't thinking clearly."

"How could it be a mistake? You saved a man's life."

His grip loosened, and reluctantly she let him go.

"Good did come from it," he agreed slowly. But he didn't sound completely convinced about it. Tabitha wondered what he wasn't telling her.

A new thought came to her mind. "What did your parents say? You were going to work on the farm, you said."

"They understood." The familiar, shuttered look came down, masking the bleakness in his eyes. "They always supported me, no matter what I did."

"I can see that they were proud of you. I can tell by looking at the picture of the three of you together."

He sat quietly for a long moment, and then he said in a low voice, "They were."

"Then why do you look so sad?"

"We all have our regrets, Tabitha." His walls were back now. He was finished exposing a little of his heart and his past to her.

Tenderness swelled in her. She wished she could help ease the hurt he was carrying inside him every day.

Tabitha didn't know what to say to express all she was feeling and thinking. And then she realized what Arnie had done. By revealing his pain, he'd taken her mind off of her father for a little while.

Tears prickled her eyes. "Thank you." Unthinkingly, her fingers curled around his forearm. She felt his strong, corded muscles tense, and then relax through the soft flannel. "And I'm sorry. I didn't mean to make you suffer through all that again."

"It's okay," he said roughly. "It happened a long time ago."

Maybe so, but clearly, he was still suffering.

Slowly, piece by piece, she was constructing a picture of what had happened to turn him into this lonely, hurting man. She wanted to help him, if she could, but first, she must find the remaining puzzle pieces to his past. Something wasn't right, and she intended to find out what it was.

Chapter Sixteen

AT SIX O'CLOCK, just after Tabitha helped Arnie light candles and set them on the mantel and the coffee table, the lights flickered on.

"Yes!" she cried out, and sprinted across the room to see if the phone was working. The dial tone buzzed in her ear. "I'm going to call my mom," she tossed over her shoulder. "Is that all right?"

"You don't need to ask." Humor lurked in his deep voice. "Do you need the number for the hospital?"

"I remember it."

Arnie watched her swiftly punch in the digits. One brow raised in surprise.

Tabitha grinned as the phone rang on the other end. "I have a thing for numbers," she confessed. "Give me any number, and I can memorize it. I write them in my mind so I see them, like a picture. Then they're always in my head."

After a number of delays, because apparently her father had been moved to a new room, Tabitha finally spoke to her mother. "Is Daddy okay?"

"So far, so good, honey." Nancy McCroy sounded weary. "He came out of surgery a little while ago. They haven't let me see him yet, but apparently he came through just fine."

Relief swept through her. "Thank goodness!"

"Apparently the first twenty-four hours are critical. I'll be watching him every single minute, you can be sure of that."

"You need to rest, too, Mom. Is there a place where you can sleep?"

"A chair." She sounded rueful.

"Can you get a hotel room—once Daddy's out of the woods, I mean?"

"We'll see. How are you, honey? Is Arnie taking good care of you?"

She glanced at her host. He slowly moved about the kitchen, preparing dinner. "He's taking wonderful care of me, Mom," she said softly.

A beat went by. "He is?" Interest sharpened Nancy's voice, and Tabitha flushed, realizing how that must have sounded.

"I mean," she said quickly, "he knows everything about surviving blizzards, and he grills a mean steak, too."

Her mother laughed. "So you'll be okay there another day or two? Did you get more time off?"

"I need to check my e-mails. But it's not as if I can get to work tomorrow. My boss will have to understand."

"I'm sure he will, honey. You're his best analyst. He knows what side his bread is buttered on."

"Mom."

"Well, it's true. You let that man work you to a nub!" Annoyance sharpened Nancy's voice. And then, "I'm sorry. I know how much your career means to you."

"Yes. But you and Daddy mean more. I love you guys." Tears hovered. "I can't wait to see you."

A pause elapsed. Her mother said in a choked voice, "We love you, too. I'll call tomorrow, okay?"

"Okay, Mom. 'Bye."

Tabitha hung up, and blinked back the tears. She loved her parents so much, and she was relieved that her father had made it through the surgery.

Arnie looked over one shoulder. "Your father's okay?"

"So far, so good." She joined him at the counter. "But Mom says the next twenty-four hours are critical."

"Then we'll keep praying."

Tabitha nodded. "What are you making?" She felt comfortable at the counter with him, watching him prepare their meal. So much had changed since Saturday night, when she'd first arrived on his doorstep, and he'd acted like a growly bear.

"Spaghetti."

"Can I help?" Water already boiled on the back burner, and he pulled down a jar of sauce.

Amusement tugged at the corners of his mouth. "You told your mother I make the grade?"

Tabitha's cheeks warmed. "I didn't mean it like that."

His smile edged higher, and she realized that he was teasing. "A man like me couldn't make it over your horizon back home. Is that what you're saying?"

"A man like you could make any woman's horizon." He eyed her with surprised interest. "I *mean*," she said, but then floundered. What *was* she trying to say?

Arnie watched her as he dumped spaghetti sauce in the pan. Amusement and a darker something else flickered in his eyes.

She willed her warm flush to subside. What was she, fifteen? "I mean, you're a terrific man. And your cooking skills are a bonus. I know most of my friends would snap you up just for that."

"If I lived in New York City." He turned his attention back to the stove and dropped a fistful of pasta into the boiling water.

"I guess that would be necessary," she agreed, dipping her finger in the sauce to taste it.

"None of your friends care for the country life?"

"Are you looking?"

"No, I'm not looking, Tabitha." An edge sharpened his words. After a pause, he asked, "What would they miss most about the city, do you think?"

"Dressing to the nines everywhere," Tabitha said promptly, thinking of several of her friends who lived for fashion. "And restaurants on every street corner. And Broadway shows, of course. And lights and action twenty-four hours a day."

Tabitha sensed that he'd withdrawn. Teasing, and then closed. He was impossible to figure out.

"I'd better check my e-mails. I'm expecting one from my boss."

He made no move to stop her.

❈ ❈ ❈ ❈ ❈

Tabitha returned to the kitchen a little while later, filled with excitement over the e-mail she had received from her boss. Delicious, warm smells of oregano and spaghetti sauce tantalized her nose.

"Get your e-mail?" Arnie had relaxed again, she was glad to see.

"Yes. And guess what?"

He smiled as he drained pasta into a metal colander in the sink. "You got a promotion?"

"Yes!" Tabitha spun on her toes, not caring at all how ridiculous she might look. "I'm promoted to the investment division!" She hugged herself.

Instead of waiting to tell her the news in their rescheduled meeting, Robert had dropped the piñata in her e-mail. It felt like Christmas all over again.

"Your dream job?"

"I've been working toward this for seven years. At Brown's Bros., everyone starts in research analysis, and if we show promise, we're moved up. Only one promotion is given each year to the investment division. It's a huge deal. It means I'll work with big clients, or even better, help run a mutual fund. Either way means a lot more money and options." She fell silent, unable to fathom how her life was about to change.

Arnie patiently waited for her to continue as he pulled down plates. She said at last, amazed, "He trusts me. You won't believe what else he told me."

He raised an eyebrow.

"I'm not sure what you know about *Barron's*. It's a financial publication."

"I've read it."

Tabitha smiled. "Then you probably know that every January they publish a Roundtable discussion. They publish it over the course of several weeks. Anyway, the people invited for this Roundtable discussion are the best on Wall Street, and it's an honor to be invited. Well, apparently one of the original panel members couldn't attend this year, so they asked my boss to join."

"That's great for him."

"I haven't told you the best part. My boss got picked partly because of me, he said. Brown's Bros.' research reports are rated top quality now. People who invest using our star rating system have done unbelievably well over the last seven years—even through corrections in the market."

"And you're one of his analysts."

"Yes." Then she said, "Okay, don't think I have that big head you were talking about, but my boss has told me over and over again that I'm the best he has. Anyway, the whole point is that Robert—my boss—wants me to send him my stock picks for this next year! And he'll report them at the Roundtable. Can you believe what an honor that is? He's going to put his whole financial reputation on the line and trust my opinion."

Arnie remained silent for a moment. "Sounds like he's doing himself a favor."

"What do you mean?"

"Sounds like he's riding on your coattails."

"No. It's my job to help the company...to help him. He's a Brown, you know."

"Is he going to credit you with his picks?"

"Of course not. That's not necessary."

He said nothing.

"You don't know how it works in the financial world."

"Sure, I do. And it sounds to me as if it's about time you got that promotion and pay raise."

Tabitha felt giddy again, thinking about the future. "I had to prove myself. It's all a part of the process. Everything is working out just like I dreamed."

"I'm glad. Did he give you the time off you wanted?"

"Yes. I'll have to be back next Wednesday. In the meantime, he asked me to finish up two projects and e-mail them by Friday."

"I thought you were on vacation."

"I'm not doing anything else right now. It'll keep my brain active."

He nodded, and she saw nothing but his broad back as he prepared the last of the meal. He said nothing more, but Tabitha suddenly wondered if he thought she'd meant his company and their time together was boring to her. Nothing could be further from the truth.

She set the table, and in short order they'd served up a meal of spaghetti, toasted garlic bread, and microwaved green beans. Arnie said grace, and Tabitha fell to her meal. He didn't look upset. But then, as she knew so well, he was hard to read. He kept all of his feelings tucked up inside.

"This is delicious," she offered.

"Thanks."

Hesitantly, she said, "I really appreciate that you're letting me stay here."

His eyebrows rose. "Why are you thanking me again?"

"I want you to know how much I appreciate everything you've done for me. And...and...this time with you has been special. I don't want you to think...." Goodness, she was not saying this well.

"You're not bored with me?"

"No! You definitely do not bore me. But I'm used to working all the time. It's hard to stop, even for a vacation. My mind wants to run on, still doing and thinking all the things I usually do."

"I understand. I feel like that during planting, the entire growing season, and harvest, too."

"So you know."

"We're not so different. We both want to be the best at what we do. For me, it's bringing in a good, productive crop. I get satisfaction from that. You get satisfaction from seeing your stocks go up. And your research validated."

Tabitha smiled. Of course he understood. He was a deep, intelligent, hardworking man. A wonderful man...

A wonderful, lonely man.

Her smile faded, thinking about him being alone, day after day, when she left. And that would be soon. An empty feeling opened up inside her. Would she see him again after that?

She couldn't think about that. Besides, she wanted to help him, if she could. He couldn't be alone forever. He needed a wife.

Discomfort pricked her at the thought of him being with an unknown woman. But it wasn't as if *she* was the woman for him.

Tabitha swallowed hard on a green bean that didn't want to go down properly. *Bite the bullet,* she told herself. *Put it out there. Make him think about it. It's for his own good.*

Drawing a breath, she spoke before she could reconsider, "You need a wife, Arnie."

CHAPTER SEVENTEEN

ARNIE FROWNED and leaned back in his chair.

"I know you loved Theresa. I know you still do. But do you think she would want you to be lonely for the rest of your life?"

"Tabitha." Warning growled in his voice.

"*Okay.* I know I'm being pushy. But I'll leave soon, and I hate the idea of you eating dinner alone for the next fifty years. Wouldn't it be nice to have someone here who loves you? Someone with whom you could share your life?"

"Why do you care?"

"You try to hide it, but you have a big, warm heart. You have so much to give, Arnie."

"No, I don't. I could never love anyone else the way I loved Theresa. A woman deserves her husband's whole heart. I don't have one to give."

"Yes, you do. And you have plenty to give. Look at how you've cared for me ever since I got here."

"Caring for a stranger is not the same thing as loving a wife."

That hurt a little. "I'm still a stranger to you?"

He drew a slow breath. "You know you're not. But you don't know me. You don't know what you're saying."

"What deep, dark secret are you hiding, then? Why are you so sure that you can't fall in love again?"

He lifted the napkin from his lap and set it on the table. His fist clenched around it. "Let it go." His brown eyes had turned black, and tense lines grooved the sides of his mouth. She'd upset him. Again, she had pushed him too hard.

"I'm sorry," she said softly. "But please, will you at least tell me why you close off like this?"

"Tabitha," he growled.

She knew she should drop the subject, but found it impossible. He'd taken her in and helped her. And he was hurting. The least she could do was try to help him. While that sounded noble, it wasn't the complete truth. Plain and simple, she hated to see him in pain. "Arnie..."

"I don't have what it takes," he said with a fierce frown.

"Why not?"

"Tabitha!" He stood abruptly and moved faster than normal to the counter. He blasted water into the sink and shoved his glass under it. His cup overflowed. Tension stiffened his shoulders.

"Please tell me. Why are you hurting so much? And why do you think you have to spend the rest of your life alone?"

He turned back to her. "Who are you spending your life with, Tabitha?"

She bobbled for a moment, startled to have the conversation turned back on her. "I...I don't have time for a relationship. But if I met the right man..."

"Would you?"

She stood, too. "Attack me if you want..."

"You want the truth from me? Then tell me the truth first."

"Okay, no. Probably not. My career comes first."

"Before everything else."

"I know it shouldn't be that way. I've been wrong to put my parents at the bottom of the list. But I plan to change that."

"How?"

"I'll visit more."

"Your dad misses you."

"He told you that?"

"No. But it's plain. And it's clear he's proud of you. He told me his daughter is a big, hotshot money girl in New York."

"I do want to be there for him. But I can't be two places at once. My job is in New York City."

"Then make a plan. You have a chance to make things right. Don't blow it."

For a second, she felt offended. And then insight dawned. "Did *you* blow it? With your parents, or with Theresa?"

"Let it go."

She searched his eyes. Although his words had hurt a little, he was right. Now it was his turn to come clean.

"Please tell me," she said softly.

A long moment passed, and she wondered if he'd speak at all.

"Today would have been my eleventh wedding anniversary."

She drew a startled breath. Eleventh! Not exactly an answer, but clearly another piece of the puzzle. "Why did you choose the twenty-sixth, again?"

"Theresa loved Christmas. She always hated to see it end. So she wanted to get married on the twenty-sixth. That way she'd always look forward to the day after Christmas."

"Did it work?"

Roughly, he said, "She didn't live to see our first anniversary."

"You weren't even married for a year?" Still newlyweds, and he'd lost her. She couldn't fathom how awful that must have been.

A muscle clenched in his jaw.

"I'm so sorry."

He drew a heavy breath. Pain vibrated from every tense sinew in his body. Rigid, bottled pain.

His eyes had dilated almost black, but she could still see a hint of the warm amber. A hint of the tender man who lived hidden inside his wall of ice, pain, and grief.

Tabitha's heart broke for him. She couldn't stand to see him suffer any longer.

Mentally prepared to accept his rejection, and with her heart suddenly beating hard with nerves, she stepped forward and wrapped her arms around him. After a hesitation, she put her head on his shoulder, too. She held him tightly, saying nothing, offering the only comfort she could give.

She felt the slow thunder of his heart, and the warmth of his body. She felt the tension in his muscles, and the rigid control he held over himself. She waited for him to reject her.

He did not.

His strong arms closed around her and his deep, ragged breaths stirred her hair. He wasn't crying, but he needed to. He held her tighter, his fingers digging into her side and her shoulder, and a deep shudder quaked through his big frame. Tabitha said nothing, but just held him tighter. Silent tears slipped down her cheeks, as if somehow she could weep for him.

They stood that way for a long time. Arnie's silent shudders stilled, and Tabitha sniffled softly against his shoulder. Finally he pulled back a bit. Only warm brown remained in his eyes. "You're crying for me?"

She wiped her cheeks. "I can't help it."

"Thanks."

"You're a terrific guy. I mean it."

He scanned her gaze. What did he see? Did he see half of what she saw in him—even though he tried so hard to hide it?

"Thanks, Tabby," he said again, and his warm lips settled across hers. A jolt of surprise went through her, and then a streak of fire. Before she had a chance to respond, he ended the caress.

He regarded her without smiling. Perhaps he was already regretting his impulsive action. She stepped back and strove for a normal tone. "Well, I don't know about you, but I'm hungry."

She returned to her chair and forked up a bite of spaghetti. Arnie sat too, and she felt his gaze upon her. For a second she didn't look up, hoping instead to cool the flush on her cheeks.

She had enjoyed his kiss again. Too much. But clearly, he'd meant it only as a "thank you." A gesture of gratitude. So she'd take it as no more, and she'd prove that to him now.

Affixing a bright smile to her lips, she said, "Want to play Clue after dinner? Or Uno?"

❋ ❋ ❋ ❋ ❋

Arnie looked at Tabitha' smile. She was trying so hard to keep things on an even keel between them. And she was determined to be friends, even when he was as touchy as a bear and sending her mixed signals.

For some reason, she truly seemed to like him. He felt as if he didn't deserve it. After all, he threw up walls, pushed her away, and to what end? To protect his heart?

He'd told her that he couldn't feel anymore. If that was true, then why did he kiss her again?

He did like her. A lot. If he was honest with himself, he wanted to relax his guard with her and see how their relationship might develop.

Dangerous thoughts. And appealing ones.

But maybe it wouldn't be dangerous. Wouldn't she leave in a couple of days? What harm could it do to open up his heart a little, and see if it could warm up? It wasn't as if he'd fall in love in two or three days. He'd known Theresa for years before he'd fallen in love with her.

So what would be the harm? It would be an experiment. A safe one. Tabitha would leave soon, and the relationship would end before things went too far.

Maybe if he could feel something for her, then he might be able to fall in love again.

Arnie had never considered remarrying. He'd failed Theresa, and he couldn't take the thought of failing someone else.

But Tabitha was right. He didn't want to live alone anymore. He longed for someone to love him.

Was that so selfish?

Pain and longing gripped him. When Tabitha had held him, a broken piece inside of him had stopped hurting.

He didn't want to spend the rest of his life alone. He wanted to love someone.

Was it possible? For years he'd thought it wasn't. But Tabitha had given him hope.

Would it be wrong to see if his heart could thaw a little? Because he did want to live again. He hadn't realized how fiercely until he'd kissed her the second time.

Time to stop hiding in the foxhole, buddy, he told himself. *What's it going to be?*

She waited with a hopeful smile tugging at her lips.

An unexpected jab of tenderness jolted through him.

So, he couldn't feel anything?

He was lying to himself.

He took a deep breath. Okay. He'd see where it went. One slow step at a time. "Feel like losing again? I'm all for Uno."

She grinned, clearly up for the challenge. "Get ready to eat your words."

❊ ❊ ❊ ❊ ❊

Tabitha finally said goodnight. As she readied for bed in her ice cold room, she realized that Arnie had finally relaxed this evening. It was as if he'd deliberately decided to lower his guard with her. She wondered why as she gathered up her heavy blankets and pillow and dragged all of it out to the living room again.

Arnie's door was shut. Again, she wondered how it was possible that he wasn't turning into a popsicle in his freezing room.

Near the pellet stove, she snuggled beneath the heavy blankets and thought about their embrace. And their kiss. A warm feeling slid through her, and she told herself to stop it. Warm feelings for him...*those* kind of feelings had no place in her life. They were foolish and self-destructive. That's all she needed—to lose her heart to him. No, thank you.

She remembered back to when he'd surprisingly let her hold him. He'd needed comfort, and she had been too happy to provide it.

He still felt terrible pain, eleven years after Theresa's death. He had loved her completely. Tabitha wondered if she'd ever find a man who loved her that much.

Her thoughts turned to something else he had said. *"I don't have what it takes."* Did he think he had failed as a husband for Theresa? She found this hard to believe. But perhaps there was another, undiscovered wound festering beneath his deeply buried pain.

What were the circumstances surrounding her car accident? And why did he think that joining the military had been a mistake?

Arnie needed to heal. He needed to be loved, too. Maybe she wasn't the right person for the last job, but she might be able to help a little with the first.

Perhaps it would help him to tell to her, a person he'd never see again, what was truly troubling him. Maybe then he could let the rest of the pain—or guilt—go, and he could live and love again.

It would make her happy to see the shadows leave Arnie's eyes. To see his handsome face relaxed, and his heart open to give all of the love hidden deep inside of him.

Then he'd be completely irresistible. Pain twisted through her. The perfect man for some lucky woman.

Chapter Eighteen

"Good morning," Tabitha said cheerily as Arnie entered the kitchen the next morning. She'd woken up at five a.m. and decided she wanted waffles. It was six o'clock now.

"Morning," he mumbled, and headed for the coffee maker. This morning he wore his usual blue jeans and a dark blue shirt that emphasized the breadth of his muscular shoulders. Its crisp lines somehow emphasized the angles and planes of his jaw and cheekbones. His buzz looked damp from the shower, and stood straight up on his head.

Eyeing it, she said, "Does your hair do that naturally? Or do you use gel?" It was a question she'd always wondered when she'd seen men with a similar hairstyle, although she'd never had the gumption to ask.

His lips twitched. "Didn't know my personal grooming was so interesting to you."

"It's not *you*," she told him. "I've always wondered how men get their buzzed hair to stick straight up. I mean, it's probably a half inch long, isn't it? It's defying gravity."

He grinned and eyed her for a long moment. Tabitha began to feel uncomfortable. She said, "Well, never mind, then, if it's some ancient Chinese secret."

Laughter lines crinkled. "You remember that old commercial?"

She smiled. "I saw it on TV Land."

He ran a hand through his hair, and to her fascination it sprang back up. "Guess."

"I'd need to feel it to make my best guess."

"All right." He dipped his head a bit so she could touch it.

Heart skipping faster than normal, she patted the top of his head with her palm. "Springy. Spiky."

"Ready to guess?"

"Not yet." Bolder this time, she ran her fingers through his hair. It felt soft and spiky at the same time. An unusual combination. And nice. That realization disturbed her, so she quickly withdrew her hand. However, she rubbed her fingers together, and sniffed them.

He gave her an unreadable look. "Well?" The word sounded gruff.

She smiled and sniffed her fingers again. "Nice. Definitely gel."

"Now you know all my secrets."

"Hardly."

He pulled out two mugs. "Should I be flattered? You're fascinated with my hair, and you want to know every detail of my life."

Embarrassment warmed her cheeks. What was wrong with her? She hadn't blushed this much since high school. What was it about him that made her feel vulnerable, and even uncharacteristically shy, like now?

It felt as if he might be flirting with her. The idea made her pulse skitter and her spirit take wing.

"You're a complex man. I told you I like puzzles."

"So when you've found your answers, will you be finished with me?"

"Of course not. I don't use people, and then discard them. I like you. That will never change."

He leaned back against the counter as the coffee maker bubbled behind him. The delicious smell of freshly perked coffee tantalized her nose.

It felt so intimate to be standing here with him first thing in the morning. He was fresh from his shower, and the coffee brewing smelled heavenly. Tabitha liked it all. She liked it a lot.

Although she'd previously claimed to be bored at his house, right now there was nowhere else she'd rather be.

"So we're friends," he said.

"Of course we're friends. Or do you still want to chase me off with a ten foot pole?"

"No." The coffee was ready, and he poured a mug and handed it to her. His fingers grazed hers as she accepted it. Alarmingly, she liked the contact and his glance, too, which held hers afterward.

She took a tentative sip. Boiling hot. Being burned was not in her plans. Not now, and not in the future, either. "Thank you. You know I owe you big. When this is all over I'll take you out to dinner. Is there a good restaurant in Newbough?"

"One. And you owe me nothing."

"Except for my life."

"Make more apple pies, and we'll call it even."

She couldn't help but smile. "You're awfully easy to please."

"I know what I like." His dark amber gaze held hers.

For once in her life, she was at a loss for words. Oh, she liked him. She liked him a whole lot more than she wanted to admit.

Biting her lip, she turned back to the waffle maker. Smoke curled upward.

"Oh, no!" She pried out the black waffle with a spatula.

"Toss it to me." When she did, Arnie tossed it over his shoulder and into the trash.

"Good shot," she complimented, and poured more batter into the waffle iron. "Luckily, I can start over fresh. Out with the old, and in with the new. If only life could be so neat." She closed the waffle lid.

"People are messy."

"I know. They don't stay in the metaphorical waffle iron, where they belong. They leak out the sides and create all sorts of problems."

Arnie was like that. If not for this storm, he would never have mixed into the batter of her life at all. Now here he was, less than two feet away, and she couldn't imagine her life without him in it. Or without his warmth and humor, his deep compassion, and his strength, too. And without his wonderful kisses that licked an unwanted flame through her blood.

He was messy all right. Messy and dangerous.

❀ ❀ ❀ ❀ ❀

Tabitha wanted to complete both projects for her boss today. A tall order, but not impossible. First, however, she called her mother and learned that her father had held his own all night, but was still in critical condition. Nancy promised to call back that evening. Tabitha breathed a prayer to God for her father's swift healing.

Then she set to work at the kitchen table with her laptop. If she worked steadily all day, she should finish by the evening. Thankfully, before she'd left work on Friday she'd downloaded all of her research onto a flash drive. Now she'd finish sifting through the information, and then type up her reports and configure the data into graphs.

Snow still swirled outside, but the wind didn't seem quite as furious as it had yesterday. Snow drifted as high as the windows in a few places, and covered the porch in a deep white blanket.

The storm would end soon. And then she'd have to leave.

Tabitha forced herself to concentrate on the numbers on her screen. *Think about work,* she told herself. *Don't think about Arnie. You're getting too attached to him.*

Pearls of wisdom. Too bad her gaze kept straying to him all morning long.

Eventually, he disappeared into the frozen wasteland at the back of the house. He returned after a bit to grab his coat, and then retreated again. Craning her neck to peer down the hall, Tabitha watched him disappear into his study. What was he doing in there? Bills? Or farm business, perhaps.

She struggled to focus on her own work. The numbers, which in the past had always gripped her with a mystical sort of appeal, failed to sing to her today. Logically, she parsed through each paragraph of her report, but when it came time to give her star rating for the company, her fingers stilled, and her mind went blank.

What was wrong with her?

It was lunch time. Maybe she needed a break. After saving her work, she turned off the computer and mixed up several cans of tuna salad, and then fixed Arnie two sandwiches and put two of the pickles he liked on his plate. Munching on her own sandwich, she brought his down the hall to the study. The temperature seemed to drop five degrees with every step she took.

Arnie sat in his chair, looking bigger than usual, bundled in his blue winter coat. His ears tips were red.

"I thought you might be hungry."

He darted a startled glance at her, and smiled when he saw the plate. "Thanks, Tabby."

"Do you want your hat and gloves? It's an ice box back here."

"I'm okay."

Crossing her arms to keep warm, she glanced at the screen. "Is that a financial report? ...If you don't mind me asking."

"Yes. I'm reading over balance sheets from the last few years. I'm thinking of buying a couple hundred acres. I want to see if I can afford it."

She moved closer, shuddering now with cold. "I'm a whiz with numbers, you know. Do you have them saved on a flash drive? You could bring it to the kitchen. After lunch I could help you evaluate the data. I mean, if you'd like my help."

"I would. Thank you."

"Good. I'm going now, because I'm turning into a popsicle."

His chuckle followed her down the hall.

Humming happily, Tabitha finished eating her sandwich and loaded up her report again. She zipped through the numbers again, and suddenly the star rating was clear. Why hadn't she seen it before? Quickly, she finished the report. By the time she'd finished the graphs, too, Arnie entered the kitchen bearing his empty plate and a flash drive.

"Pull up a chair when you're ready," she invited.

He washed the dishes, and then hooked a chair backwards and straddled it beside her. "I know you're an analyst, but what is your job, exactly?"

"I research companies and study their financial reports. Sometimes I go on location and meet the manager and tour the facility. I talk to the workers, too. But mostly I concentrate on the financial data and see how strong the company is. I evaluate how much risk an investor would take on to buy shares. I'm usually right," she said, without conceit. "Although the stock market doesn't always agree with me in the short term."

"You recommend long term investments."

"I recommend investing in a company for as long as it's strong, healthy, and has the potential to grow."

"So you assess risk?"

"Yes."

Slowly, he said, "I could use your advice, then. I'm thinking about buying five hundred acres from a neighbor."

"How many acres do you have now?"

"Almost two thousand."

"*Arnie*. And you farm all that by yourself?"

"No. I hire help. You're sure you wouldn't mind looking through my financial statements?" Tension laced his words. Clearly, he was not used to asking for help. "I could pay for your advice."

She only smiled. Bit by bit, he was opening up to her. He'd just offered her another olive branch of trust. Did he realize that? A glance into his direct, measuring gaze told her he did. "I owe *you,* remember. Besides, my policy is 'no money between friends.' Let's check out your drive."

After pulling up his financial records, Arnie showed her the page where he'd estimated the costs of the expansion and the improvements he'd need to make. Then he showed her the files of his yearly business statements.

Tabitha read the first file, and then scrolled quickly through the others, and jotted down notes. The first business statement shocked her speechless. No debt at all. And the profit margins...she couldn't believe it. The following reports collaborated the first. She stared at him. "You're rich!"

He smiled. "I've invested most of it in low risk bonds because I've wanted to expand for a few years. Do you think the expense for the land is worth it?"

She scanned her notes again. "Frankly, you can afford to take on any risk you want. I think you know that. As far as expenses weighing against future profit... It'll take a few years to come even. But corn prices are stable. If the land produces like you think it will, you'll be sitting pretty before you know it."

"I can afford to take on any risk I want?"

"Yes."

"Taking a risk doesn't come easily to me."

"Me, either," she admitted, and grinned. "But I'm good at evaluating them for other people."

He smiled. Slowly he began to tell her about other plans he had for the farm, and he scratched out numbers on a paper before them. Tabitha listened, warmed by the enthusiasm in his voice and the small smile he gave her as he detailed innovative new ideas for his farm.

She forgot all about the reports she wanted to finish. The afternoon flew by with both of their heads nearly touching over the papers. She felt amazed by his sharp business insight. More, she felt privileged that this reserved man had decided to trust her with his dreams. She wanted, more than anything, for him to succeed. And to be happy.

❄ ❄ ❄ ❄ ❄

By the time evening rolled around, Tabitha had detailed a few investment ideas for Arnie's free cash, as well.

"Thanks, Tabby." He gathered together all the papers they'd scribbled on and his flash drive, too. "In the real world, I'd owe you a fortune for the advice you just gave me."

"Oh, nonsense." She lifted her palms, as if to weigh something. "Let's see, what's worth more? Saving my life, or a few scraps of advice? No contest, if you want my opinion."

"I interrupted your work," he reminded her. "How much do you have left?"

"One report." Tabitha glanced at her watch. Already five o'clock.

Return to work? Or quit for the day? Normally, the question would be simple. Work. Disturbingly, she wanted to cook dinner for Arnie instead. It was her turn, after all.

"Maybe I'll work a few more minutes," she said reluctantly. "What do you want to eat tonight? It's my turn to cook, don't forget."

He regarded her with faint amusement. "Didn't know we were taking turns."

"Now you do. What do you want?"

"Know how to make beef stroganoff?"

"I do. I'll start at six."

He moved away, and Tabitha became absorbed in her next report. When she next came up for air, Arnie was in the kitchen, and meat sizzled in a pan.

She leaped up and scurried to his side. "What are you doing?" she exclaimed. "This is my job. Please go and relax. I'll take over now."

He didn't move, so she frowned up at him. "You're not being very cooperative."

"Finish your report."

"I have hours of work left. I told you I'd do this, now kindly vamoose!"

A smile tugged at his lips. "Step out of my kitchen, madam. Or I'll remove you."

Warmth flushed through her body. "Are you threatening to manhandle me?"

"Promises work better than threats."

"You are a maddening man."

"Because I won't do what you want?" He chuckled.

Sweetly, she said, "I promised to make dinner. Now, will you make me welsh on that promise?"

He chuckled deep, from his belly. "Good try, Tabitha." Then, to her shock, his warm hands closed around her waist and her feet flew off the floor. She found herself deposited beside the table.

Tabitha gasped with astonishment at the ease with which he'd carried her. And she trembled with quick temper, too. "Don't do that."

His smile vanished. "I'm sorry."

She crossed her arms. "Please don't do that again."

"I won't. But why won't you let me help you with dinner?"

"Because... And this is *not* about control issues."

"It isn't? You really don't have to do everything."

The phone rang, and Tabitha sprang to answer it. "I want to," she said, and snatched up the phone. "And that does not mean I'm a control freak!"

Chapter Nineteen

"TABITHA?" Her mother sounded faintly surprised. She must have heard Tabitha's last words to Arnie.

"Mom." She struggled to switch tracks in her mind. It was difficult. She turned her back on Arnie so he wouldn't distract her. "How's Daddy? Is he okay?"

"He's doing well, but his doctor wants him to stay in intensive care for another day."

"Why, if he's doing well?"

"I'm not sure. You know how it is with doctors. Always rushing in and out, and by the time they leave you realize you've forgotten half the questions you wanted to ask."

"Write them down."

Nancy laughed. "That's just what your father said."

"So he *is* fine." She felt relieved.

"I think so. But I'll feel a lot better when he's out of ICU. He looks so fragile with all those tubes and IVs in him."

"I'm praying he'll be okay."

"Good, honey. He needs that. How are you, by the way? Have you been having a discussion with Arnie?"

'Discussions' were how her mother referred to the arguments she had with Tabitha's father. Usually the term made her smile. It didn't now.

"He thinks I'm a control freak."

A small pause elapsed. "You do like to have your own way, honey. You have since you were a little girl."

"So *you* think I'm a control freak, too?" A whisper of sound came through the receiver. "Are you *laughing* at me, Mom?"

"Of course not, sweetie. It's just...well, you're an awful lot like your father. You know how he has to have his own way. And he won't listen to anyone..."

"I listen!"

"Sometimes you do. And other times something has to hit you over the head so you'll slow down enough to notice. If you want to know the truth, I think this time with Arnie is doing you a world of good."

"Why would you say that?"

"Arnie's a calm, reasonable man. He's got his head on straight about deep things. Things that really matter. I know he's riled you up somehow. But he's a strong man, and you won't be able to push him around. Now, do you really want to stay mad at him?"

"No," she muttered.

"Then go make up. Your father and I are hanging in here. I'll call you again tomorrow."

"I love you, Mom."

"I love you too, honey." Laughter colored her mother's voice. "Say hi to Arnie for us, will you?"

"Will do." Slowly, she hung up.

At the stove, Arnie glanced over his shoulder. "Is your mother mad at me, too?" He looked sheepish.

"No. Of course not." She joined him at the counter.

"Tabby." To her surprise, he put an arm around her shoulders and hugged her close to his side. "I'm sorry. Please don't be mad at me."

With relief, she turned into him and slipped her arms around him, cheek to his chest. "I'm sorry, too. I know you just want to help."

He dropped a kiss on top of her head, and for a moment she felt his warm breath caress her skin. "Are we good again?"

She tightened her grip, and then let go and smiled up at him. "Yes. But I'd love to help you with dinner. Maybe I could make the salad?"

"Be my guest. I definitely won't stop you." He chuckled, and the sound brought her joy.

❀ ❀ ❀ ❀ ❀

After dinner, Tabitha worked for four solid hours on her report, but it still wasn't done. She stretched her neck and rolled her shoulders. Arnie had the T.V. on low volume over in the corner. Presently it was tuned to the eleven o'clock news, and she listened to the weather forecast.

"The snow should slow to intermittent flurries tomorrow. On Friday the storm will finally move east."

She should feel relieved by this good news. Soon, she'd be able to visit her parents in Buffalo. But that meant leaving Arnie.

The thought made her feel unhappy, so she plowed back into her report. In a couple more hours, she would be done. This report was trickier than the first one, and there were stacks of footnotes to read and also to double-check in the company's annual report.

She didn't like what she was discovering. Long ago, she'd realized that footnotes often held unexpected gems for the dedicated miner. Some detailed good news, some bad. All vital to understanding the future facing the company.

In one corner of her mind she heard Arnie turn off the television and head for the hall. "Goodnight," he said.

"'Night," she mumbled, deep in another footnote.

She ended up giving the company two stars. Failing, in her opinion. On the surface, they appeared okay for the short term, but their products were building up in their warehouses faster than they were selling them. Accounting tricks made it seem as if they had a lot of orders, when in fact sales were recorded before they were paid for. Many products were returned. A big red flag, in Tabitha's books.

Her shoulders ached, and she felt a knot in her neck when she finished the last graph. She saved it all to her flash drive as a precautionary backup, and decided to wait until tomorrow to e-mail it to her boss. But she did compose the letter and attach the files so it would be ready to go, first thing in the morning. She'd check it one more time, too. Her boss would be pleased to receive it so early.

She reread the quick note to her boss. The words blurred a little, and she rubbed at the painful spot in her neck.

"Still at it?"

Arnie's words made her jump. He wore charcoal gray sweats and a pillow crease imprinted into his cheek. She smiled. "What are you doing up, sleepyhead?"

"I saw the light under my door. It's two o'clock, did you know?"

"I wanted to finish this tonight."

He hesitated, and then glanced her fingers, which were still probing her neck. "You have a knot?"

"Yes."

"Want me to try?"

With relief, she said, "Would you?"

His warm fingers touched her neck, and a thrill of pleasure slid down her spine.

"Tell me when it hurts." The ball of his thumb gently massaged up her vertebrae, testing the muscles between each joint.

"Nothing...no... Ow!"

His strong fingers went to work. It felt painful, and yet delicious at the same time. Tabitha sighed and let him work his magic.

"Did you finish your report?"

"Huh? Oh, yes." She turned off the computer. The small movement caused a sharp stab of pain beneath her right shoulder blade, and the breath hitched in her throat.

"Am I hurting you?"

"No. My neck feels a lot better. I just felt a twinge in my back."

"Where?"

Tabitha twisted her arm up behind her, trying to reach the spot. "Here."

His strong hands went to work kneading that area too, and she sighed in pure bliss. It felt good. Too good. Nerves were tingling in unrelated areas.

She pulled away from his touch. "That's good. I mean, that's wonderful. But I think I'm good now." She stood, closed her laptop, and scooted away from him, so her chair stood between them.

Belatedly, she said, "Thank you. That was awfully nice." Her face felt warm.

Arnie's warm gaze ran over the color on her cheeks. It didn't seem to put him off. In fact, she received the distinct impression that it gave him satisfaction to see it.

With a faint smile, Tabitha strove for normalcy. "I think it's time to hit the hay."

After a short beat to acknowledge the change of subject, he nodded toward her computer. "Why did you want to finish tonight? I thought it was due on Friday."

"Better sooner than later. I hate to have things hanging over my head."

Slowly, he said, "So you did it for you, not your boss?"

"Yes. Why?"

"I don't like to see you pushing yourself so hard. You're on vacation."

"That's life sometimes."

"Is this how you push yourself all the time at work?"

"I work as hard as I need to, to stay ahead of the game. If that means an all-nighter, that's what I do. Please don't judge me."

"I'm not being judgmental, Tabitha." His voice deepened. "I'm concerned."

"Why?"

He remained silent for several long moments, as if trying to decide whether or not to speak what was on his mind. "I think you've set some pretty high standards for yourself. Your boss says you're his best analyst. That took a lot of work. And a lot of determination."

"That how I got where I am today. I know it's a lot of pressure. My new job will require a lot more time and work. And I'm prepared to give it. I want to be the best."

"And you can do it," he told her. "I have no doubt. You're smart and determined. You're an amazing woman, Tabitha."

She felt a warm glow from his words. "You think so?"

"I know so. And it's not because Brown's Bros. says you're their best analyst. It's you, Tabby, just the way God made you."

She wanted to accept his words. Finally, she shook her head. "No, Arnie. Research and results have made me their best analyst. Not just me, as a person. I appreciate the thought that you like me just as I am, but in the business world, things are different. Results are what count."

"Results are important—to a point," he agreed. "But when push comes to shove, we all have to accept that God made us, and he loves us, just as we are. Whether we succeed or fail."

"I'll accept myself when I'm perfect," she tried to joke. Arnie had tried to tell her this same thing the other night... What had he said? That she, just being herself, had already made a difference to him. Could that be true?

The idea flew in the face everything she'd learned in school and in the workplace—that accomplishments equaled self-worth. Success meant you were worth something in this life. Triumph equaled success. God's view of a person and his love did not enter into the equation.

"What if you fail?"

"What?"

"I'm worried about you, Tabby. Who are you trying to please?"

"Myself," she said. "And my boss. I want to be successful."

"The stock market is fickle. How do you feel when your stocks tank?"

"Not good."

"Do you think God accepts you because you're successful at your job?"

"Of course not!"

"Then why does success matter? What's really important in this life?"

She felt momentarily at a loss. "I don't know. Loving people?"

"And loving God. You'll never be perfect. You'll never be successful all the time. But God accepts you just as you are. Believe that, and you'll find rest."

In a low voice, she said, "You have all the answers, don't you?"

"No. But I've learned the hard way that my self-worth has to be based on God's love for me; just as I am, right now. Success comes and goes. The highs are high, and the lows can destroy you. If you tie up your value in your career, sooner or later, it'll eat you up."

Tabitha hugged the laptop to herself. "I'll think about what you said. Good night, Arnie."

"'Night."

A few minutes later, she curled up in front of the stove, blankets cocooned around her.

Could he be right? Why *did* she push herself so hard? Who was she trying to please? Ultimately, shouldn't she pursue the things that matter the most? Loving people. Loving God. Could it all be so simple?

As she lay there, Tabitha realized that she'd accomplished none of the goals she'd laid out last night, and now she probably only had one more day left with Arnie. She'd made no effort to discover the reasons for his deeply buried hurt. And why?

Because she'd been engrossed in her reports. She hadn't had time to think about anything else. Of course, she had helped him with his financial questions. That had been good, at least. But if he hadn't asked for her help, Tabitha knew she would have ignored him all day, buried in her work. Just like in New York, when she'd turned a blind eye to the seriousness of her father's health problems. Was she truly that person—lost in her own little world and cocooned from reality? Maybe she was the one with the heart problem.

Another uncomfortable thought followed; when a choice came between work and caring for someone, how did she typically respond?

Guilt prickled. Work had engulfed her for the last two years. What would happen when she returned to New York? Especially with her new promotion? She'd already admitted to Arnie that the new job would require more time and concentration than her old one. Well—it would if she wanted to be the best. And of course, she wanted nothing else.

Didn't she?

Who *was* she trying to please? And what did she want from life? Troubled, she fell into a restless sleep.

CHAPTER TWENTY

THURSDAY

WHEN ARNIE MOVED, soft-footed into the living room the next morning, snow still spit outside against the windows. His best guess was that the snow plow wouldn't make it out until tomorrow morning.

He was glad it wouldn't be today.

His gaze lingered on Tabitha, still sleeping on the floor, blankets bundled over her, and dark hair fanned out on her pillow. Sleep flushed her cheeks. Tenderness kicked him, like a punch in the gut. His gaze ran over her again, wanting to memorize every detail. He'd felt that soft, slippery hair when he'd massaged her slender neck last night.

Tension tightened inside him, and he quietly turned away to make coffee. He didn't want to wake her. It was eight o'clock, but she needed to sleep.

Only one more day left with Tabitha. It wasn't enough. He didn't want to think about her leaving.

Just a few days ago he'd decided to open up his heart a little. Already he felt more for her than he should. Seeing her pale and exhausted last night, finishing that blasted report—if he'd thought her boss had demanded it, he'd have wanted to punch the guy. To know she'd done it to herself...

It disturbed him, deeply. If that was a taste of her driven life back in New York, he was worried about her health.

How long could people push themselves before they cracked? And she'd admitted that she hadn't seen her parents in two years. Somehow, he had to make her see the light. The protective part of him demanded it. And his own experience refused to let him walk away from the problem.

He'd lost all of his chances, but Tabitha still had plenty ahead of her. He didn't want her to make the same mistakes he'd made...or pay the terrible cost he still paid.

❄ ❄ ❄ ❄ ❄

Tabitha woke to the wonderful aroma of coffee perking. She sniffed, and poked her nose out of her blankets. She felt deliciously warm and cozy. Hearing soft shuffling sounds, she peered over the lip of her gray, fuzzy blanket to see Arnie in the kitchen. He pulled out a black skillet and set it quietly on the stove, and then swung open the refrigerator and retrieved a carton of eggs and some bacon.

A yawn caught her unaware and she sighed. The warm puff of air drifted down inside her blanket cocoon. Her watch said nine o'clock. And Arnie was just now making breakfast? He must be starving.

Tabitha opened her mouth to tell him that she was awake so he wouldn't try so hard to be so quiet anymore, but then last night's conversation rushed into her mind.

Today she'd finally get her priorities straight. She still wanted to e-mail her boss, and research and send him her picks for the Roundtable meeting, but she intended to accomplish her other goals today, too. Namely discovering answers to the remaining questions about Arnie's past. And the root of his unending hurt. She wanted to help him feel better, if she could. The weather forecast had promised that the snow would end today. Tomorrow she would go home.

A lump of dread filled her heart at the thought. Of course she wanted to see her parents, but she couldn't bear the thought of leaving Arnie, and maybe never seeing him again. Even if she did see him again, it would never be like it was now, spending close, intimate time in his house. If they saw each other, it would likely be a fluke—strangers waving "hello" if they glimpsed each other in Newbough. Or maybe at church, when she visited her parents in the summer.

Pain sliced through her, as sharp as a blade, and Tabitha closed her eyes to hold back the tears that sprang to her eyes. *Stop it*, she told herself. *Just stop it.*

Finally, she pushed back the covers. Time to face the day. She'd enjoy every minute she had left with a certain strong, stubborn, wonderful farmer.

"Morning." Another yawn escaped, and she clapped a hand over her mouth to cover it.

He approached. "Did I wake you?"

"No. You were quiet as a mouse. Thanks for letting me sleep." She climbed to her feet.

His gaze ran over her face, and her heart beat a little faster at its steady, appraising look. A very masculine look. "Coffee?" he asked.

She put a hand to her hair. "I must look like a mess. Maybe I should get a shower first."

"You look fine the way you are."

He meant it. She could see it in his calm gaze.

"Thanks." Her cheeks warmed, and she glanced down at the gray sweats she'd taken to wearing at night in Arnie's house. Wearing a nightgown, especially in his living room, had seemed inappropriate.

She smiled. "You must be hard up to think that I, with my wild, uncombed hair and baggy, rumpled sweats, look 'fine.'"

"I think we both see deeper than the surface now, Tabby."

She liked it when he called her Tabby. And she also liked how he looked this morning, too. He wore another flannel shirt today. It was a warm, caramel color, with darker brown crisscrosses which complemented his dark amber eyes. And of course his inevitable jeans and brown leather belt. Today he wore brown socks.

"Goodness, you're color-coordinated this morning." She accepted a mug of coffee and sat at the kitchen table, her feet curled together for warmth under the chair.

He sent her a faintly surprised look.

She said, "I mean your socks and shirt and belt. Put on some brown shoes and you might pass muster with my fashion police friends. Though the flannel may not cut it with them."

"What about with you?" The bacon sizzled as he turned it in the pan.

"I like your flannel. It has charming qualities." Basically, that the man who wore it took her breath away. Tabitha briefly closed her eyes, appalled that this was true.

He glanced at her over his shoulder, his white teeth flashing in a smile, and her heart beat harder. Maybe she should change the subject. "So what's your plan for today? Do you think the snow will stop?"

"Yes. Probably this afternoon." He set a pan of sizzling bacon and another of scrambled eggs with cheese on the table between them. Tabitha jumped up and grabbed plates, silverware, and napkins. "I'll clear a path from the front door to the driveway later."

"Will you need to shovel your whole driveway?" She helped herself to the delicious smelling breakfast.

"Scully or one of his guys will plow it for me when they come out."

Melancholy slipped through her heart. "When do you think that will be?"

"Tomorrow morning, most likely."

Tabitha nodded, glad it wouldn't be today.

She wondered if he'd miss her as much as she would miss him. "Soon you'll get your house back." She tried to smile.

"Are you glad you'll be able to leave soon?" he asked quietly.

"No. But at the same time, I want to see my parents..." Words failed her. "I think I'll miss you." Quick tears blurred her eyes. Her fork tines poked into a yellow, fluffy lump of egg. "Who would have thought, huh? We didn't start off so well, but now..." To cover her inability to finish the thought, she took another bite.

A long moment elapsed. "Do you have plans?"

"Do you mean for today?" When he didn't answer, she said, "I'll e-mail my boss. Maybe do a little research for the Roundtable. But only for a little while this morning. That's it."

"Good." Arnie ate silently.

Tabitha sensed something was amiss. "What's wrong?"

Quietly, he said, "I'll miss you, too, Tabby."

She bit her lip. "Don't say that. You'll make me cry."

His warm, calloused hand covered hers. "I'd like to drive you to Buffalo tomorrow to see your parents."

"You would?" Her spirits leaped at his offer.

"Yes."

"But why?" She could have bitten her tongue. *Just accept his wonderful offer, Tabitha!*

"I'd like to see how your father's doing. And I'd like to get out of this house, too. I've been cooped up long enough."

He wanted to drive her all the way to Buffalo. Tabitha smiled. "I'd like that a lot. If you're sure you don't mind."

He smiled. "My pleasure."

Tabitha's spirits lifted at the thought of spending an additional day with him. And she'd get to see her parents, too. What could be better?

"We'll leave as soon as the snow plow comes."

"Great." Then Tabitha thought about returning to Arnie's house tomorrow afternoon. She couldn't stay with him any longer—not when the roads were plowed. Maybe her parents would give her a key to their house. "I guess when we get back I'll need to dig out my car. Do you think it'll start up?"

"It's a rental?"

"Yes."

"Then it'll probably be fine."

"I'll make sure I'm packed up tomorrow morning. When we get back I'll be ready to go to my parents' house. After we dig out my car, of course."

A silent moment elapsed, and then he said, "Sure."

"I won't need to take advantage of your hospitality any longer," Tabitha explained. "I mean, not when we're not snowed in anymore."

"Sure," he said again, but he didn't look too pleased about it.

"It's all set. Tomorrow we'll break out of here!"

"Freedom." He smiled. But it told her that he was enjoying the time with her, too.

❄ ❄ ❄ ❄ ❄

After breakfast, Tabitha took a shower and tried to call her mother, but received no answer. She'd try again later, and in the meantime would pray for the best.

Next, she e-mailed the reports to her boss, and then accessed her files on the Brown Bros. server for stock picks. A few months ago, she'd culled the best from her list, and now she only had to narrow the choices down to the best five or so. She also perused her research files, steeping herself in notes she'd taken about different sectors of the economy. Robert may already have his own opinion about which sector would be hot next year, but it wouldn't hurt to put in her own two cents, backed by research, of course.

Four hours flew by before she knew it. Only her rumbling stomach distracted her. That, and the sound of Arnie stomping his boots outside the front door. A blast of cold air goose-pimpled her skin when he shut the door. He pulled off his boots and hung up his snow sprinkled coat.

"Brrr!" She crossed her arms and blinked over at him.

His face was ruddy, and he strode toward her, radiating masculine vitality. "Still at it?"

"Another paragraph to Robert, and I'm done." She crossed to the kitchen window. Intermittent flakes still swirled down. Arnie had dug a long trench through the three feet deep snow. It stopped at the top of the driveway. "Wow! You did a lot. You must be exhausted."

"I could use some food." He pulled open the refrigerator and set to work building a double-decker sandwich. "Want something?"

"Leave out the lunch fixings. I'll make something when I'm finished." Tabitha returned to the table and reread her e-mail, making sure she'd included all the facts Robert would need. By the time she sent the e-mail and sat down with her lunch, Arnie had already wolfed down his sandwich.

"You're done?" he asked.

"Unless he asks me to do something else."

He frowned.

"He won't," she assured him, taking a big bite.

"If you were my employee, I'd add two days of vacation to your account."

"Really? Why?"

"You've worked sixteen hours over the last two days. Those weren't vacation days for you."

"It's my job. Besides, that was nothing. You should see my 'in' box at work. It's overflowing."

"I thought you were getting a new job," he said gruffly. "Who'll take your old one?"

Tabitha hadn't thought about that yet. "I guess I will, until Robert hires a new analyst. It shouldn't take more than a few weeks. Maybe a month."

"For a month you'll be expected to do two jobs?" His voice deepened with displeasure.

While his protectiveness warmed her heart, she had to make him see the reality of the situation. "I know I'll have to sacrifice. Maybe I'll go with a little less sleep for a while. But I can do this. Robert believes in me. It's a great honor, you know, to move to the investment division."

"Didn't the SEC rule that Lehman Brothers and other investment companies have to keep the research and investment departments separate?"

Tabitha fell silent in surprise. "You're right. I'd forgotten about that. I guess I won't be doing my old job. Just as well, because I'm sure the new job will keep me really busy."

Arnie drew in a slow breath. Somehow, she got the feeling that he was girding himself up for an unpleasant task.

"How busy? Tabby," he said gently. "You told me you want to visit your family more. But it sounds as if this new job will take just as much time as your old one. If you didn't have time for them then, how will you now?" He drew a harsh breath. "I'm afraid for you. I want to help you. To warn you. I don't want you to make the same mistakes I made. Mistakes I'll regret every day for the rest of my life."

CHAPTER TWENTY-ONE

TABITHA SAID GENTLY, "What happened?" She guessed he was about to tell her more about his past. She hoped so. If she knew what mistakes he'd made—what pain he still carried with him—maybe she could finally help him, too.

He glanced away, as if loathe to talk about it, even though he'd brought up the subject. After a pregnant pause, he gritted, "I wasn't there for my parents. Not when they needed me the most."

"What do you mean?"

"I told you I planned to become a partner with my dad on the farm after I finished my Master's degree."

"Yes."

"I came back that awful Friday night intending to do just that. But when Theresa died, I lost it. My whole life blew apart." He drew a harsh breath. "So I ran."

"You ran?"

"I ran away from the pain. I couldn't stay in Newbough. I couldn't take the memories of seeing Theresa everywhere."

"So you joined active duty," Tabitha remembered.

"I left my father high and dry."

"But Arnie..."

"I was selfish," he interrupted, "and thinking only of myself. Just like I'd been selfish with Theresa. I didn't listen to her. I wouldn't let her follow her dreams."

"What do you mean?"

"Theresa hated Newbough. Her family was poor. She wanted nothing more than to escape. When we started dating, she moved to Syracuse and worked as a waitress, just to be close to me. And she loved it there more than she'd expected. In my last year of school, Theresa decided she wanted to go to beauty school. She finished just before our wedding, and she starting working in a salon."

Arnie ran a hand through his hair. His expression looked tortured. "She was good. She started to build up her clientele. She wanted to stay in Syracuse, Tabby. But I wouldn't hear of it."

He turned away and began to pace. "She begged me," his voice roughened, "to stay a little longer after I graduated in May. Maybe another year, so she could get more experience and learn more tips from her hairdresser friends and take more classes. I know she hoped I would want to stay forever. I couldn't. I'm not a city man, and I'd promised my father..." His voice broke. "I promised my father..."

He fell silent, and Tabitha moved closer. "You promised your father that you'd come home."

"Yes." He turned to her. "And then, when Theresa died, I broke that promise. Just like that." He snapped his fingers. It sounded harsh in the stillness. "I was selfish, do you see? I said I loved Theresa. I said I loved my parents but I failed them both. I didn't care enough about Theresa's hopes and dreams. I broke my promise to my father. It was all about *me!*"

"But..."

"No buts. I'll always wonder if I was the reason why Theresa died." Although Tabitha felt confused by this statement, he plowed on before she could speak. "I wasn't there for my parents when they needed me. When my mother was dying of cancer, I was stuck in Afghanistan. When I got home, she was dead. And when my father needed me then, I still had two months to serve."

"Wouldn't they let you out? Give you an exception?"

"I didn't push hard enough for it. I figured I'd be out by the beginning of June. Dad had help with the planting. He said he'd be fine. I should have come home sooner. I should have."

Arnie sat down hard on the coffee table and visibly crumpled before her. He buried his head in his hands. Tabitha put a hand on his trembling shoulder, wanting to comfort him.

"It was a mistake." His words ended in a gulp, and a harsh sob shuddered through his great frame. "I got out on

June seventh. He died June fourth." Another sob gulped out. "I failed him, Tabby. I failed them all!" He began to cry, and Tabitha sat beside him and held him as tightly as she could.

❈ ❈ ❈ ❈ ❈

Tabitha held him for a long time. After a while, Arnie wordlessly turned to her and buried his face into her hair. His strong arms held her close to him. She felt content to hold him forever, if need be. She gently stroked his broad back, wanting to comfort him.

She was glad that he'd finally broken down, and wondered if she the first person to whom he'd told his guilt and pain. How long had he carried this ugly, awful load? Close on eleven years, likely. No wonder he'd isolated himself.

He unfairly blamed himself. And apparently no one else knew that or had tried to set him straight before now.

Well, she would, and as speedily as possible. But first, she had one more question to ask. She hated to hurt him still more, but like a rotting tooth, she reasoned it might be better to get it all out at once. Then the healing could begin. She hoped.

He finally pulled away, and swiped his face on his sleeve. Tabitha sat quietly beside him and waited until his breaths quieted. He leaned forward, forearms resting on his thighs. With a feeling of trepidation, she boldly curled her hand over one of his.

"Arnie," she said softly, "please tell me one last thing."

"What?" He sounded tired.

"You said you'll never know if you're the reason why Theresa died. What did you mean?"

He pulled his hand free and abruptly stood. She watched him walk away and wondered if he intended to answer. Had she pushed him too far?

He paced the kitchen, and finally faced her. "You don't need to know. I told you how I ran off on my parents. How I always followed my own way without counting the cost to the people I love. I told you all of this so you could learn from my mistakes. Don't let anything—work, or your career—pull you away from the people you love."

"I hear you."

"Do you?" he asked grimly. "I learned the hard way I can't have it all. Something always ends up being sacrificed."

"Is that why you've decided to live alone forever? Why you won't consider marrying again? Because you think you failed Theresa?"

"I *know* I failed Theresa."

"I don't see how," she said. "Didn't she know before she married you that you intended to go back to the farm?"

"Yes, but..."

"She knew the score, Arnie. Sure, maybe she was disappointed, but she could have cut hair in Newbough. I'm sure you would have supported her taking classes in Buffalo or Syracuse when they became available."

"Well, yes..."

"Then why are you blaming yourself?" She rose to her feet. "You were planning to fulfill your promise to your father. How was that selfish?"

He looked taken aback. After a quiet moment, he said, "I was selfish because I wouldn't consider Theresa's wishes. It was always about what *I* wanted. What I thought was best. And she died."

"And that's another thing. How could you *possibly* be responsible for her death? She died in a car crash. You weren't even at the scene. Or were you?"

"No." His fingers clenched. "You don't understand."

"Then make me understand, I *want* to understand."

"Why?" His voice rose. "How is any of this your business?

"I care about you, Arnie. You're broken and hurting...and...and I hate to see you living under all this guilt. Bogus guilt. *None* of it was your fault!"

Hope flashed in his eyes. But then he shook his head. "I should have been here. I should have driven her to her birthday party. Not Doug."

Tabitha raised a hand. "Wait a minute. I'm missing pieces. Theresa was here, but you were still in Syracuse. Is that right?"

"I asked her to go home to Newbough during finals week and look for an apartment or house for us to rent. I said I'd get there Friday night, pick her up at her parents' house out in the country, and bring her to Newbough. Friends were throwing a party for her."

"Did you say you got home late Friday night?"

"Yes. It was not planned. My C.O. at the base had me on the line, trying to convince me to go active. Then I had to finish moving and closing up the apartment. It took longer than I expected. I called and told Theresa I'd be late. She laughed and said it was no problem. Doug would take her to the party."

"Doug, her high school boyfriend?" Another memory hit surfaced. "And your best friend."

"Yes. So I said, 'Fine. See you later.' That was the last time I talked to her. I didn't even tell her I loved her."

"Did she tell you that she loved *you*?"

"No. She was mad. Theresa didn't get mad often, but she was angry when she left Syracuse Wednesday night, and she was still upset when I talked to her on Friday afternoon."

"Because you sent her home. Because you wouldn't stay in Syracuse like she wanted."

"Yes."

Tabitha still didn't see how Arnie could possibly have had anything to do with Theresa's accident. She pressed, "And so she drove to the party with Doug."

He glanced away, and his hands briefly fisted again, obviously in remembered pain. "Doug was wasted. His drinking got worse after Theresa dumped him. I should have told her not to drive with him. I'm not sure why he offered, and I don't know why she agreed to go with him. Maybe she wanted to make me jealous."

He fell silent for a moment. "They crashed out on Highway Sixteen, and that was it." Bleakness entered his eyes.

Tabitha decided it was high time to give Arnie her two cents worth. This blind, stubborn man needed to see the truth, and quit blaming himself.

"How could her death possibly be your fault?"

"She was mad at me, and for good reason. She wasn't thinking clearly, so she got in the car with Doug. I should have told her to ride with someone else. Or to drive herself. She had her own car."

Tabitha could not believe what she was hearing. "Unfortunately, Theresa made a bad choice. She chose to drive with a drunk man. That is not your fault."

He slammed his hand across the back of his neck. "I should have been there for her!" His voice thickened. "If I had been, none of this would have happened."

"I know you wish you could change things. But you can't. Terrible things happen. Theresa died. Your mother got cancer. How could you possibly have known your father would suddenly pass away like that? You couldn't know any of those things. You suffered through three unimaginable tragedies. But please, you have to see that none of it was your fault!"

"You're wrong, Tabby. I could have handled it a whole lot better. I could have listened to Theresa, and stayed an extra year or two in the city. Then I could have come home and helped my parents with the farm. I would have been here when they'd needed me."

"Hindsight is always twenty-twenty. You say I should stop trying to be perfect. To accept that I'm enough as I am. How about you?"

He looked away. "I know God accepts me. I know he's forgiven me."

"But have you forgiven yourself?"

He heaved a quiet breath. "Learn from my mistakes, Tabitha. That's why I told you all of this."

"You need to forgive yourself," she insisted. "You've closed yourself off from love, and you're all alone. It's a shame..."

"I accept what happened, and I accept that this is the way things have to be now."

"What is that supposed to mean?"

"Farming is my life."

"Your whole life, you mean. You've boxed yourself up in your secure little world. I imagine it's comfortable and safe there."

Arnie frowned. "I'm content."

"But are you happy?"

"I've accepted my life."

"But are you *happy?*"

He scowled. "As happy as I need to be."

"What kind of an answer is that? Have you given up?"

"I've grown up. A long time ago I thought, like you, that I could have it all."

"You still can."

"No, Tabitha. Life is not that way. I've learned that sacrifices have to be made, big and small, to keep what's most important to you. I was selfish, and I chose my own way over everyone I loved—twice. Now I'm living with the consequences."

"That is ridiculous!" she sputtered.

"Listen to me," he said quietly. "You have a chance now to do what I've always wished I could do. Get your priorities straight. Love your family while you still can."

"I will. I'll do everything I can."

But Arnie was wrong to think he had to live under that crushing, lonely guilt. And she also believed that he was wrong to think that sacrifices were needed in order to keep what was most important to her. Just because it had been true for him didn't mean it would be true for her. She wanted it all, and she intended to get it.

"The difference between you and me, Arnie, is that I'm going to keep pushing to get everything I want. And in the long run I'll get it, somehow, someway. You, on the other hand, will get nothing except for this farm, because that's all you're pursuing. I know you feel like you've failed, and I know you've been through an awful lot of pain. But please, you have to see. It's time to live again!"

Arnie plucked his jacket off the hook. With slow, leashed movements, he shoved his arms in the sleeves. "I'm going out." And then he was gone. The door slammed behind him.

CHAPTER TWENTY-TWO

TABITHA HAD PUSHED him too hard, yet again. She'd wanted to help him. However, she'd also said the last part because she had felt defensive, and it seemed clear it had upset upset him. She felt bad about that.

She hadn't liked Arnie implying that she might have to sacrifice in order to keep her parents a priority in her life.

Frankly, learning how suddenly his parents had died scared her silly. Perhaps a part of her had wanted to think, like when she was a child, that her parents were indestructible. That they'd always be there when she needed them.

Life held no guarantees.

She drew several deep breaths. He was right. She did need to visit her parents more than twice a year. Unfortunately, her new job would undoubtedly require more time than her old one. She buried her head in her hands. What a mess! And Arnie. She'd meant to make him feel better, but she hadn't handled the end of that conversation very well at all. She'd apologize when he came indoors.

Tabitha moved into the kitchen and put water on to boil for tea. For a moment, she watched Arnie outside, standing hip deep in snow, shoveling great clumps of white stuff and sending it flying. He'd forgotten his hat and gloves again. His ears looked red, and he worked fast and furiously, clearly working out his frustration on the snow.

She crossed her arms tightly, watching him. He was in so much pain—from the past, and perhaps from her words, too.

Somehow, she had to try to make things right, but she sensed that for now, he needed to be left alone.

It felt quiet inside. Too quiet. She perused the pantry, with the vague idea of planning dinner. Instead, she saw the sack of leftover of apples. Maybe she could bake a cinnamon apple streusel cake.

Arnie seemed to have a sweet tooth. The thought of pleasing him lifted her spirits, and she hurried to retrieve the recipe from her computer. After jotting the basics down on a scrap of paper, she poured a cup of tea. The cake was her mother's secret recipe. She was sure he'd like it.

Tabitha stopped mid-swallow and tea burned her throat. Her mother! She'd forgotten to call back. Again she'd become engrossed in her work. Now it was three o'clock. Quickly, she punched the remembered numbers into the phone and waited to connect to her mother.

"Hello?" Nancy McCroy's voice sounded faint, and a little vulnerable.

"Mom, it's Tabitha. How's Daddy?"

"Better. I was just going to call you. He's been out of ICU since last night, and the doctor is pleased with his progress. We might be able to come home on Saturday."

"So soon?" Tabitha was surprised. "I mean, that's wonderful, but Daddy just had major surgery."

"Staying four or five days in the hospital is typical after a bypass."

"Will he be able to take care of himself at home?"

"The doctor says he'll be able to walk. In fact, he'll need to walk in order to get better. You know they took an artery or vein or something out of his leg to fix up his heart? Well, he needs to get that leg moving. But of course he won't be doing much for a while. And I'll need to keep a close eye on him and watch for complications."

"Still. That's wonderful news."

"How are you doing, honey? Things all patched up with Arnie?"

She sighed. "Yes, except we just had another discussion."

A pause. "A fight?"

"No. He told me some things about his past. Mistakes he doesn't want me to make, too. He's hurting so much, Mom."

"He's a quiet man, but I've sensed that. So he opened up to you?"

"Yes. But then I was defensive about something and the conversation didn't end the way I wanted it to."

"You'll make it right."

"Yes."

Another pause elapsed, and then Tabitha said, "He's going to drive me to Buffalo to see you guys tomorrow."

"Wonderful! It'll do your father good to see the both of you. He thinks the world of Arnie, you know."

Her throat tightened. "He's a special man."

"Sweetie," her mom said softly, "is everything okay between you two? Besides your latest 'discussion,' of course."

Everything except that she liked him altogether too much. She swallowed past the lump in her throat. Softly, she said, "It'll be strange to leave. I've been here for so long."

"And you've become close."

"Closer than we probably should be."

Her mother digested this. Hesitantly, "You don't mean..."

"No, Mom!" A hot flush suffused her cheeks. "Certainly not!"

"Good. That would certainly complicate matters—and not in a good way."

"I know. I already hate the thought of saying goodbye to him."

"Do you have to?"

"I'm driving back to New York on Tuesday. I don't live here."

"But you could still see him when you visit us."

Tabitha feared that wouldn't be enough. She was afraid that as far as her heart was concerned, it was either all or nothing with Arnie. She expelled a long breath.

"That's a heavy sigh, sweetie."

"Tell Dad I love him, okay? We'll see you tomorrow, probably late morning or early afternoon, depending upon when the plow comes. I'll call when we're close."

"Can't wait to see you, and Arnie, too. He's a fine man, Tabitha. I can't say it bothers me that you're developing feelings for him. New York City is fine, but sometimes you find the best things in life at home."

"'Bye, Mom."

"'Bye, honey."

Home. Why did Arnie's house feel like home? Home was New York and her studio apartment. But the lights of the city seemed very far away right now. They even seemed unreal, compared to the sight of Arnie shoveling snow outside, and the cup of tea warming her hands. And an apple cake she wanted to make, just to see him smile.

❅ ❅ ❅ ❅ ❅

Tabitha chopped apples, mixed up the batter and set the cake in to bake. It was close to five o'clock by then, and dusk was deepening fast.

Still, Arnie was working outside—slower now, but just as steadily. He'd reached the driveway, and now he seemed to be clearing a path toward the side of the house. Maybe toward that shed that she'd seen. She wondered if he kept his vehicle in there, because she hadn't seen any sign of one outside when she'd retrieved her suitcase on Sunday. Briefly, she wondered what he drove. An SUV? A truck?

The smell of the baking cake reminded her that she should start thinking about dinner, and she returned to the pantry to peruse the shelves.

Tabitha was working on a chicken pot pie when the front door opened and Arnie finally came inside. He'd been working in the pitch black for at least a half an hour.

She poured the sauce into the crust and looked up to see him hang up his coat. His cheeks and ears were red, and his hands looked chapped and cold, too.

The timer dinged, and she turned and grabbed the potholders. With quick finesse, she pulled out the aromatic cake and set it on the back burner to cool.

"What are you doing?" His deep voice was right behind her. Tabitha spun around. He was closer than she'd expected, and his brown eyes looked warm. He wasn't upset any longer, and she was glad.

"I baked a cake. I hope you like it."

Unreadable thoughts flickered. "Why did you make it?"

"Because..." She struggled for words. "Because I hate the way we ended our talk. I'm sorry. I didn't mean to hurt you."

"You didn't. You wanted me to wake up."

"I want you to *live*," she said softly. "I want you to be happy."

"You care about me."

"Yes. You know I do. Thank you for telling me what happened."

He nodded and moved to get a mug. After pouring hot water into it, he added a tea bag. Carefully, he swallowed the hot water, obviously trying to warm up.

"Want a slice of cake?"

"Thanks."

She served him a healthy portion, and then put the finishing touches on her pot pie. She slipped it into the oven, and leaned against the counter, trying to decide if she should join him at the table. They'd already had enough deep discussions. She didn't want another.

Arnie finished the cake and tea. His ears were a normal color now, and so were his hands. He glanced at her as he deposited the empty dishes in the sink.

"Why are you staring at me?" he asked in a mild tone.

Warmth blossomed on her cheeks. "I'm not. I'm waiting for my pot pie to bake."

He smiled. "Have cake if you're hungry. It's great, by the way. Thank you."

"I'm not hungry." She crossed her arms, feeling unnervingly aware of him.

"Do you want me to leave?"

She frowned. "Don't be ridiculous."

"You seem prickly."

"I am not." Never mind that it was true...and for reasons she didn't care to guess.

"Don't you want to talk to me anymore?"

"I do want to talk to you. But not about anything deep. I think we've done enough of that today. And I don't want to make you feel sad again."

"It wasn't because of you, Tabby."

"You were upset."

"But not because of you. Those old feelings took a while to work through. And I thought about what you said, too."

"That it wasn't your fault?"

"I deserve some of the blame."

"No!" she whispered fiercely. "Arnie..."

"Tabby." One warm finger brushed her lips, and she went very still. "You're right. I need to let it go. It's hard to accept, because I want to think I could have changed the past. I wish that somehow I could have kept Theresa alive."

"It's hard to accept that we don't have control over everything," she agreed softly. "But God does, right?

Sometimes bad things happen, but doesn't he turn them around for good? Isn't there a Bible verse about that?"

"Romans eight, verse twenty-eight. 'And we know that in all things God works for the good of those who love him, who have been called according to his purpose.'"

"See? God still has good things planned for you, Arnie Arnold III. Will you tell me that you'll pursue something good for your life?" She whispered, "Love, even? You deserve it."

His warm brown eyes scanned her features. "I want that."

Why couldn't she look away from him? She swallowed. "Good." The word sounded breathy. To cover, she joked, "No more deep discussions necessary."

A beat went by. "I wouldn't be so sure of that."

"Why not?"

"I've been in over my head ever since you got here."

Her heart beat a little faster. "You have?"

"You've broken through my walls. I'm not sure how to protect myself anymore."

"Do you need to?" Without thinking, she touched his arm. "You must know that I don't want to hurt you. Not ever." She bit her lip to keep from spilling out more of her feelings to him. About how she thought he was a warm, wonderful man—the most terrific man she had ever met.

"Thanks for caring about me."

"I do," she said. And suddenly it was important that he knew how much. Without words, she wrapped her arms tightly around him. Peace and wholeness filled her when his strong arms closed around her, too. She felt his warm breath in her hair, and Tabitha wished she could stay there forever.

Long moments ticked by, and at last she pulled back a little, believing that she had been there long enough. It felt wonderful—too wonderful—and she was starting to feel things that maybe she shouldn't. He didn't release her, so she glanced up. Her heart beat faster at the look in his eyes.

His warm lips brushed hers. A sizzle flashed through her and her fingers fisted involuntarily into his soft shirt. He kissed her again. And again, deeper, as if searching for answers to the questions between them.

She could lose herself in his kiss, a panicked part of her warned. But when his warm hand slid down her back, urging her closer to him, she melted into him, unwilling to stop.

Finally, he lifted his head. His eyes simmered with dark, unsettled passion, and his heart beat with heavy, strong pumps beneath her palms.

Tabitha couldn't think for a few long moments as she struggled to catch her breath. Then reason finally surfaced. What was she doing?

She couldn't lose her heart to him. Their worlds would never have collided if not for that snowstorm. And their lives would part ways again after their trip to Buffalo tomorrow.

Tabitha pulled free, although she didn't want to. This realization caused further panic. She'd kissed plenty of men in her day, but none compared to this.

None compared to Arnie.

He regarded her, his brown eyes seeming to read into the depths of her soul. Tabitha didn't know what to say. She couldn't deny what she felt, but...

"Maybe that wasn't the best of ideas." To her chagrin, her voice shook. At home she could hunt down and slay the unknown with facts. But here, with feelings she couldn't define and clearly had no control over, she felt lost.

Quietly, he said, "I won't apologize."

"I don't want you to apologize! It was wonderful." Abruptly, she turned away and grabbed a potholder. "Maybe too wonderful," she muttered, checking on the meal. It was a welcome distraction, and she felt relieved when he retreated to his recliner in the living room.

A little while later the browned, bubbling chicken pot pie was ready. Soon it was dished up and they sat across from each other at the table. Arnie said grace, but didn't pick up his fork. He watched her until she reluctantly lifted her eyes to his. "What?" she said.

"I won't kiss you again, if that's what you want."

Tabitha struggled to find the right words. "I...I just don't think it's the best idea. Tomorrow's our last day together. We shouldn't start something we can't finish."

"We've already started."

"I know." Quick tears blurred her eyes, and she glanced down at her food. "But let's not make it any harder than it has to be, okay?"

"If that's what you want."

She didn't answer. It was not what she wanted. She wanted to kiss him again. She wanted to live close to his heart forever. But that was impossible. So she'd settle for second best—enjoying every single minute they had left together. Twenty-four more hours. Not nearly long enough.

She lifted her juice glass in a mock toast. "To our road trip."

"To sunny skies ahead." His glass clicked against hers.

"Amen." Tabitha did wish for sunny skies...and for the impossible. For her heart to stop aching with dread at the thought of saying goodbye to this wonderful man tomorrow.

❄ ❄ ❄ ❄ ❄

Arnie watched Tabitha eat with her head bent, as if determined not to look at him. She'd made up her mind. She was smarter than he was, then, because he did not want things to end between them.

Not now. His feelings for her were quickly growing stronger. He couldn't escape them, and foolishly, he didn't want to.

But Tabitha was right. Tomorrow they would part ways.

And yet he couldn't accept it. She had finally broken through his walls, and for the first time in years, he felt hope. Foolish or not, he wanted to get closer to her. To see how deep the feelings could go between the two of them.

His head knew a future between them was impossible, but his heart demanded that he try.

She wasn't leaving for New York until Tuesday. He would take every opportunity over the next few days to spend time with her, and see if there might be a fighting chance for the two of them.

Probably that was out of the question, but then again, he'd never thought he could feel again, either. That alone was a miracle. God's Christmas miracle. God had brought her into his life on that snowy night, and now Arnie wanted her to stay with a fierceness that scared him.

He wanted to live again. He wanted Tabitha.

CHAPTER TWENTY-THREE

TABITHA AWOKE FRIDAY MORNING with a feeling of dread, but also of acceptance. It was her last day in Arnie's home. It was also the beginning of the end. Soon she'd return to her real home, New York City. A life she loved, and one which would keep her separated from Arnie forever.

Last evening she had enjoyed every minute they'd played board games together. He hadn't pushed things between them, and she told herself she was glad.

Arnie was nowhere to be seen this morning. Quickly, she folded all of her blankets and stacked everything neatly in the guest room. Then she showered and dressed. She realized she needed to do laundry. Perhaps she could do it at her parents' house tonight. Or maybe Arnie had a washer, and she could do a load now. The snow plow might be a while in coming.

When she returned to the kitchen, Arnie had started waffles. She poured a cup of coffee and peeked into the bowl next to the waffle maker. Chocolate chips swam in the creamy batter.

"Yum," she said. "You're spoiling me, you know."

He smiled. "I want to."

A warm feeling filled her up inside. At the moment she was of two minds. She was trying to decide whether she should move away from him, and try to treat him with that ten foot pole he'd employed when she'd first arrived, or perversely walk straight into more heartache and enjoy every single second with him.

Something else caught her eye. "The snow has stopped." In fact, was that a ray of sunshine peeking between two clouds? It was! She rushed to the kitchen window. "Look," she cried out. "Sun!"

He chuckled. "Want to go out and play after breakfast?"

She spun back, eyes narrowed. "You betcha. I want a rematch."

"You're on."

Tabitha savored every bite of the scrumptious waffles. After cleaning up, she shrugged on her flimsy coat and hot pink mittens while Arnie pulled on his own winter gear. "You'll freeze in that," he told her.

"Nonsense. I'll live." She flung open the door and blinked with delight. Brilliant sunlight sparkled over the white snow as far as her eyes could see.

She moved onto the porch, boots crunching on the white stuff. Miles of white snow lay before her, broken only by a few bare, scraggly trees or telephone poles. It seemed as if she and Arnie were the only living creatures in this quiet world.

"It's so beautiful!" She inhaled the clear, crisp air. "It's like heaven must be. It's so bright and clean. Full of unlimited possibilities."

Arnie tugged her close to his side, and she smiled up at him. When he smiled back, a warm glow filled her. It felt right to stand so close beside him. She felt secure next to his solid frame. And complete.

Against her better judgment, she slipped her arm around his thick coat. It was impossible to get too close, but she liked the sense of intimacy.

"When I was a boy, I felt invincible on days like this. As if I was only limited by my own imagination."

"It must have been nice to grow up here, with all this space to run and play in. I grew up in New Jersey. The burbs. All concrete and little yards. The most grass I ever saw was at the park. And there were people everywhere. It's so quiet here."

"Like it?"

"I love it."

His arm tightened around her shoulders. "Still sure you want that snowball fight?"

"Afraid you'll lose?"

"I'm a gentleman. I don't want to see you suffer." He grinned.

She pulled free. "Oh, bring it on, buddy. Those are fighting words."

They engaged in a brief, furious snow fight. Again, Arnie was swifter, but Tabitha managed to hurl her snowballs with perfect accuracy, too. White marks sprayed across his dark blue jacket. Unfortunately, far more dusted her own long coat. She backed off, planning to regroup and find cover, but she only saw one avenue of escape—the path Arnie had dug. The only other option would mean floundering through hip deep snow.

So when she reached the end of the path to the driveway she darted around the corner, heading up the path he'd dug to the large shed. Her thought was to either find cover, or get far ahead and start building a stack of snow balls.

Unfortunately, Arnie kept coming, tossing snowballs underhanded at her. Squealing, she dashed for the shed and fumbled with the door latch with the thought of hiding inside. And then he was upon her, with one last ball of snow in his hand.

"Uncle?" he suggested.

"I am *not* eating snow." With one lightning fast move, she knocked it from his hand.

He only smiled down at her. "Give up?"

She lifted her last snowball. "Hungry? Or maybe 'thirsty' would be a more appropriate word."

His thumb easily pushed the snow out of her palm. Smiling, he murmured, "Can I take my prize now?"

"Depends on what prize that might be."

With a breath of a laugh, he kissed her. His lips felt warm after the cold of the snow and she curled her hands into his shoulders, and leaned into him. It didn't matter if he had vanquished her in the snow fight. She wanted this. She wanted to be close to him. She felt a joy in his arms that she'd never felt before.

Only the faint, growing rumble of an engine interrupted their kisses. Unfortunately, the house blocked their view, so they couldn't see what was coming down the highway.

Arnie took her hand and they hustled down the path like children on Christmas Day. An orange vehicle slowly moved down the road, pushing aside a pile of snow.

"The snow plow!" Tabitha flung her arms around Arnie's neck. "We're free. At last."

"Free," he agreed, looking down at her, his eyes dark...with what?

"Free to do whatever we want."

❄ ❄ ❄ ❄ ❄

Tabitha packed while Arnie waited for the snow plow outside. She didn't want to leave. But what *did* she want? To stay with him forever?

Logically, she knew that was impossible. And goodness knew, she knew how to be logical.

She thrust her dirty clothes bag in a corner of the suitcase. All thoughts of laundry would have to wait until she reached her parents' house. Good thing she'd over-packed. A bad habit that had finally paid dividends. Her lips twitched at the poor stock pun.

The rumble of the snow plow sounded very close now, and she popped out to the living room in time to see the giant beast churn up and funnel snow to the sides as it lumbered up the driveway. Arnie seemed to be directing the driver, who was a burly man wearing a blue cap with ear flaps.

Just like that, all of the snow holding them hostage curled aside, and the path was clear for her to return to her old life.

Just like that. Tabitha felt a clutch of loss in her heart and returned to her room to finish packing. *Stop it,* she told herself. She would not break down because she was free to join civilization. Freedom was a good thing.

She zipped her case shut, but decided to leave it in the guest room for now.

The sound of the snow plow faded. She knelt on the couch and peered out the living room window. Sure enough, the vehicle had returned to the main road. Arnie lifted a hand in farewell to the driver, and headed back up the drive toward the house. He was smiling.

No doubt the driver was one of his friends. Tabitha suddenly bet he had a lot of friends. How could he not? He was a wonderful man. Compassionate, deep, and considerate. Tender when he kissed her. She flushed with the

direction her mind was taking her. She watched him stride
steadily closer. He'd make a good father one day.

Now where had that thought come from?

He grew steadily larger, closer. He raised his hand to
adjust his cap, and suddenly Tabitha saw something else...

*Arnie with a small child perched on his broad shoulders,
tiny hands held tight in his own. The well-bundled child and
he were laughing.*

*A surge of love, so strong Tabitha thought her heart
might burst, rushed through her.*

Heart thumping heavily, she gripped the back of the sofa
and blinked. Now she only saw Arnie. Alone. Where had that
picture come from?

Still feeling a bit breathless, she watched him enter the
front door. He stamped his feet and she stared at him, heart
fluttering. Her breath caught with expectation...but of what?

His gaze pierced her. "What?"

Her spirits deflated. She drew a shaky breath. What was
wrong with her? Perhaps she'd seen—or imagined—a snow
mirage. Were there such things as snow mirages? She
certainly couldn't tell him what she had been thinking.

"The drive looks good." And she mentally rolled her eyes.
What an inane thing to say. But better than saying, *I just
imagined you carrying our child on your shoulders.*

She must be going stir crazy. She'd been cooped up here
too long. This forced intimacy was making her imagine all
sorts of things. The image she'd seen hadn't been real. It
wouldn't ever *be* real, either. No, when she finally went to
her parent's house, all of this would be the mirage.

"Ready to go?"

"Of course. Let me grab my purse."

Arnie had gathered up his keys and wallet by the time
she'd shrugged into her coat. He opened the front door for
her, and then locked it behind them. It all felt pleasantly
domestic. And right.

Disturbingly so. Tabitha tried to shake off this feeling as
she followed him to the shed. She stood clear as he pulled
open the massive door.

A huge, steel blue, two ton truck was parked inside.

"Nice!" She stroked the shiny paint. Arnie smiled. "Is it
new?"

"A year old. My old one gave out."

"I sold my car when I moved to the city. I don't need it, but I miss it."

She climbed inside. Clean, and well cared for, obviously. The plush cloth seat felt comfortable. She sniffed. "No more new car smell. Unless hay is a new scent."

He chuckled as he slammed the large door shut. He turned the key in the ignition and a heavy rumble flared to life beneath her feet.

Tabitha grinned. "Now *this* is a truck."

A small smile tugged at his lips. "You like it?"

Her grin widened. "I do. It's a monster truck. Definitely a man's truck. It suits you to a 'T.'"

His smile deepened. "I'll take that as a compliment."

"As you should." She wouldn't say so, but it thrilled her to ride in his powerful truck. It was a mirror image of the man she knew he was, inside and out. Powerful, deep, and strong.

Out on the main road, Arnie drove at an unhurried pace, because a layer of snow still covered it, and ice could lie beneath that. Tabitha was glad she wasn't driving. She had no experience in these types of conditions. Look how she'd ended up in the ditch!

Which reminded her of the rental. They appeared to be passing it now, if the extra huge white lump on the side of the road was any indicator. Unfortunately, the snow plow had mounded extra snow on top of it when it had cleared the road, so now it resembled a tiny mountain.

"That'll be a big job later," she said.

"Your car?"

"It'll take a while to dig out."

"It won't be too bad. I'm a good shoveler."

"Yes, you are," she agreed with a smile. "I don't know how you shoveled so much snow yesterday." When she'd first arrived at Arnie's house, she'd wondered if his bulk was from a solid build or from muscle. Now she knew, without question.

They passed through Newbough, and ten minutes later Arnie pointed out a drive to their left. It led to a small house about a quarter of a mile away.

"That's your parents' place."

It was hard to see much about the house. Snow covered the roof and more snow partly buried the house in a sea of white. The driveway had been plowed.

Thirty minutes later they turned onto a busier highway. Route 16, she noted. The road here had been salted, and Arnie upped the speed up to sixty. A thought tugged at her mind, and when the next road marker passed, it finally broke free.

"Didn't you say Theresa and Doug died on highway sixteen?"

Grim lines etched into his features. "Yes."

"But..." she turned around to look behind them, "I thought the party was in Newbough. Did her parents live out this way?"

"No," he said tersely. "They lived near your parents."

She tried to make sense of these facts. "Then why were they driving all the way out here?"

"I don't know."

She didn't like the thoughts entering her head. Namely, Theresa driving to an unknown destination with her ex-boyfriend. Clearly, he hadn't taken her directly to her party.

Harshly, Arnie said, "You're not thinking anything I haven't thought a million times over. I've wondered if she was through with me. If she wanted to go back to Doug. Or if driving with him was her way to lash out at me."

"She loved you," Tabitha said softly.

"I want to think she did." A pause elapsed while he passed a slower vehicle. "Doug had decided to move to Buffalo. They crashed halfway there."

She gasped.

He said in a low voice, "Sometimes I wonder if she was planning to leave me."

Tabitha could not believe what she was hearing. "Was luggage found in the car?"

"No."

She felt relieved. "Well then, there you are. To me it sounds like she was mad, and decided to go for a joyride. Maybe it was her way to thumb her nose at the world for a while."

"I think so. I hope so."

Arnie would never know, though—no wonder he was so confused by guilt and pain. He believed he'd failed Theresa.

She had run off with her ex-boyfriend, for who knows what reason, and been killed. What a tragedy, on all counts.

"I'm sure she loved you, Arnie. She married you. Not Doug."

"I hope she did. I believe she did. But sometimes, when I can't help it, I think about how she'd always wanted a ticket out of Newbough. Her family was poor. Doug had plans to go to school in Buffalo, but then he dropped out and went back to Newbough. She broke up with him right afterward. Maybe she thought I was her ticket to freedom."

Tabitha couldn't believe her ears. "Doug started drinking," she exclaimed. "That's why she broke up with him. And of *course* she loved you. A woman doesn't marry a man just to escape from her home town. If you want my opinion, Theresa was in a snit with you and went on a joyride with Doug. I really don't think she meant to leave you. What woman in her right mind would want a drunkard for a husband? If I wanted a better life, Doug would not be my first choice, that's for sure."

He smiled. "All logic, aren't you?"

"That's my job. Arnie, I know you loved Theresa, and I'm sure she loved you, too. Please quit beating yourself up over this."

"I feel a little better," he admitted after a minute. His gaze held hers for a long heartbeat. "Thanks, Tabby."

Deep joy lifted her spirit. Somehow, she'd helped him. She gazed out at the clear, cerulean blue sky. *Thank You, Lord.* She hadn't felt such complete happiness in a long time. Not since she'd abandoned her walk with God. And she had Arnie to thank for helping her to find her way back.

Had God allowed her to crash into that snow bank for a reason? To help her and Arnie find their way back on the right roads in life? Their time together was a gift. Like snowflakes drifting through an hour glass. Unfortunately, time was running out.

Chapter Twenty-Four

TABITHA GENTLY PUSHED OPEN the door to her father's room at the hospital in Buffalo. Her mother sat with her back to the door on a black, padded stool next to her father. She wore a rumpled pink and gray sweat suit, and her cap of dark blond hair looked tousled—unusual for her.

Her father lay still and pale on the bed. IVs dripped into his arm.

The room smelled of antiseptic, and a small window with the blinds twirled open softened the harsh fluorescent lights. The other bed in the room lay empty.

"Mom. Dad." Quietly, she moved inside. Her mother turned quickly, and then flew over and wrapped her in a hug.

"Honey, it's so good to see you!" Nancy's bright blue eyes, the same color as Tabitha's own, glanced at Daniel.

Tabitha's father smiled. It was faint shadow of his normal one, and it scared her to death. He looked so pale, lying under that white hospital sheet. Fatigue dimmed his hazel eyes and his wavy, iron gray hair looked washed out against the pillow.

"Daddy." Tears sprang to her eyes. She rushed over and kissed him and gripped his hand. To her relief, his grip felt stronger than she'd expected. "Are you keeping those doctors and nurses in line?" she said, wanting to see him smile again.

Daniel rewarded her with a faint grin. "You know I am, sugar. They fuss too much. Can't wait to get out of here."

"Tomorrow, right?" She glanced at her mother.

"So far, that's what the doctor said."

"I'm glad you're okay. You're looking good."

"Don't lie to your old man. I know I look like drowned fish bait. I'll feel better when I can get home and sit in my old chair."

"I'm sure you will."

"Those fluorescent lights aren't too flattering, either," he muttered. The twinkle in his eyes eased her worry, but only for a moment. The obvious fatigue in his pale face clawed at her heart. How fragile he was, this man who had run beside her, teaching her how to ride her bicycle. The man who had taught her how to drive a car, and laughed when she'd accidentally blown through a stop sign and was pulled over by the police.

She hated seeing him like this. And she realized all over again, like a shot through her heart, how deeply she loved her parents. Wasn't Arnie right? This was what life was all about. Loving her family and friends...and God.

Visiting them again in the summer wouldn't cut it. They needed her support right now. So she'd come once a month, especially while he was recovering. Maybe more. She wasn't sure how she'd work it out, not with her new job and the new demands on her time. But somehow, she'd figure it out. She had to.

She suddenly realized that she hadn't seen her brothers. "Where are Jake and Steven?"

"They went back to school. They say 'hi.'"

"I missed them." Disappointment licked through her.

"They'll be back for your father's birthday in two weeks." Her mother glanced at her with sharp eyes. "I'm not sure if you can make that, of course..."

"I will." Tabitha promised. Somehow, she'd make it.

Pleasure lit her mother's eyes, and Daniel smiled, too. He said, "I've been lying here thinking about what's important in life these last couple of days. Guess you've been doing the same."

"We all need a wakeup call sometimes, Daddy. I'm just glad mine didn't come too late." Tears filled her eyes, and Daniel patted her hand with a rough palm.

"None of that. Not for your old man. You know I'm a tough bird. I'll be around a lot longer. Plenty of time to give your mother fits." He smiled at Nancy, and Tabitha saw the love in her gruff father's eyes. "That's what it's all about, right, hotcakes?"

Tabitha giggled at her father's old endearment for her mother. "Arnie's here, Dad. Let's not embarrass him."

He moved forward then and his large, tanned hand engulfed the older man's in a brief, firm shake. "Good to see you, sir."

Daniel smiled and extended the grip for a moment. "You taking good care of my girl?"

"I'm doing my best, sir."

Daniel sent him a keen look. "She's something else, isn't she?"

Arnie looked at Tabitha. "Yes. She is."

She smiled. A soft, warm feeling glowed within her. "Of course," she said, unable to help herself, "he has to say that, Dad. I cooked him apple pies."

"You have a sweet tooth, too?" her father grinned. "Welcome to the family."

A breath of alarm licked through her. "Dad..."

"Far as I'm concerned, Arnie's like family now, angel. He took care of my little girl during a blizzard. You've always been a man I respect. Now I'm grateful to you, too."

Tabitha had never heard her father talk so frankly about any of his feelings before. She gaped at him.

Her father patted her hand. "Angel, I found out life's too short. Say what you mean. Don't let a chance slip you by. Tell people what they mean to you. What's the point of clamming up? I don't want any regrets."

"Neither do I." She cast Arnie a quick glance.

The next hour passed quietly. By the end of that time, Daniel was visibly starting to tire.

Tabitha rose. "I'll see you tomorrow at home. Just call, so I'll know what time to expect you. Or if something happens, let me know. You have my cell number, of course."

"Of course, honey."

"And...oh." Tabitha suddenly remembered. "I need the key to your house. Arnie and I still have to dig out my rental car, but I can drive to your place later tonight."

Nancy frowned. "Why? Is that necessary?"

Surprised, she said, "Where else should I go? It's stopped snowing..."

"You can stay at our place, of course, honey," Nancy agreed. "But I hate to think of you in that cold, lonely house tonight. And we won't be home until late tomorrow. And that furnace has been acting up."

"Tabitha can stay with me tonight," Arnie said.

Tabitha glanced at him, and then at her mother. If she didn't know better, she'd think the two of them had cooked up this idea together. For some reason, staying at Arnie's had never crossed her mind. She'd had it in her head that once the snow stopped, she'd need to go home.

Nancy's smile looked relieved. "You're a dear, Arnie."

"Are you sure?" Tabitha asked him.

An unknown expression crossed his features. "Your suitcases are there." Quietly, he said, "Do you want to stay with me?"

She definitely did, and too much. "I would like that a lot. Thank you."

"So it's settled!" Nancy exclaimed. "Arnie, you're a double life saver. I don't know how to thank you for all you've done for our dear Tabitha."

He glanced at Tabitha. "The pleasure has been all mine."

Her cheeks warmed, and she turned to hug her mother. "Call me when you leave the hospital, Mom."

"I will. Your daddy will be glad to get home. No doubt he'll be a bear!" But she smiled when she said it.

"Take my cell number, too." Arnie pulled a business card from his wallet and handed it to Nancy. "Just in case."

❄ ❄ ❄ ❄ ❄

"Feel better now?" Arnie said, on the freeway heading home.

"Yes. But he looked so fragile. It scares me because he's always been so strong. Bigger than life."

"Yeah," he murmured. She wondered if he was thinking about his own father.

"You're right, you know," she told him.

"I am? What about this time?"

She rolled her eyes and laughed. "You are pretty smart," she admitted. "But I mean about priorities and making a plan. I'm going to visit my parents every month—at least until Dad's feeling better."

"Good idea."

Unspoken words remained between them. Would she visit Arnie when she came? Could their relationship progress? Realist that she was, she knew that was unlikely. But the thought of leaving him in a few days to go back to

New York City stabbed like a knife through her heart. The pain felt unbearable.

At least she'd get to stay with him tonight, and she'd see him for part of tomorrow, as well. Maybe she could even stop by his house on her way home on Tuesday.

Definitely unsatisfactory. They drove in silence for a while.

"You know," she said, "I owe you dinner."

"For what?"

"Now, don't start that again. We've already discussed this. You took me into your home, fed me, and put up with me for almost a week. I owe you. I want to take you out."

Arnie drove without speaking for a while. "I owe you," he said at last. "You gave me all that financial advice. I probably owe you a thousand bucks."

"You bullheaded man. I *want* to take you out," she told him. "Or is that hard on your manly ego?"

He glanced at her. "I feel like I owe you ten thousand times more than the little I gave you. You've kept me company. You've baked me apple pies. You helped me to think about living life again."

"I'm glad, but still..."

"Please, Tabby. I'd like to take you out when we get home to Newbough. A friend of mine helps manage a pretty decent steakhouse."

He had totally turned this around on her. Exasperation was a mild term for how she felt. "Would this friend think it's strange if you let a woman pay for your meal?"

"Ellen's not like that."

"Ellen?" Tabitha felt unprepared for the tiny stab of jealousy. Then she told herself to quit it. What was with her? From exasperated to jealous in the space of two seconds. Her emotions were all over the board. She took a breath and spoke reasonably, "I appreciate your offer, but I'm sure Ellen, as a working woman—a manager—would agree that a woman can buy a man's dinner. We *are* equal with men, you know."

"You're right. But I guess I'm an old-fashioned man at heart. I appreciate you and I like you, and a man likes to pay for a woman. Especially if that woman is his date."

"Date?" Tabitha blinked. "You're saying this is a date, now?"

His gaze held hers for a long moment. "I want it to be. I'd actually planned to ask you out to dinner when we got closer to Newbough."

"You were? You did? I mean, you do? Want it to be a date, I mean."

He smiled a little. "Do you, Tabby?"

"Sure. I mean, yes. I would." Heat warmed her face. "I'm just so unprepared. I haven't done a thing with my hair. And I'm wearing jeans. And my makeup..." She smiled, to let him know she was joking.

He chuckled. "Marty's has a powder room. I'm sure you can make yourself beautiful there." His warm, brief glance took in her appearance. "You don't need it. You look beautiful just the way you are."

"Thank you," she said softly.

He ran a hand over his spiky buzz. "What about me?" he asked with a grin. "Do I need to stop by the powder room?"

With a laugh, she playfully swatted his arm, and spoke without thinking, "You're the handsomest man I know, Arnie. How can you improve on perfection?"

He shot her a surprised glance. "Really?"

Her heart beat faster, but she wouldn't recall her words. After all, what had her father said? "Tell people what they mean to you." Softly, she said said, "Yes, really."

"Wow." His voice deepened a notch. He cleared his throat. "Never been told that before."

Tabitha just smiled. It was true. And it also felt nice to be feel wrapped in the warm knowledge that he thought she was beautiful, just the way she was. And he'd felt that way even even when she was fresh out of bed with rumpled hair and old gray sweats, like yesterday. It was a nice feeling to be accepted for who she was, with no extras involved. No perfect make up, hair, clothes, or perfect performance on her job, either. Arnie liked *her,* period, and it felt terrific.

CHAPTER TWENTY-FIVE

By the time they reached Newbough, it was dusk. Arnie had had to slow down again when they reached the rural highway that serviced the town, and Tabitha felt stiff from sitting for so long when she finally climbed down from his truck in front of Marty's Steakhouse. The building was made of old, weathered wood. Snow capped the roof and the restaurant sign glowed neon pink and green.

He opened the wooden door for her. "Don't judge until you go inside," he said in her ear. "It's not New York, but it's not half bad."

The instant she stepped inside, the warm smells of baked potatoes and grilled meat greeted her. The interior was warm and beautifully decorated. Polished, honey-toned wood planks covered the floors and paneled the wall up to the chair rail. The room was painted a warm, muted gold, swirled with a darker tan color. A canoe had been mounted on the wall above the hostess stand, and other outdoorsy knickknacks decorated the interior of the restaurant.

"Do you have a reservation?" asked the hostess. She wore a beautifully tailored black dress. Tabitha felt self-conscious that she was wearing jeans. But Arnie wore jeans, too.

"No reservation. Is Ellen here tonight?"

"You know Ellen?" The girl smiled. "I'll seat you in her section. Right this way."

"I thought Ellen was a manager," Tabitha whispered, following the hostess to a booth in a secluded corner.

"She wears different hats."

No one else in the packed restaurant appeared to be wearing jeans. Tabitha felt better once she sat down, menu in hand. At least her cream-colored, cashmere sweater looked presentable.

"Ellen will be right with you." The girl swept away, and Tabitha smiled at Arnie.

"You're right. This place is definitely high class."

"At least middle class." Arnie sipped his water.

She was deep in her menu, trying to decide between a New York steak or salmon when a cheerful voice said, "Arnie! So you dug your way out."

"Even Scully makes it to the back of beyond," he chuckled, and Tabitha looked up. A woman with shoulder length blond hair stood beside the table. Darker blond streaked through her straight locks. It looked natural, as did the relaxed, casual way she stood, pad and pen in hand. The woman turned her attention to Tabitha, and she realized that Ellen was older than she'd first thought. Maybe mid-thirties, like Arnie. Smile lines crinkled around her eyes.

"Hi, there." Her smile appeared genuine. "Any friend of Arnie's is a friend of mine. I'm Ellen, by the way, since Arnie is slipping on his manners."

"Tabitha McCroy. My parents live nearby."

"The McCroys! We all go to the same church. Have you been home for long?"

"She's been staying with me. Her car got stuck outside my farm just before the blizzard."

"Aha!" Ellen regarded Tabitha with sharper interest.

"Back off, Ellen," Arnie said gently.

Ellen only smiled. "You must have become well acquainted then, staying together for what...six days?"

Embarrassment warmed Tabitha's cheeks. "It's not what you think. We're just..."

"I'm not thinking anything. I know exactly who Arnie is, and frankly, I think it's time a little jolt upset his placid life."

Tabitha couldn't swallow her giggle of surprise. "That's exactly what I thought when I first met him."

Ellen smiled, and glanced at Arnie. "All the better. How about it, Mr. Arnold? Will you invite her to our annual New Year's Eve party?" She turned back to Tabitha, "You will be in town, won't you?"

"Well, yes, but..."

"Give me a chance, Ellen," he said mildly.

"Mmhm. I know you. You move as slow as molasses. Tabitha, you're welcome to come. It starts at eight, and it's at my house. People from church come, too. And of course my family will be there, and our dogs."

Tabitha wasn't surprised to learn that Ellen was married, with a family and dogs. She emanated the warmth of a mom, and the way she'd addressed Arnie projected the concern of an old friend. "I'd love to come—that is, I'm sure my parents won't want to stay up to celebrate the New Year. I'll come after dinner."

"Terrific! I'll see you both then. Now, what can I get for you?"

When Ellen left with their orders, Tabitha lifted a questioning eyebrow at Arnie as she stirred her drink.

"Ellen's a friend from high school. Her husband is my foreman."

"She seems really nice. How many kids does she have?"

"Two. Annie's seven, and Josh is nine. And they have two Labradors. New Year's Eve is always crowded, but fun."

Tabitha sipped her drink. "Do you mind if I come?" she asked diffidently. "They are your friends, and..."

"Tabby." His warm hand covered around hers. "I want you to come. I'll pick you up, if you'll let me."

"Another date?"

"I wish I could have asked you first," he growled. "You women are taking all my thunder."

She smiled. "I'd love to go with you."

"Good."

Tabitha had chosen the salmon. The meal tasted delicious, and the time sped by. She enjoyed talking and laughing with Arnie so much that she was surprised to learn it was eight-thirty. He helped her on with her coat and they headed for the door, after promising Ellen they'd be at her party on Sunday night.

"Good." Ellen looked at Tabitha, and then back at Arnie. A pleased smile curved her lips. "Have fun, you two. Good night."

The cold air felt like a brisk slap in the face when they left the warm restaurant. Tabitha quickly climbed into the equally cold cab of Arnie's truck. "Quick," she shivered, rubbing her hands together, "turn on the heat!"

He set it blasting on high, and by the time they turned onto the highway a little warmth blew onto her cold hands.

The miles unhurriedly slipped by. Arnie drove slowly, since snow still covered the road in thick patches. At least visibility was excellent. Light from the full moon spilled over the glistening white landscape.

"It's so beautiful," she said. "I never understood before why my parents decided to move here, but now I do."

Arnie glanced outside, as if trying to see it for the first time himself. "I love it," he said simply. "It's my life."

She nodded, but sat silently, again thinking about the differences in their lives. He belonged here, in this quiet, serene beauty, while she belonged in bustling New York City.

No happiness filled her at the thought of returning home to the twenty-four hours of lights and hustle bustle. She hadn't missed it at all, she realized with surprise. But she would miss this. She'd miss Arnie.

She silently stared out the window, watching the glittering snow slide by. How could her life turn upside down so quickly? One week ago she'd considered this the uncivilized boondocks, and now...now it felt like home. Part of her wanted it to be home. Just as she wanted Arnie to stay in her life.

More miles slid by in silence. "You okay, Tabby?"

"Sure." Her voice sounded tight, just like the ache in her throat. "Sure, I'm fine. Are we almost home?"

"We just passed your car."

"I guess we'll have to dig that out tomorrow."

At the house, Arnie parked his truck in the shed and they crunched through the snow together to the house. They'd forgotten to leave the porch light burning, so he fumbled with the door lock for a minute, and then finally pushed it open and switched on the lights.

The house felt cold.

"I let the stove burn out."

"Could we have a fire tonight?" she asked. "It's only nine-thirty. Maybe we could play games for a while."

A slow smile pulled at his lips. "Sure. I'd like that. I'll get some logs."

Before long, he'd returned with logs and kindling, and then knelt and skillfully set a fire blazing. He fired up the pellet stove, too, while Tabitha made tea in the kitchen.

Since she knew where he kept the games, she carried their favorites to the coffee table. Then she sat cross-legged on the floor, her back to the warm, crackling fire, while he sat on the couch.

"Okay," she said with a grin. "What game do you feel like losing?"

"Let's make it interesting."

"Interesting?"

"Loser makes breakfast."

"That's easy," she scoffed, and dealt out the Uno cards. "I thought for a second you meant *really* interesting. Like living dangerously. I guess I was wrong about that."

To her surprise, he didn't retreat like she'd expected. Instead, he said, "What stakes do you want?"

"I want a reward for every game I win."

His eyes darkened. "What kind of reward?"

"I'll let you choose that."

He smiled. "You want me to lose on purpose?"

"What stakes do you want?"

"I want more of those pancakes you made on Sunday. A whole stack of them."

"You're easy to please."

"That's for the first game I win. For the second..." A grin curved his lips. "Another apple pie."

"You're losing now," she told him. "I don't have time to make another apple pie. By the way, do you mind if I use your washing machine in the morning?"

"I'll dig out the dryer vent outside for you. Want that to be your reward?"

"My first one. We can go from there," she promised.

They'd each won a game—Arnie at Uno and Tabitha at Clue—before she started yawning. "It's almost eleven," she said. "One more game. We need to have one grand winner, don't you think?"

"Absolutely. Uno. Draw to see who goes first."

"You're on." She drew the highest card, and then they both tossed down cards, hard and fast. Giggling, she finally threw down her last card. "I'm the *winner!*" She spoke into her card as if it was a microphone, "And what do you plan to do now? Collect my reward, of course!"

Arnie smiled a little when he handed over his remaining card. On impulse, she checked it before tucking it into the deck.

A wild card draw four. Accusingly, she flicked it up to show him. "You lost on purpose."

He smiled. "Sure about that?"

"Yes, I'm sure! Why?"

"I'm satisfied with my winnings." He gathered up the boxes and retreated to put them away in the study.

Tabitha deposited the tea mugs in the sink and returned to the living room at the same moment Arnie did. She hesitated, in order to let him pass. Instead, he closed the distance between them.

Heart beating suddenly faster, she said, "I'm satisfied with my winnings, too. Clean clothes are hard to beat."

"Are you sure?"

"What could be better? Well, besides a vacation on a tropical island, with miles of white sand beaches…"

"All alone?"

"Well, no. Of course that wouldn't be much fun." She easily slipped into the spirit of the impromptu game. "But maybe I'd get trapped on some tropical isle with a handsome, very handy man. He'd know how to make a fire and keep us warm on those cold nights." More softly, she said, "And I'd be very happy."

His warm hands settled around her waist, and the breath caught in her throat. He said, "What does this guy do for a living?"

"He harvests coconuts," she improvised. "Yes, he has a whole plantation of coconuts and bananas. So we'll never go hungry. That's important, you see, on a deserted island."

Arnie tugged her closer, so his belt gently touched her belly. "And what sort of a guy is this? Will he take advantage of you? Or can you trust him?"

Tabitha looked up into his warm, dark brown eyes. "I trust him. I can definitely trust him."

"Trust is a reward, too. Not easily given, and fragile, like a perfect, one-of-a-kind snowflake." His gaze settled on her lips.

"He won't hurt me," she said softly, and feathered her hands over his broad chest. "Ever. And I would never hurt him."

Huskily, he said, "Trust is important. It's fundamental."

She nodded fractionally. "Vital…"

Arnie kissed her, and her mind spun under the assault of his slow, warm caresses. Molten warmth licked through her, and she suddenly realized she was in trouble. She didn't want him to stop.

He broke away first. His bristly jaw gently slid by her cheek and she felt his warm breaths in her hair.

"Arnie," she whispered. Her heart thundered in time with his, and she suddenly knew that every intimate moment they spent together from now on would be playing with fire.

"Arnie."

"What?"

Her fingers curled into his shoulders. "I...I..." She couldn't say it, or put a name to the feelings burgeoning up inside her. "Maybe we should be careful."

"Yes." His deep rumble reverberated through her. Reluctantly, it seemed, he slowly released her. His gaze searched hers...for what, she could not guess. It was on the tip of her tongue to blurt out her feelings for him, but she was afraid to give them voice. To make them real.

She whispered, "Maybe I'd better say goodnight."

He nodded, and stepped back.

As Tabitha moved toward the hall to fetch her blankets, she sent him a smile over her shoulder. "By the way, that was a pretty awesome reward."

She changed into her sweats, but lingered in the chilly guest room until she heard him close his door across the hall. Then she quietly gathered up her blankets and bedded down near the pellet stove, as usual.

Her feelings for him were growing too fast. In fact, they seemed out of control, and that scared her.

She had always liked things to be labeled and put in their appropriate boxes or columns. It was one reason why she loved her job so much. Facts, and knowing where things belonged—those things made her feel secure. Swiftly snowballing feelings for Arnie did not.

She could not lose her heart to a man would not fit into the world she'd so carefully fashioned for herself.

Lord, why do I have these feelings for him? We can't fit together. I don't want to leave here with a broken heart.

How could she feel such unspeakable joy when she was with him? How could he already have a grip on her heart? Tomorrow she'd have to be careful. If she grew any closer to Arnie, and she'd lose it completely.

"Help me, Lord," she whispered. "I don't know what to do."

❋ ❋ ❋ ❋ ❋

Arnie lay awake late into the night, unable to sleep. A long while ago, he'd heard Tabitha gather up her blankets and return to the living room. He thought about her lying there now, sleeping peacefully.

He did not feel peaceful. Strong, unstoppable feelings filled him—things he hadn't felt so intensely since Theresa. He shoved his hands over his face. What was he going to do? He'd wanted to see if he and Tabitha had any sort of foundation to build upon, and he'd found it. Trust, respect, and more—much more than he'd ever expected to find again.

Was he a fool to want to pursue a relationship with her? Did they have any sort of a chance together, or was he hoping for a pipe dream?

Tabitha felt something for him. He sensed it in her kisses, and in the way she looked at him and spoke to him. The attraction was mutual. Their feelings were mutual.

He wanted her to stay in his life. But how?

He rubbed his hand over his temple, and stared up at the inky black ceiling. Wasn't God the God of the impossible? All things were possible with him.

Maybe he and Tabitha could have a chance together. He'd keep trying. He'd gone too far to back off now.

And he prayed to God for a miracle.

Chapter Twenty-Six

THE NEXT MORNING, while Tabitha made hotcakes, Arnie dug out the dryer vent, and then she glimpsed him walking down to the main road to shovel out her car. She had tried to insist that she wanted to help, but he refused to listen. Just like him. The stubborn, wonderful man.

She threw her clothes in the wash, and then served up the pancakes when Arnie returned and stamped his snowy boots on the porch. Snow clung to his jeans, and crusted around his calves.

"Did you already dig the car out?" she asked, surprised.

"Most of it." He hung up his jacket and peeled off his black gloves. "After breakfast I'll put chains on it and try to pull it out with my truck."

"Thank you. I really appreciate it."

He gave her one of his slow smiles. "You're welcome."

Tabitha deposited a plate of steaming hotcakes before him. Ten of them, each lathered in butter and dripping with syrup. And a fresh cup of coffee.

His face lit up. "A feast fit for a king."

She only smiled, and surreptitiously watched him enjoy his breakfast while she ate her own. The washer buzzed as she finished, and she dashed to transfer the clothes to the dryer. After her clothes were done, all she had to do was pack, and she'd be ready to leave.

On second thought, why the big rush?

She found Arnie washing up the dishes when she returned. "That wasn't part of the plan," she protested.

"We're partners," he told her. "I help you with this, and then you can help me get your car out of the ditch."

Tabitha enjoyed the quiet harmony of drying the dishes while he washed. Afterward, she rode in his truck to the main road, rental car keys in her pocket.

The car still had quite a mountain of snow on top and on its sides. Arnie had mostly cleared the front and the driver's side door, and went down on his knees in the snow to attach the chains. Tabitha unlocked the car when he asked her to.

"Okay," he said, heading for his truck. "Stand back." He pointed to the other side of the road. "I don't want you close if a chain breaks." He swung up into the cab of the truck and Tabitha moved to a safe distance.

The big truck's engine fired and Arnie slowly moved forward so the chains drew tight. The smaller car edged forward, and then seemed to get stuck. For an alarming second, the truck's tires spun.

Arnie eased off and tried again. After long, nail-biting moments, her black car finally emerged from its cocoon of snow, although mounds of white stuff still covered the top. When all four tires were on the highway, he took off the chains.

"I'll follow you back to your house." Tabitha slipped the key into the ignition while he stood nearby, obviously waiting to see if everything was okay. She turned the key. Nothing happened. Again, and nothing.

She opened the door. "It won't start."

He frowned. "I'll give it a jump."

The engine caught after he hooked the two vehicles together with jumper cables.

He ducked down to speak in her window. "When we get home, leave it running. The battery needs to recharge."

"Okay." With care, she executed a three point turn, and then cautiously drove up Arnie's driveway. She left it running, just as he'd asked, and followed him inside the house.

"I don't like it," he said, shrugging off his coat. "The battery shouldn't be dead. I think it would be best if you bring it by my friend's garage."

"I'm not sure if the rental agency will pay for it."

Arnie dismissed this with a shrug and headed for the phone. "He owes me a favor. He'll check it for free."

"That would be wonderful."

He nodded, and after a few words with his friend said, "Okay," and hung up.

"Thank you," she said. "How will I find the garage?"

"I'll follow you to Newbough."

"I feel like I've put you through enough trouble already."

"I'm glad to help," he said quietly. "And after you drop it off, you'll need a ride to your parents' house."

"Why are you frowning?"

Tabitha didn't realize she had been. "I appreciate everything you've done. I guess I just wish I could return the favor."

He smiled. "You've done plenty. These last few days have been special. And it's all thanks to you."

"Well." Now things were getting mushy and tender. Not a good idea, when she planned to leave Newbough soon. All the same, she couldn't help but smile back. She said softly, "It goes both ways."

❋ ❋ ❋ ❋ ❋

When Tabitha emerged from her room with her suitcase and assorted odds and ends a while later, Arnie was waiting, coat in hand, flipping through a large stack of mail.

She paused, and just watched him for a second. A lump formed in her throat. It was the end of the quiet, magical world that had cocooned the two of them during the snowstorm. Never again would she see him like this. Never.

He shrugged into his coat and approached her. "Ready?"

She couldn't speak. "I..."

Even though she didn't know what to say, he knew what to do. Arnie enfolded her in his strong arms and held her close to him. Wordlessly, she clung to him. Her cheek rested on his soft flannel shirt, open at the throat, and she breathed in the scent that was uniquely him.

She remained in that blissful, protective embrace for as long as she could. Finally, she drew a fortifying breath and pulled back. "Are you ready?"

His eyes were a warm brown. "No," he said, and gently kissed her.

His warm caress was nearly her undoing. Helplessly, she melted against him. Her head spun and her heart filled with overwhelming tenderness for this man.

I love him.

She pulled back and managed to affix a wobbly smile. That couldn't be true. Surely it wasn't. "Well. That's quite a sendoff. Which bag would you like to carry?"

He smiled.

❄ ❄ ❄ ❄ ❄

Rodney, Arnie's mechanic buddy, promised to check out the car later that afternoon. Tabitha left behind the rental car information in case he needed it and her parents' number, too, and then Arnie drove them both to her parents' house.

The green house's porch was a bit higher than Arnie's, so snow hadn't drifted against the front door. He had brought his shovel, though, and cleared a path from the driveway to the porch, and then carried her suitcase inside the cold house.

Tabitha immediately recognized a number of old, familiar items from her childhood: the old brown leather couch and recliner in the chilly living room, the bright, circular rag rug on the floor, and the family pictures on the mantel. It felt just like home, and smelled like home, too. The scent of her mother's perfume lingered, and so did the aroma of chocolate chip cookies.

Her cell phone rang when Arnie returned from depositing her suitcase in the guest room. She answered it.

"Honey, it's your mother."

"Is everything okay?"

"We won't be home today. But the doctor said he'll release your father tomorrow, for sure. Are you still at Arnie's?"

"I just got to your house. Is Daddy all right? Why can't he come home today?"

"The doctor wants to observe him for another twenty-four hours. He says it's just a precaution. He'll discharge him tomorrow morning. We should be home by one o'clock."

"I'll see you then," Tabitha said, and disconnected the call.

"Your dad will come home tomorrow?"

"Yes."

After a pause, he said, "You don't have to stay here alone, you know."

Her heart leaped at the possibility of returning home with him again. But then she realized that would be silly. "I might as well stay. My suitcase is here. I'm here." She glanced up and saw the concern in his eyes. "I'll be fine."

He shoved his hands in his jeans pockets. "I don't like it."

"Why not? What could happen?"

"Your mother said the furnace has been acting up."

"I'll be fine," she assured him, although she didn't want him to go, and she didn't really want to be here alone, either. "I've imposed on you for long enough."

"It's not an imposition. I care about you, Tabitha, and I don't like the idea of you being here by yourself."

"Thank you. I'll be all right for one night alone in the country. You don't have any murderers on the loose, do you?"

"No. But you never know who might stop by on the highway in the middle of the night. Strange things happen. I don't like it, Tabby. Come home with me."

He was concerned and protective. She appreciated that. But she was afraid that if she returned to his house, it would be even harder to leave tomorrow. She had to stay strong now, because they had already become too close. It was time for her to stand on her own two feet again.

"Thank you. But I think it would be best if I stay here."

He stared at her, his features tight, and clearly troubled.

She said, "I'll see you tomorrow night."

He still didn't move, and for a moment she wondered if he would argue about the subject. Then he abruptly headed for the door. Outside, he faced her.

"Call if you need anything. And I mean *anything*." Concern and frustration colored his tone. Tabitha bit her lip. She didn't want him to leave. But this was for the best. Wasn't it?

She made herself say, "'Bye, Arnie."

"Goodbye, Tabby," he growled. He pulled a business card from his wallet and pressed it into her palm. Then he strode down the steps and was gone.

Tabitha heard the rumble of his truck grow faint as she leaned against the closed door. Tears ached in her throat, but she fought to ignore them. The crisp business card dug into her fingers, but she couldn't look at it. She thrust it into her pocket.

First order of business—heat up this frosty house. She found the thermostat in the hall and raised the temperature from fifty degrees to sixty. Nothing happened.

Perhaps the furnace took a while to start up.

Arms crossed to ward off the chill, she entered the living room, still trying hard not to think about Arnie.

She noticed that her parents had a pellet stove, too. She plucked a magazine from the coffee table and tried to read. It didn't help. She felt colder by the minute. The furnace didn't appear to be working.

Worse, it bothered her as she thought about how she had pushed Arnie away, and how he had left. What a fool she was! With him or without him, she still missed him.

Tears threatened again. *Stop it,* she told herself, and stood up and paced. Exercise was a good way to warm up, right? Surely the furnace would start soon. She'd give it a few more minutes.

❄ ❄ ❄ ❄ ❄

Arnie drove faster than normal for home. Stubborn. That description fit Tabitha to a "T." She'd given him that level look and basically told him to leave.

Well, he'd left, and he didn't like it. He'd hated leaving her there by herself. He didn't want her to be alone tonight. Logically, he knew she'd probably be fine. All the same, worry gnawed at his gut. It was freezing cold outside. And what about the furnace? What if it didn't start?

He drew a harsh breath. He'd been a fool, running off in a fit of frustration like that. He should have at least started the furnace for her. And now he wouldn't see her until tomorrow.

As he drove, worry continued to plague him.

Familiar landmarks appeared. He was nearly home, and it surprised him to realize it. The speedometer hovered near seventy. Seeing it, he eased up on the gas. The last thing he needed was to kill himself by spinning out on a patch of black ice.

Buddy, you're losing it. Call her. Make sure she's all right.

❀ ❀ ❀ ❀ ❀

Twenty minutes had passed. Tabitha shuddered, arms crossed tightly over her flimsy winter coat. When she got back to New York City, she'd buy a parka! She never wanted to feel cold again. Fashion could take a hike.

She glanced from the unresponsive thermostat to the cold, dark pellet stove. It looked different than Arnie's. She wasn't even sure where to light it. But clearly the furnace wouldn't start, so she'd need to tackle the pellet stove next. Otherwise, she'd freeze to death.

She needed matches.

Tabitha retreated to the kitchen. Her mother had always kept matches in a cupboard above the refrigerator when she was a child. She stood on her tiptoes and flipped open the cabinet. Sure enough. A red box of matches.

She returned to the living room and found a bag of pellets in a corner. Good. Next, she opened the door of the stove and peered in. It was pitch black inside the dark cavern.

After lighting a match, she surveyed the mysterious interior of the pellet stove. What on earth was she looking for? Should she directly light a pellet? What if she started a fire where one shouldn't be? What if smoke poured into the house instead of out the chimney?

Frustration mounted. If only Arnie had taught her how to light his pellet stove!

She drew a trembling breath and tried to keep calm. It was difficult, because the unhappy feelings lingering from Arnie's abrupt departure combined with the incompetency she felt, being unable to light a simple piece of equipment. It all gathered together to create a knot in her stomach.

The phone rang behind her. With relief, she hurried to answer it. Maybe it was her parents, and she could ask their advice about lighting the stove. "Hello?"

A loud noise roared in the background. It sounded like a truck, or a piece of heavy machinery. Then a deep, familiar voice spoke in her ear. "It's Arnie."

Tabitha clenched the receiver so tightly she was surprised it didn't break. "Hello."

"You okay?" he asked gruffly.

"No!" She took several deep breaths, trying to calm her upset feeling. "But I *would* be if I knew how to light a pellet stove."

Silence from the other end. Then, "I'm coming back."

"That's not necessary. Just tell me what to do."

"I'd feel better if I could show you. Be there in twenty." The line clicked dead in her ear.

Tabitha glared at the receiver. He still wouldn't tell her what she needed to know. She was freezing cold right now, and she wasn't going to wait twenty minutes for him to arrive.

She was a grown woman, and she could take care of everything herself.

She shuddered harder inside her coat.

First, she'd see if her mother had a spare warm jacket. Then she'd find a way to warm the house.

Her gaze landed on the fireplace. Of course! She had matches, and she saw a few logs in the hearth. She could start a fire. When Arnie arrived, he'd find her sitting warm and comfortable in front of the fire. Of course she'd first need to get a few more logs to last through the night.

But first things first. A coat.

Tabitha pawed through the closet by the front door and found a scarf and mittens, a sweater, but not a jacket. Her mother must have worn it to Buffalo. Well, that couldn't be helped. She pulled off her own coat, pulled on the sweater, and then buttoned her trench coat over it.

There. Already she felt a little warmer. Now to find more firewood. She wanted to look competent and fully prepared when Arnie arrived. That meant she needed to find a small stockpile of wood quickly.

Whipping the pink scarf around her head, and pulling on her own hot pink mittens, Tabitha emerged into the frosty afternoon. Brilliant sunshine sparkled off of the deep snow. Now, where would her parents keep wood? Not outside, where it would get wet, that was for certain.

She took several mid-thigh deep steps through the snow and peered behind the house. Aha! A shed. The perfect place to store wood.

Tabitha floundered and battled through the heavy snow. By the time she reached the gray, weather-beaten shed she was exhausted. Snow had found its way up her pant legs and down inside of her boots. Great. She'd better make this snappy, or she'd get frostbite.

Unfortunately, the shed door opened to the outside, and the thick wall of snow prevented it from opening. Fortunately, however, she noticed a window on the side, which was slightly cracked open. She pushed. After a stiff squeak, it opened.

Tabitha peered into the dark interior, and her heart leaped with triumph. A small mountain of firewood lay piled against the far wall.

Now, just to get inside.

One advantage of the deep snow was that it gave her a small boost in height. The window was at waist level. She grabbed the sill and hooked one leg through the opening. Although it was narrow, she thought she could make it. Getting the other foot through, however, would be the tricky part.

Holding on tight, she struggled, scrunching up her body, and trying to shove her other foot through the narrow opening. The hard window ledge bit into her legs, and her hampering long coat didn't help matters, either.

Finally, she slithered inside, dragging her coat and a shower of snow along with her. She shivered, and waited a moment for her eyes to adjust to the dim light.

It was bigger inside than she had thought. In the back of the building she saw the outline of a work table and a pile of lumber. Neatly arranged tools hung on the wall. Her father probably spent hours here in the summertime. The floor appeared to be concrete, and it looked glossy near the window. A polish of some sort? Or maybe old spilled paint.

Not that it mattered. Time to gather up a few logs for the fire. Tabitha hurried forward. Suddenly, her feet skidded out from under her. With a cry, she twisted sideways and fell hard on the floor. The impact knocked the breath from her lungs.

Pain shot from her ankle all the way up to her hip. Gasping, she blinked back tears. After a few shaky breaths, she surveyed her body for damage. Her arms felt fine, and so did her back and her other leg. *I'll be fine,* she told herself, and lay quietly for a moment, hoping for the pain to ease.

The pain in her hip subsided after a long moment, but her ankle still hurt. Tabitha put her mittened hands on the floor and attempted to push herself up. Her hands slipped, and she fell hard on her shoulder. She gasped with pain. Ice! That's why the floor looked so glossy.

More carefully this time, she maneuvered into a sitting position. Her left ankle throbbed unmercifully. She must have twisted it. *Now* what was she going to do? She still needed that firewood. And it would do her ego a lot of good to get back to the house before Arnie arrived. It would be mortifying to have him find her lying here, incapacitated.

Carefully, she maneuvered onto her knees. Sharp pain stabbed up her leg every time she moved her foot, but she tried to ignore it. She needed firewood.

Determined, she crawled over to the stack. The floor here was dry. No more ice, thank goodness. Now she only needed to stand. Tabitha grabbed at the stack of firewood for balance, and very quickly discovered that she could put no weight on her left foot. Putting her left knee on the floor, she stood on her right foot, clutching a log for support.

Not the best of ideas, she realized when the piece of wood moved in her hand. A shudder went through the entire stack of logs. Terror streaked through her.

With a rushing, mighty thunder, all of the logs barreled down, crashing into her. She toppled over, landing on her stomach, and protectively clutched her arms over her head.

Logs battered her back and legs and arms. Terror and pain billowed through her. This was it. She was going to die. She'd never see Arnie again. Never. A sob seized her, and a block of wood hit the back of her head. Everything went black.

❅ ❅ ❅ ❅ ❅

An unexplainable urgency filled Arnie. He watched his speedometer needle climb higher. Only fifteen minutes from the McCroy house now. It felt like a lifetime. He wanted to push the gas to eighty, but that would be stupid. The roads were still icy and treacherous.

Tabitha wouldn't freeze before he got there. So why did he have this gut feeling that she needed him *now*?

The last miles passed by with excruciating slowness. At last he spotted the turn for the McCroy place, and he took the corner faster than he normally would. The truck jounced violently. *Easy,* he told himself. *You're here.* He threw on the parking brake and jumped out of the truck.

He walked fast for the front porch and pounded on the door with his fist. "Tabitha?"

Nothing.

He tried the knob. Unlocked. He strode inside and called her name again. Silence.

"Tabitha, where are you?" he bellowed. Moving fast, he did a quick check of all the rooms. Empty.

He returned outdoors. Where could she have gone without a car?

It only took a moment to note the footprints heading left, toward the back of the house. Zipping his jacket higher, he plowed after them. They ended at Daniel's shed. A window stood open, but all was silent and dark inside.

He didn't like it. Not one bit.

"Tabitha!" He stuck his head in the window. It took a moment for his eyes to adjust. Then he saw her still body, lying face down on the floor. Logs covered half of her body.

Fear slammed through him. "Tabitha!" he roared.

Chapter Twenty-Seven

TABITHA HEARD A FAINT SOUND. Her head hurt. Her body hurt, and especially her ankle hurt. She felt like she'd been battered by a thousand fists. She groaned. Something pounded in her head.

Or was it outside?

Neck feeling a bit stiff, she twisted her head and saw the door shudder. Strange. Didn't the person know it opened to the outside? They'd never get inside that way. As her bleary eyes watched, the door shuddered, and then splintered right before her eyes. A massive shoulder shoved through it. Another body slam, and the entire door ripped off its hinges and fell on the floor.

A man's large frame filled the doorway. *Arnie.*

Relief trembled through her, followed by a flare of fear. "Careful," she whispered.

He moved toward her, probably not hearing her.

"Ice!" she choked out. "Careful."

Arnie slowed down and walked with careful deliberation toward her. Within seconds, he knelt beside her. Weights lifted from her legs. And then she felt his warm fingers on her cheek.

"Are you okay, Tabby?"

"I'm...I'm not sure." Tears of relief and reaction dripped across her nose and down her cheek, toward the floor. She flexed her elbows. Maybe she should get up.

"Don't move. Let me check for broken bones." His firm, gentle hands moved over her body. "Tell me when it hurts."

She whispered, "Are you a doctor, too?"

"I'm trained for search and rescue. EMT, too." His fingers touched her left ankle, and she yelped. "That hurts?"

"I think I twisted it when I fell on the ice."

Arnie continued to check her body, and she lay very still, grateful that he knew what he was doing.

"Try to roll over," he told her. "I think your ankle got the worst of it."

Tabitha moved her shoulders and groaned. Her whole body ached, but she managed to carefully turn over as he asked, and even attempted to sit up. She made it to her elbows.

Arnie's strong arm went around her shoulders, supporting her. His face was very near, his eyes a dark, shadowed color in the dim shed. "What are you doing out here?" he said quietly.

Tabitha gestured toward the logs. "Getting firewood. I wanted to prove that I could take care of myself." More tears welled. "How useless am I?"

"It was an accident."

She shook her head, and bit her lip. "I'm freezing," she whispered. "I want to go to the house. Will you help me up?"

"You can't walk," he told her. One arm slipped under her knees, and in one swift movement, he pulled her close to his chest and rose to his feet. Tabitha gasped with surprise. She flung her arms around his strong neck, and held on for dear life.

A chuckled rumbled from deep in his chest. "I won't drop you."

"But no one's ever...I'm too heavy!" she squeaked, as he moved toward the door.

He hefted her in his arms, making her gasp still more. She felt his warm, quiet chuckle in her hair. "Two sacks of grain. No problem."

They stepped out into brilliant sunshine again. "I'm worth two sacks of grain?" she wanted to know. Arnie chuckled again, and she smiled, too.

She liked being held so close to him. He was strong. He held her as easily as he would a child, even tramping through the deep snow.

Inside the house, he set her on the couch and knelt to unzip and pull off her boots. She yelped when the left one came off. A shower of snow fell onto the floor.

His fingers gently probed her ankle. It looked twice its normal size. She gritted her teeth, enduring the pain, as he finished his evaluation. "I'm pretty sure it's sprained," he said. "But we should get you to a doctor."

"Not right now." That was the last thing she wanted to do. "He'll say the same thing you have. Then he'll give me two aspirins and tell me to lie down."

His frowned. "You're a stubborn woman."

"Yes," she agreed. "But if it's not better by tomorrow, I promise I'll call Dr. Callahan."

"All right. I'll see if your parents have an ace bandage." He disappeared down the hall. After a short absence, he reappeared and wrapped up her ankle, and then applied an ice pack. "I recommend ibuprofen. It'll reduce the swelling." He handed her a tablet, along with a glass of water. Tabitha gulped it down.

Arnie rubbed his hands. "Now I'll start the stove." He still wore his heavy navy blue coat. Tabitha felt colder than ever. She noticed the afghan on the back of the couch and pulled it over her legs and cold feet.

If only she could move, she could watch him start the stove. Would starting a pellet stove forever remain a mystery to her?

Soon warmth emanated from the stove, and he turned his attention to the malfunctioning furnace. He disappeared down the hall. Tabitha was just starting to feel warmer when he returned.

"Did you find the problem?"

"No. But it feels nice in here now." He shucked off his jacket and glanced at the recliner.

Tabitha blurted, "Sit over here. With me. ...If you want to, I mean," she said. "This blanket is nice and warm."

An indecipherable look crossed his face, and he slowly moved toward her. "You want to share a blanket with me?"

Her face warmed. "Only if you're cold."

It was a small thing, but they'd never sat beside each other before. At his house, he always sat in his recliner.

He eased himself down beside her.

"Do you want the blanket?" she asked shyly.

"No. You keep it." He stretched his arms across the back of the couch. She glanced at him, and saw he was looking at her, too. His brown eyes looked warm, and a little cautious.

"Thank you," she said. "For rescuing me, I mean."

"I broke the speed limit getting here," he admitted gruffly. "I had a feeling you were in trouble."

She absorbed this. Arnie, who was always so careful, had broken the law because he was worried about her. "I'm sorry for earlier. Before you left." She offered the truth. "I think I wanted to push you away. I'm not looking forward to leaving Newbough."

Understanding flickered in his gaze. The hair stirred at the nape of her neck.

She said, "So, will you forgive me?"

"Only if you'll forgive me. If I'd shown you how to light a stove, this wouldn't have happened."

"Thank you for coming back."

"I'd like to stay here tonight, if you'll let me."

Joy filled her. But she said, "Why?"

"Because I want to be with you. I want to know that you're safe."

Tabitha didn't know what to say to this. How could this man make her feel so secure and protected, and yet exasperate her a tiny bit, too? "I can take care of myself," she told him, conveniently forgetting the shed incident.

"I know."

"Really?"

"Yes, Tabitha. You're one of the strongest women I know. But I want to be here and protect you because I care about you."

"You do?" She smiled.

"So will you let me stay?"

Soft gratitude filled her. "I would appreciate it. Thank you."

"Good," he smiled.

Peaceful moments passed, and then his fingers brushed the skin on the nape of her neck. She drew a quick breath, and flashed him an unsteady smile. "Are you making a move on me?"

He watched her for a long moment, as if trying to make up his mind. "Maybe," he growled huskily.

Tabitha lay her head on his shoulder. His arm went around her, securing her close to him. She wanted nothing more.

"Now what?" she whispered.

He took a deep breath. "Take it slow," he suggested. She nodded, and remained where she was, snuggled up against him. Peace and comfort filled her heart. After a long while, she felt his warm breath stir her hair, and then a fleeting caress brushed her temple.

She looked up into his warm brown eyes, and her fingers curled into his flannel shirt when she saw the need and longing there. She wanted the same, and moved closer. He kissed her. The slow, exploring kiss burst Tabitha's nerve endings into flame. She melted against him, wanting to be closer to him. She loved the feel of him, the taste of him—everything about him. Her head spun with the potency that was all Arnie.

She worked her fingers into his collar, and somehow she had been divested of her coat and extra sweater when he at last pulled away, breaths harsh. "Tabitha." His voice sounded rough. She clung to him, unwilling to let go. "Tabby, this is not slow."

She gasped, and realized that she was plastered against him. She jerked away. "I'm sorry! I didn't mean to...to..."

"It wasn't only you." Arnie looked down at his hands, as if he'd never seen them before, and then at her coat and her mother's sweater, pooled on the floor. "I'm sorry. It's been a long time..."

"Don't apologize," she said fiercely. "It was wonderful. But I agree that we need to stop." After all, she shouldn't have been kissing him at all. Hadn't she warned herself?

But she wanted to kiss him again. Right now. Tabitha bit her lip and scooted away at the same moment Arnie rose to his feet. Abruptly, he headed for the kitchen. "I'll make dinner," he said over his shoulder, and disappeared.

She elevated her foot on the arm of the couch, and again draped the ice pack over it. She lay back on the cushion which was still warm from Arnie's body heat. She thought about their kiss. And about how she'd felt in his arms. And how she felt about him. Warmth. Tenderness. Respect. The depth of her feelings frightened her. He was the most wonderful man she'd ever met. Why did he have to live here, and not in New York City?

She couldn't be falling in love with Arnie, a farmer. A man whose life was as different from hers as night was from day.

❄ ❄ ❄ ❄ ❄

Arnie stood in front of the open refrigerator, trying to cool down. He didn't even pretend to look for food.

He'd lost his head with Tabitha. He'd gone too far, and his visceral response scared him. Was it truly because it had been a long time since he'd held a woman? Or was it Tabitha?

Knowing the answer, he growled in his throat. So he'd wanted to know how deep his feelings could go? Here was his answer. A flame licked inside him for Tabitha.

He was falling in love with her.

If he was a swearing man, no words could express how he felt right now. Hopelessness. Despair, and the familiar aching, scorching pain.

"You're a fool!" he whispered, clenching his fist. He slammed the refrigerator door, pulled open the kitchen door and headed into the bracing cold of twilight.

He strode to his truck and pulled out the sleeping bag he always kept behind the seat. He'd asked Tabitha if he could stay tonight. Maybe it wasn't the best of ideas, but he still felt determined to do so. He wouldn't leave her alone here. He'd protect her...perhaps especially from himself.

He clenched his sleeping bag in his freezing arms and returned to the house. He could not kiss her again. His heart was already too far gone. No more sliding down that slippery slope to the hell of love he knew too well. He couldn't live with that kind of pain ever again.

❊ ❊ ❊ ❊ ❊

Tabitha heard the kitchen door slam and wondered where Arnie had gone. His coat still lay on the arm of the couch.

She swung her legs to the floor. Her ankle still hurt, and aches and pains remained from the battering the logs had given her, but she wanted to go into the kitchen and see what was going on. Grabbing the couch arm for support, she levered onto to her feet.

So far, so good. Lifting her injured foot off the floor, she slowly hopped toward the kitchen, first by holding onto the end table for support, and then the recliner. Five feet of open space remained between where she stood and the kitchen door. Once inside, she could use the counters for support.

She steadied herself by clutching the back of the recliner. Good. Now, perfect balance, perfect hops... After first imagining success in her mind, she hopped for the doorway. The first two hops went well, but then she began to wobble dangerously from side to side. The last thing she needed was to fall again.

With a burst of speed, Tabitha hippity-hopped to the swinging door and grabbed the door frame before she could topple over.

Heart racing, she paused for a moment, regaining her breath and her balance, and then pushed into the kitchen. As she'd suspected, Arnie was nowhere to be seen. She hopped in and leaned against the counter. Before she could decide what to do next, a large shadow moved outside the curtained kitchen door and Arnie stomped back inside, shaking with cold.

"What were you doing out there?" she exclaimed.

He frowned, looking none too happy to see her. "Getting something from my truck."

"Without your coat?"

Arnie didn't answer. His arm tightened around his sleeping bag, and then he shoved it onto the counter. "Why are you up? You're not supposed to be walking."

"I'm hopping," she informed him. Clearly, he was in no mood to speak. Would he retreat behind his wall again? Tabitha hated the thought. She didn't want their relationship to regress again. "Don't do this, please."

He really looked at her then, and she felt unnerved by the dark pain in his eyes. "Things are going way too fast, Tabitha."

She said nothing for a moment. "I know we shouldn't be romantically involved." It hurt to say it, but logically, it was true.

"Then what's happening between us?"

"I don't know. I like you so much, Arnie. That wasn't planned. This past week I've never felt so up in the air and uncertain...and cold and warm...and exhilarated and frustrated and...and...wonderfully happy, ever. And it's all because of you. You've made all the difference to me. You've helped me to see life more clearly." She raised her hands helplessly. "When I'm with you, everything makes sense."

"And without me? When you go back to New York?"

Softly, and with an ache in her throat, she said, "I don't know."

He raked a hand over his buzz cut. "Let's stop this now, Tabitha. Friends. No more kissing or touching."

"Okay." She bit her lip. "If that's what you want."

He stared at her, and then slowly advanced toward her. His movements now seemed dangerous and predatory. Entirely unlike the Arnie she knew and loved.

Her breath caught. *Loved?* No.

He stopped a spare foot from her. His presence electrified her senses. So did a small thrill of danger.

"Is it what *you* want?" he growled.

Goosebumps prickled up on her skin. She moistened her lips. "Kisses...well, they're probably not the smartest thing."

An unspoken "but" hovered on her tongue. Appearing to sense it, his gaze licked over her like white lightening.

Her breaths slowed in response, feeling thick and heavy as sweet tension spiraled in her. She swallowed. "What do you think?"

"If I kiss you again tonight, I may not be able to stop."

Her heart beat like thunder. "Okay," she said softly.

"Okay?" His eyes narrowed, shocked, and then heat scorched them, lighting the dark amber to flame.

"I meant," she said shakily, raising her hands to his chest to ward him off, even though he had come no closer, "you're right. No more kissing."

The intense fire in his gaze banked to burning embers. "So we're agreed?"

"Yes." Her mouth said the logical thing, but her heart said another. Not that she wanted to...to... Her face flamed at the thought. "We'll be friends. I don't want you to go all reserved and prickly on me again."

"Tabitha." He sounded frustrated.

"Please, can we just talk and enjoy ourselves?"

He heaved a breath. "If that's what you want."

"I do." She smiled. "Now, how can I help with dinner?"

He put an arm around her shoulders and firmly guided her to the kitchen table. There, he pulled out a chair for her. "Sit," he told her. "I'll cook dinner."

She obediently sat, and pulled out another chair to rest her foot upon.

Arnie moved about the kitchen with his usual slow grace and economy of movement that were his trademarks. Her gaze lingered on how his jeans hugged his lean hips, and how his plaid flannel stretched across his broad shoulders. Arnie was definitely the most handsome man she had ever met.

And he was also strong, honorable, smart, and deeply compassionate. He possessed a depth and integrity of character that she'd never seen in anyone else. A depth that fascinated and thrilled her.

She did love him.

The intense, sweet feeling flooded her, catching her breath. It was true. She wanted to stay with him. In fact, she didn't want to leave him—not now, not ever.

She was head-over-heels in love with Arnie.

On the heels of that knowledge came despair. She'd lost her mind.

She couldn't leave New York City, and he couldn't leave his farm.

What a mess! Pain welled within her. How could she have fallen in love with the wrong man?

Maybe it wasn't love. Maybe it would all go away when she went home. Maybe she'd forget about him. Maybe their enforced closeness had forged an illusion of powerful intimacy.

Or maybe she was just about to suffer through a broken heart.

❀ ❀ ❀ ❀ ❀

Tabitha and Arnie spoke politely at dinner, but took great pains not to touch each other again. When it was time for bed, she briefly put an arm around his waist for support as she hopped to the bathroom door, and then managed on her own.

When she hopped out to the living room, using the wall for support, she discovered that Arnie had found blankets and pillows and set up two sleeping areas for them on the floor near the pellet stove. Since the furnace still wasn't working, it would be too cold to sleep in the back part of the house.

Without a word, he put an arm around her shoulders and helped her maneuver to her pile of bedding.

"Thank you," she said lowering herself to the floor. "You're awfully chivalrous."

He smiled and flipped off the lamp. In the darkness of the room, she heard rustling movements as he slid inside his sleeping bag.

"I think I'd better see the doctor tomorrow," she said. "I need crutches."

"Good idea." He fell silent, and Tabitha lay in the dark, thinking about the eventful day, and about Arnie.

Although the two of them had agreed they should back off and just be "friends," who was she trying to fool? She couldn't be just friends with him. She loved him. Pretending only friendship wouldn't change the truth. Vowing not to kiss him again would not change her feelings.

She loved him. And in a few days she'd leave him. At last, overwhelming pain scorched her. Hot tears slipped into her pillow. She sniffed quietly, so he wouldn't guess that she was crying.

CHAPTER TWENTY-EIGHT

NEW YEAR'S EVE

THE NEXT MORNING when Tabitha awoke, Arnie's sleeping bag was empty. Her ankle still ached, and so did the bruises on her back and legs. She'd call Dr. Callahan this morning. Her ankle should be evaluated, and she needed crutches, too. Hopefully the elderly doctor would agree to see her today, on a Sunday.

A pan clanked in the kitchen and she relaxed a little, knowing that Arnie was nearby. Probably making their breakfast. Afterward, she was sure he'd drive her to Dr. Callahan's.

Driving reminded her of the rental.

Arnie's mechanic buddy hadn't called yesterday with a report about the car, and she wondered if the garage would be open on New Year's Eve.

After showering as best she could, she joined him in the kitchen. He'd set two places at the table with coffee, eggs and bacon, and he already forked food into his mouth.

Carefully, she slipped into her chair, wincing a little. Her ankle hurt a little less than yesterday, but the bruises seemed to hurt more. In the mirror she'd counted seventeen covering her back and thighs. Many looked angry and purple, and the knot on her skull felt tender. She swallowed another ibuprofen and hoped it would help.

"How are you feeling?"

"I've been better. I took another pain pill, just like the doctor ordered." She offered him a smile, hating the distance she still sensed between them. Part of her, however, wondered if Arnie might be right—if pulling back, or maybe even pushing each other away before she left would make her departure less painful.

It seemed unlikely. She already loved him. How could leaving possibly become less painful? But the distance between them now hurt, and she wanted it gone. "We haven't heard from Rodney. Does he work today?"

He pulled out his cell phone. "I'll call him at home."

During his short call, Tabitha tried to piece together the story from Arnie's terse, "You're sure that's it? ...Great. Thanks, buddy." He hung up.

"It's fixed?" she guessed.

"Needed a new battery. The car agency okayed it. Rodney says we can pick it up anytime. He left the keys behind the tire."

"Is that safe?" And then she smiled. "I forgot. This is Mayberry."

"Not quite. But it should be safe."

"I'll call Dr. Callahan after breakfast. Hopefully he'll see me. Maybe we can do all of our errands at once."

He nodded and fell to his breakfast again.

The silence felt awkward. "My parents should be home by around one o'clock."

"I'll be out of here as soon as you're set."

"It sounds like you're eager to run off."

"It's for the best, don't you think?" He put his plate in the sink.

"Ignoring the problem won't solve it."

"Do you have a better plan, Tabby?"

The "Tabby" encouraged her. "We only have a few days left. It'll hurt a lot when I leave. I don't want it to start now."

"I don't know if I can handle it. In some ways, this feels like Theresa, all over again. I don't want to lose you, too."

"I understand."

A moment passed, and then he slowly pushed away from the counter. "*Do* you?"

"I do. But denying our feelings won't make them go away. And it won't make leaving any less painful."

"Things can still go a whole lot deeper between us." Pain tightened his low words. "I can't take it. Not again."

"So we'll treat each other like strangers now? Is that it?"

"No." Frustration bit through the word.

"But you're putting up that wall again." Her voice caught. "Frankly, that hurts a whole lot more than saying goodbye."

He straddled his chair and faced her. "What do you want, then?"

Tears threatened, but she blinked them back. "I don't want this wall, or this distrust between us."

"I trust you," he said quietly. "But I can't take another broken heart."

"I don't want to break your heart." To her dismay, tears slipped down her cheeks. Impatiently, she dashed them away. "I lo..." She stopped. She couldn't tell him she loved him.

Not now. It would only complicate matters even more. She drew a fortifying breath. "Maybe I'm foolish, but I want to enjoy our last days together. Every single minute. Is that so terrible?"

Long moments passed, and she feared he wouldn't say anything at all. But of course he did. "I really want that, too, Tabby. But I want to go slow. We've been speeding."

"I agree."

"No kissing for a while." His broad palm covered hers. "But we can hold hands, if you want."

She covered his hand with her left one. "I want that, too."

He growled, "I hope we're not making a mistake."

"Since when is it a mistake to care for someone?" With a smile, she finished her eggs. Arnie's hand still covered her right one, which made it difficult to eat, but his smile leant wings to her heart.

"Okay, gimpy," he said, plucking up her plate and rising. "I'll clean your dishes while you call Dr. Callahan."

She stuck out her tongue. It felt good to be back on more secure footing with him. She loved him so much. And she *would* enjoy every minute they had left together. She'd deal with the pain later.

❄ ❄ ❄ ❄ ❄

Dr. Callahan cheerfully agreed to meet Tabitha at his office. The quick visit confirmed that she had a sprain, and he outfitted her with crutches and a caution to continue the ice packs and anti-inflammatories.

After retrieving her car, they caravanned back to the McCroy house so Arnie could collect his sleeping bag and head home. Tabitha's spirits fell at the thought.

When they arrived, her father's dark blue Bronco was parked the driveway.

"They're home!" She swung on her crutches as fast as she could for the front door.

"Easy," Arnie murmured when the end of her crutch caught in a small snow hole and she teetered off balance. Only his quick hands around her waist prevented her from falling. He gently tugged the crutches away from her and gripped them in one hand. "Put your arm around me. These crutches aren't much use in the snow."

Tabitha was happy to do so. Holding onto him tightly for balance, she hopped up the porch and inside.

"Mom! Dad!" she called out. "We're home!"

"Tabitha!" Nancy McCroy hurried from the kitchen and enveloped her in a warm hug. "Did you spend the night here? I notice the stove is burning. That furnace!" She expelled an impatient breath. "Your father is insisting on fixing it right now."

Daniel shuffled into view in the hallway. He had a hand on the wall for support.

"Looks like you need crutches, too, Dad." Tabitha retrieved hers from Arnie and swung over to give him a hug.

"What *happened* to you?" Nancy demanded.

Tabitha laughed a little. "You don't want to know." She glanced at Arnie. "Good thing my knight in shining armor rescued me."

"Sit down right now," Nancy fussed. "You too, Daniel."

Daniel shuffled instead for the utility closet. "Doc told me I need to walk. I'm gonna take a look at this cantankerous piece of equipment."

To Tabitha's relief, Arnie moved to assist her father. Soon she heard clanking noises and the low murmur of the two men's voices.

Nancy plopped down beside her on the couch. "I see the two beds on the floor. Arnie spent the night?"

Tabitha explained yesterday's drama, and Nancy exclaimed every few moments.

The furnace gave a clank and a hiss, and then rumbled to life.

"Thank the Lord!" Nancy exclaimed, and the two men returned to the living room. Daniel clung to Arnie's arm, his face gray, and Arnie gently helped him into the leather recliner.

"How about a drink?" he suggested.

"Scotch?" Daniel said, with a weak bark of laughter.

"Water," Nancy said firmly, and Arnie retrieved a glass for Daniel.

Daniel eyed him over the rim. "You're a lifesaver, son."

"You don't know the half of it," Nancy said. "Arnie, we are forever in your debt. Could you possibly join us for dinner tonight?" She glanced at Tabitha. "Of course, it is New Year's Eve. Perhaps you have plans."

"We're going to a party tonight," she said. "But that's after dinner."

"Thank you," Arnie said. "I'd enjoy that."

"Excellent!" Nancy looked pleased. "We'll see you at six?"

He nodded. "That will be just right. I need to buy groceries and head home to change. That will give me plenty of time."

He gathered up his belongings, and Tabitha saw him to the door. Joy lifted her spirits at the thought of seeing him again for dinner, and for the party afterward. She smiled. "See you later. Thank you for everything."

His fingers curled briefly around hers. "Later, Tabby."

Chapter Twenty-Nine

The afternoon passed quickly, and Tabitha enjoyed spending time talking to her mother. Daniel dozed off in his recliner, and slept away most of the afternoon.

His frailty alarmed her. She knew he'd just had major surgery, but seeing him so weak frightened her. Again, she renewed her resolve to visit every month after she returned to work. She'd learned her lesson. Life was too short. She would spend every minute she could with the people she loved.

It seemed strange to spend an entire afternoon without Arnie. They had spent the past week practically glued at the hip, marooned in a sea of white, and now, suddenly, he was gone.

She missed him. At the same time, she realized this small break from each other was probably a good idea. They'd grown so close so fast. Maybe it was best to take a breather and see if their feelings still remained after their enforced closeness ended.

However, her five hour separation from Arnie didn't dampen her feelings at all. If anything, she anticipated seeing him more intensely as it neared six o'clock. She was ready at five forty-five, dressed in black slacks and a royal blue cashmere sweater.

Finally, the cuckoo clock chimed six o'clock, and the little yellow bird she'd watched since childhood wobbled out. She resisted the adolescent urge to dash to the window and peek through the drapes to see if his headlights were approaching. But she did hover in the living room, leaning on her crutches, and pretended to look over old photographs on the mantle. Only four quick hops, and she'd be at the front door.

Tabitha at last heard a firm, heavy knock, and her heart skipped into an accelerated rush.

"I'll get it," she called out, and quickly swung over to open the door. When he smiled at her, joy leaped in her heart. "Hi."

His gaze scanned her face, and then slowly grazed her lips. "Tabby."

Her breath caught for a second. She gathered her thoughts. "Come in."

He wore his usual jeans and dark blue heavy jacket, but no cap. His buzzed hair stood up crisp and straight, as if he'd come straight from the shower. A faint waft of spicy aftershave tantalized her nose.

He shrugged out of his jacket and Tabitha's heart fluttered. He was so handsome. Tonight, instead of his usual flannel, he wore a brown button down shirt which was a shade darker than his warm brown eyes and hair. Its clean lines emphasized his muscular physique and broad shoulders.

"You look nice." Definitely an inadequate word. Arnie looked devastatingly attractive. Her throat suddenly felt dry. "Can...can I take your coat?"

"I'll get it. Those crutches are enough for you."

When he moved by, his arm brushed hers and the breath hitched in her throat again. To cover her disturbingly flustered feelings, she said, "Dinner's ready. I think Mom wants us to sit down."

In short order, they all sat around the dining table, with her father at one end and Arnie at the other. Color had returned to Daniel's face, and Tabitha was glad to see it. She glanced at the two men in her life. It felt right to have them both here, together.

Her father sent Arnie a small smile. "You've taken good care of my little girl."

He smiled. "I tried, sir."

"She can be a handful," Daniel agreed, spooning potatoes onto his plate.

"Daddy."

"Don't pretend to be different than you are," her father said gruffly. "Wouldn't have you any other way."

She glanced at Arnie, who gave her one of his slow smiles. "She's one of a kind," he agreed.

Daniel fixed him with a narrowed glance. "You got close, did you? Not too close, I hope."

Her cheeks warmed. "Daddy! Please."

Daniel ignored her plea. "Arnie's a man who'll tell me what's what. Won't you, son?"

Tabitha remembered the sizzling kiss on the couch last night. Still, they'd stopped in plenty of time. "Nothing happened, Dad. Arnie is a complete gentleman."

"That so?" Daniel's gaze still bored into his guest.

"Sir, I wouldn't take advantage of Tabitha. I hope you know that."

"Just making sure. Or I'd have to throw you out, weak heart an' all."

Everyone burst into laughter. Her father's eyes twinkled. "Thought I had you sized up right, son. Glad to see I wasn't wrong."

Tabitha felt an urgent need to change the subject. "Mom, did I hear you talk to Ellen on the phone earlier? Are you coming to the party?"

"No, honey. I'm going to stay right here with your dad. He needs me."

"Go on, woman," Daniel growled. "I'm not sick. I can wipe my mouth and dress in my pj's, all on my own."

Nancy rolled her eyes. "Why would I choose to leave here and miss all this love?"

"You know you love me," Daniel said smugly. "That's why you want me to keep kicking a little longer."

Tabitha's mother sighed. "Just think. This is only the beginning of his recovery. The next six weeks should be a picnic! Are you sure you can't stay longer, Tabitha?"

"No, but I'll come back for your birthday, Daddy."

Daniel eyed her. "You sure about that?"

"Yes, Dad. I love you both, and I plan to visit every month from now on."

"Might get sick of us." But a faint smile tugged at his lips.

"Dad."

"We'll keep the light on for you." Daniel cast Arnie a glance. "Maybe you should, too. Just in case she gets lost again."

Tightness again squeezed her heart at the thought of leaving and hardly ever seeing Arnie again.

His gaze seemed to shutter when he looked at her. "Tabitha is always welcome at my house."

If only she could stay with Arnie when she came to visit her parents.

She blinked, aghast at her thoughts. She couldn't stay with him! Her father would have a coronary, for sure. But she'd miss being with Arnie, and talking to him, arguing with him, and being close in the same quiet room with him for long, lazy afternoons. Her heart constricted, and tears ached in her throat.

Tabitha said, "I'll visit whenever I can."

Arnie's gaze held hers for a long moment, and he gave a short nod.

Nancy turned the conversation to other subjects, to Tabitha's relief. She didn't want to think about leaving. And would everything be different when she returned for a visit? Would the closeness between them die? Would he become that remote, cold stranger again? The thought scared her, because she was afraid that was exactly what would happen.

Chapter Thirty

Arnie parked behind a long line of vehicles on one of Newbough's residential streets. A streetlight lit a far corner, and lights glowed behind a multitude of curtained windows. Sidewalks, if there were any, were still covered in deep snow. Tabitha hoped her crutches wouldn't skid on the slippery road.

Arnie walked close beside Tabitha and directed her through the moonlit dimness to a low, one-story house.

Two trucks were parked in the crunchy, lumpy driveway, and the garage door was open, but the path to the front door had yet to be shoveled. Tabitha guessed the way indoors was through the open garage. Another shadowy vehicle loomed in the dark interior.

Arnie moved through the garage and opened a door on the far side. Light streamed out. It appeared to be a laundry room, but the door leading into the house was closed. As Tabitha carefully swung inside, she discovered why. In the middle of the laundry room was a basket of wriggling puppies.

"Aren't you sweet," she exclaimed, and propped her crutches against the dryer. Grabbing the white machine for support, she knelt to the ground. Arnie went down on one knee beside her, too.

Six puppies squirmed, wriggling for attention. Three were black, two were chocolate colored, and one was white.

The other door swung open, and blast of noise erupted into the quiet laundry room. A red-haired boy appeared.

"Arnie!" he cried out, and the big man hugged the boy's skinny shoulders.

"Josh, this is Tabitha."

Tabitha smiled. "Nice to meet you, Josh. Are these your puppies?"

The boy dropped to his knees. "Yeah. But Mom says we have to find homes for them." Hopeful blue eyes peeked out from behind a drooping lock of hair. "Do you want one?"

She smiled. "I'm sorry. My apartment doesn't allow pets."

"Bummer."

"But they are so *cute*," she said, lifting the soft, white, wiggling pup into her arms.

"That one's a girl," Josh said helpfully, and watched the puppy wriggle upward to lick Tabitha's face. He grinned. "She likes you."

The puppy caught sight of Arnie then, and strained toward him, too. Tabitha handed her over, and the pup gave a little leap and eagerly licked his nose. He stroked the soft fur bundle for a minute, allowing the puppy to lick his chin and cheek.

Josh smiled in satisfaction. "She likes both of you."

Arnie gave the pup one last caress with his large, gentle hand, and lowered her to the basket.

The door flew open again and a blast of party sounds swirled inside. A woman with honey-colored, corkscrew curls appeared in the doorway.

"Arnie Arnold!" she cried, somehow managing to sound both pleased and reproving at the same time. She wore a drapy, sequined white blouse, multi-patterned teal capris and impossibly high, spiked gold heels. "Been waiting for you, big boy. Stop hiding out in the laundry room!"

The other woman flashed Tabitha what was probably meant to be a smile, but instead resembled a baring of fangs. "Don't keep us waiting," the woman cooed, and shut the door.

A faint smiled tugged at Arnie's lips. "Mitzy Mae loves a good party. The more the merrier."

She wasn't sure that was all Mitzy Mae liked. She tried to ignore a prickle of jealousy as she followed him into the crowded house. He wasn't interested. Was he?

The small house was packed. People gathered in tight clumps in the kitchen, in the living room near the bottles of soda and buckets of ice, and near the trays of deserts, too. Arnie cleared a path for Tabitha as he headed toward the drinks table, and introduced her to people along the way. Everyone seemed friendly, but most—especially the women—cast speculative glances between her and Arnie.

He poured them both drinks and held hers as they edged toward Ellen.

His friend, dressed in a black, sleeveless dress, made a beeline for them. "You made it!" she said, and kissed his cheek. She turned to Tabitha with a look of concern. "And what happened to you?"

"I hit a patch of ice. Dr. Callahan says I'll live."

She laughed and patted Tabitha's shoulder. "I like her, Arnie." With a warm smile, she said to Tabitha. "Has he introduced you to everyone?"

"A few people. I'm not sure I'll remember everyone's names, though." She laughed. "Except for Mitzy Mae, of course. She definitely leaves an impression."

Ellen rolled her eyes. "Don't let Mitzy bother you. She's just off a divorce. Now she's flexing her claws for her next victim."

Tabitha gasped out a surprised laugh and felt Arnie's hand touch her back. It felt secure. Anchoring. Suddenly she felt like she belonged at this party of all his friends. And with him.

He said, "Expecting a heat wave, Ellen?"

Ellen unexpectedly giggled. "You mean this old dress? I'm waitress, hostess, and party smoothing conversationalist. It's hot work. Speaking of which—I see more people I need to greet. See you later." She slipped off.

He said, "Want to sit down?"

All the seats were taken. "I'd rather meet more of your friends."

Arnie introduced her to many more people, and before long she found herself engaged in conversation with a young, earnest businessman who was fascinated by her job on Wall Street.

Arnie touched her shoulder. "I'll be back in a minute."

"Don't worry about me. Have fun." She smiled up at him. One of her best skills was striking up conversations with new people at parties. People fascinated her. Ask the right questions, and it was amazing how quickly they opened up. This young man, for example, began to wax philosophic about the stock market, and she smiled as she listened, and interjected a pithy comment from time to time.

❄ ❄ ❄ ❄ ❄

Arnie watched Tabitha across the room. Wearing a sweet, vivacious smile, she chattered with a new set of his friends now. The crutches weren't holding her back at all. She seemed to feel perfectly at ease in a roomful of strangers—as if she found each and every one of them fascinating. And he was certain that she did. Pride and admiration grew for her. She cared for people, and for him.

She was so beautiful. His gut clenched. So sweet and warm. She had melted the block of ice around his heart. Now he felt things again, all right. Too much.

A hand on his shoulder startled him.

Ellen smiled. "Is there hope for you after all?" She glanced at Tabitha, and then back at him. "It's about time. You deserve to be happy, Arnie."

It hurt to say it, but he did anyway. "Tabitha's not for me." His throat felt tight. He'd been wishing for the moon, hoping he and Tabitha could have a chance. But the closer it came to her departure, the quicker reality stripped away the impossible hope in his heart.

"No? Could have fooled me."

"She's heading back to New York City on Tuesday."

"And you'll let that be the end of it?"

He gulped fruit punch. "It's the way it has to be, Ellen."

Softly, she said, "It's too late, isn't it?"

"What do you mean?"

"You're in love with her."

Arnie wished his friend wasn't so insightful. "Let it go."

"You'll regret it if you don't at least try."

"Her world is New York. All the lights and glitz and hustle bustle. She thrives on it. She's one of the best analysts on Wall Street. She's going places, and I won't hold her back."

"Have you asked her how she feels? Have you told her *you* feel?"

"No."

"Why not?"

"She can do better than me, Ellen. New York is full of men. One of them will be perfect for her." Just the thought of that, however, squeezed a fist of agony around his heart.

Tabitha glanced over and flashed him a smile. It lit up her entire face.

"You're a fool," Ellen murmured. "That girl is bonkers for you."

He said nothing, and watched a dark-haired, goateed man approach Tabitha. Derek. He'd never cared for the man. Derek said all the right words, but his gut told him the guy was slime. Smiling now, Derek edged closer to Tabitha and lay a familiar hand on her arm. She flinched and discretely tried to twitch free, but he hung on.

Fury shot through Arnie, as sharp as a jab of adrenaline. His fists clenched. He wanted to stride over and shove the man's hand off of her. But would she thank him? Wasn't she always insisting that she was a grown woman, and capable of taking care of herself?

"You're sure you won't mind her getting involved with another man?" Ellen's sharp gaze scanned his face. "You want to go over and punch Derek, don't you?"

He didn't answer. His jaw ached from clenching it.

"You love her."

"No."

Ellen squeezed his shoulder. "Tell yourself the truth. And then go for what you want. I don't want to see you spend the next fifty years alone and miserable."

"Tabitha said the same thing."

"Did she? Then I like her more and more. In fact, I think I'll go talk to her right now."

"Ellen..."

She ignored him, as he'd known she would. His friend headed across the room.

Now he noticed that Tabitha had disentangled herself from Derek's octopus hands. Still, Arnie found himself moving toward her, too. Who knew what plan Ellen had hatched up her sleeve now—and he wanted to silently warn Derek to keep his distance, too.

CHAPTER THIRTY-ONE

TABITHA FELT RELIEVED when Derek finally released his grip on her arm. A groper. She'd figured him out after his first oily sentence.

He still hovered too close to her, laughing at his own poor jokes. She wished he'd go away. Unpleasant breath fanned her face, and his black eyes, half-hidden behind his black-framed glasses looked hard. He pretended to be warm and friendly, but it was an act. Those pebbled eyes suddenly glanced up. Alarm registered, and then derision.

Arnie's arm settled around her shoulders. It felt warm and secure, and relief slid into her bones. "Arnie," she grinned up at him. "You have so many nice friends." Not so unobtrusively, she angled her back toward Derek. "You're just in time. I need a sip of my drink." Arnie handed her the cup he'd been carrying for her.

As she drank, out of the corner of her eye she watched Derek slither away. Ellen appeared from nowhere, carrying a tray covered with little pastry cups filled with cream or chocolate.

"Mini cheesecakes," Ellen announced with a smile. "Want some?"

"Yum!" Tabitha reached for a chocolate, while Arnie grabbed two of the cream colored ones. He reached for another, but Ellen swatted his hand and extended the tray to Tabitha.

"Another?"

"I can't resist," she sighed, and plucked up another sweet confection.

Ellen glanced at Arnie. "We make some pretty good stuff here in Newbough."

"They're homemade?"

"The best kind."

"Everything I buy is prepackaged," Tabitha admitted. "Nothing tastes as good as it does from scratch."

"Down-to-earth, good and wholesome. That's what we offer here," Ellen remarked. "Even our men are tasty and wholesome, through and through. But maybe you've realized that already."

"Ellen!" A flush rose on Arnie's neck.

Tabitha felt a similar one warming her cheeks. "I know the best when I see it," she assured Ellen, and glanced at Arnie. He frowned at Ellen, who ignored him.

"Good!" said their hostess. "So, I see you've noticed the difference between your city boys and a down home, country man."

More unwelcome heat warmed on her face. "I certainly have. No one can compare to Arnie. I know that already." Her soft gaze lingered on his face, and he stopped looking daggers at Ellen long enough to catch it. His brown eyes melted to the dark amber again, and his arm tightened around her shoulders.

Ellen said, "When you've found the best, forget the rest." With a grin, she said, "Ta!" and glided away.

"Sorry," Arnie muttered.

"Why? Because she cares about you?" She still felt embarrassed, but it was clear that the other woman only wanted Tabitha to give him a chance. Ellen wanted Arnie to be happy, and so did Tabitha, more than anything.

"She's not one to keep her opinion to herself."

She smiled up at him. "I'm glad you have a friend like her."

"Me, too. But sometimes she's too pushy."

"That's what friends are for. To help us see things we may not on our own. You've made me realize a few things, too."

"I have?"

"You've helped me to remember what's most important in life. God. My family. And to slow down and accept myself for who I am. It's freeing and restful to know that the people who care most about me don't give a fig whether I win or lose on Wall Street."

He smiled at her, and for a second she received the strong impression that he was about tell her something. But then Rodney barged up and wanted to know how her car was running, so the moment was lost.

But she still wondered about the emotions she'd seen simmering in Arnie's eyes. Deep, like the man, steady and sure. A man she could easily trust with her future, and with all of her tomorrows. If only it could be so simple.

❄ ❄ ❄ ❄ ❄

Near midnight Tabitha leaned against a wall for support, holding her cup of sparkling cider. Across the room Arnie spoke to one of his good friends. She was beginning to feel pleasantly tired, and felt content to watch the sparkling ball on TV begin its descent in Times Square. She'd gone there to experience it once, on New Year's Eve. Never again. The crush of the crowds had been too much. For her, it had diminished the joy of the moment.

Right now, the people around her chanted, "Five ... four ... three ... two ... one... Happy New Year!"

People cheered and kazoos tooted. Tabitha sipped her bubbly cider. Arnie headed toward her, but Mitzy Mae flung her arms around his neck and went on tiptoe with brightly painted lips puckered up to kiss him. At the last second, He turned his head. Red lipstick slashed his cheek. He disentangled himself, but before he'd gone far, several more females mobbed him, apparently taking full advantage of the celebratory moment to snatch whatever kiss they could.

An unpleasant feeling slid through her. Jealousy. Disturbed, she turned away from the sight. Those brazen hussies!

The earnest businessman from earlier approached her. "Happy New Year." After shaking her hand, he said in a stage whisper, "Any time you get a tip, pass it along." Tabitha just smiled. People didn't understand that she wasn't privy to insider information.

From out of nowhere, Derek crowded close and pressed a moist kiss on her cheek. Revulsion pulsed through her, and she flinched. She wished she could move away, but her drink occupied one hand and in order to hop away, she'd spill it. She gave him a cold look.

Unfortunately, he did not take the hint. "Staying long in town?" he breathed in her ear. "If you like action, I know where to go. You probably need it, after staying at Arnie's." He gave a mean little chuckle. "The guy's dim when it comes to women."

Anger flashed. The jerk! "Apparently *you* are the one who isn't so bright," she retorted, and poured the remainder of her drink over his head. Cider ran down his longish hair, smeared over his glasses, and ran in rivulets down his clothes.

He gawked at her. "You...you..." he spluttered. "How *dare* you?"

"Women don't like being mauled. Learn some manners. And while you're educating yourself, look up 'respect' in the dictionary, too."

Derek glared.

Arnie appeared at her side, and she was glad, because she was shaking. He eyed the goateed man with displeasure. When Derek caught sight of his expression, he quickly slunk away.

"You okay?" he asked.

"I'm fine, but tired."

They said their goodnights to Ellen and her family. Ellen hissed in Tabitha's ear, "He's a special guy. Don't lose him."

She nodded, but wasn't sure how to keep him. She'd leave the day after tomorrow, and then what? New York City was almost four hundred miles away!

After driving her home, Arnie walked her to the door. A lone light bulb lit the porch.

"You have a lot of wonderful friends," she told him.

"Are you surprised?"

"Of course not. You're a terrific guy, Arnie."

"You think I'm terrific?" His grin edged up.

"I think you're the absolute best. One in a million. Maybe even one in a thousand million."

His eyes searched hers in the dim light. "The best?"

She nodded, and Arnie closed the distance between them. His strong arms pulled her close against him, and he kissed her with a quiet intensity. Tabitha's fingers curled into his shoulders and she melted into his kiss. Her world spun, and when he lifted his head, all she could see was Arnie. How had this one man grown to fill her entire world?

He said in a low voice, "I want to see you tomorrow."

She smiled, and blinked back sudden, foolish tears. "I want that, too. And on Tuesday I'd like to stop by your house on my way home."

But Arnie's house felt like her home now. She didn't want to stop, and then drive on.

More tears choked her throat and wordlessly, she wrapped her arms around him and held him close, her cheek nestled into the hollow of his throat. His arms around her felt secure and comforting.

Her throat ached from the effort of holding back the tears. The thought of leaving him so soon felt like a knife stabbing through her heart.

"I don't want to leave you, Arnie." A soft sob caught her breath, and then she could say no more. Tears slipped down her cheeks.

His arms tightened around her, anchoring her close to his heart; the one place where she wanted to stay forever. He kissed the top of her head and his warm breaths stirred her hair. She wished this moment would never end.

But of course, it did. Arnie gave her another long, lingering, kiss. "Good night," he said, his voice rough. "I'll be over tomorrow, probably late morning."

"Okay," she said softly. "Drive safely."

After seeing her through the front door, he headed for his truck. Tabitha realized she was watching him go like a love-struck teenager, so she went in and shut the door. As she leaned against it, his truck rumbled to life. Snow crunched, and the roar of the engine faded. She hated the sound of Arnie driving away. All too soon, she would be the one driving home.

Logically, she knew their relationship was about to end.

Tears burned her eyes, and she swung fast for her room. Tomorrow she'd see him for a little while. And again on Tuesday for a few minutes, but the reality was, it was pretty much over right now.

Never again would they spend long hours wrapped up in each other's company. Of course, when she visited her parents, she could stop by and see him—if his wall hadn't returned. Or they could say 'hi' in her parents' church. But that would be it. They could have nothing more, because their lives would be forever separated.

Tabitha burst into tears and flung herself on the old quilt that had always covered her bed. Childishly, she wished she had her old, worn brown teddy bear to sob into. But even Teddy couldn't comfort her now. She loved Arnie. Nothing would ever ease the grief of losing him.

CHAPTER THIRTY-TWO

ARNIE SHOWERED and dressed with care on Monday morning. All he could think about was seeing Tabitha. And finding the answers that his heart demanded.

He'd spent a restless night, thinking of their kisses and of Tabitha softly weeping in his arms because she didn't want to leave.

What was he expecting today? For her to declare her undying devotion to him? For her to say she'd chuck her job and take up needlepoint in Newbough?

Arnie raked gel through his hair. No. But he wanted resolution to their relationship. He wanted something to be decided between them. He wanted to discover how deep Tabitha's feelings went for him, and if he had any sort of a chance with her at all. He loved her. Was it too much to hope that she loved him, too?

If there was a chance—even the smallest one—for the two of them, he would take it. Even if that meant a long distance relationship for a while.

Was he was hoping for too much? Was he a fool to follow Ellen's advice?

Who was he kidding? He was blindly following his own heart.

Fool or not, in thirty minutes he'd learn his fate. Arnie shrugged into his jacket and locked the door behind him.

❀ ❀ ❀ ❀ ❀

"Is Arnie coming by?" Nancy asked after they'd cleared up the breakfast dishes.

"Yes. Sometime soon."

Silence elapsed as her mother put away the griddle. Daniel sat in his recliner in the living room reading the paper, so Tabitha and her mother were alone in the kitchen.

"What do you plan to do, Tabitha?"

"What do you mean?" She sat at the kitchen table, coffee mug warming her hands.

"What do you think I mean?" Her mother sent her an exasperated look. "You're leaving tomorrow. Do you two plan to keep seeing each other?"

She bit her lip and tried to ignore the ache in her heart. She'd spent the whole night soaking her pillow with tears. What good had it done? Now bags shadowed her eyes, and no amount of makeup could hide it.

"I want to, Mom. But what would be the point? We live in two completely different worlds. Why try to build a relationship that's doomed to die?"

"You'll give up so easily?"

"I don't want to, but I have to be logical."

"When is love is logical? Honey, if you love him... Do you love him?"

"Yes. Yes, I love him." Her voice broke, and Nancy hurried over to hug her tightly.

"Then you must follow your heart. We're lucky if we find love in our lives. You have to hold onto it with both hands when you find it, and don't let go."

"But what about my career, Mom? I can't give it up. I've worked so hard to get where I am. And what would I do here in Newbough?" She gestured toward the snowy window. "Loving Arnie is one thing, but being stuck here with nothing to do... No offence, Mom, but I would go crazy. And I'm afraid I'd end up resenting him for taking me away from the job I love."

"First of all, you would not blame Arnie. You make your own choices, Tabitha. And right now, sweetie, whether you see it or not, you're at a crossroads. You need to decide what's most important to you—your career, or a love that will last you a lifetime."

"It's not so simple, Mom."

"I know it's not, honey. But be *very* sure before you make any decision." She moved toward the counter. "I'll leave you alone to think. I'm going to the store. Do you need anything?"

She shook her head. She needed Arnie, and she needed her career. How could she possibly have them both?

After her mother left, Tabitha didn't want to sit and think any longer. She'd thought quite enough last night, and it hurt. Since her father was still deep in the newspaper, she pulled her laptop into the kitchen and decided to check her e-mails. She didn't really expect any, since it was a holiday, but she needed something to do.

An e-mail from her boss appeared. It had arrived on Friday afternoon, while she'd been in Buffalo. Robert had already thanked her for the information she'd sent for the Roundtable. What could this be about? She scanned the letter once, and then again, and then let out a squeal.

Tabitha, I'm thrilled that you want to transfer to the investment division. I've found an opportunity for you that twenty others in the company would kill for. Marty Davis is starting up a new mutual fund. He wants you to help him pick the companies for it, and help run it, too. Power, kid. A golden opportunity to prove yourself to the financial markets. We'll talk more on Wednesday. Robert

Tabitha leaped to her feet. "Yes!" she cried, and then quickly shot off a reply to Robert.

The opportunity to start a new mutual fund—to select the shares of the best companies in the country—was an unbelievable coup. And Marty was one of the best managers in the world, with thirty years of experience. He'd teach her a lot.

"Heard a shout in here." Her father shuffled through the doorway. He walked with a marked limp, and Tabitha remembered that the doctor had taken a vein from one of his legs. It must be hurting him.

"Daddy! Come sit down."

"I'm fine, angel." With slow steps he moved to the cupboard and retrieved a water glass. "What's the brouhaha about?"

She quickly explained about the fantastic opportunity, and finished with, "I can't believe it, Dad! Could things get any better?"

Daniel took a tiny sip and placed the glass on the counter. "Could it? You seemed pretty happy last night with Arnie. You saying this investment thing means more to you?"

Tabitha abruptly fell back to earth.

But really, what had changed? Golden opportunity or not, she was returning to New York. "What I feel for Arnie is separate from my work."

Daniel's eyes narrowed. "Didn't know you could divide your life into two pieces like that."

She said nothing for a moment. "It's not like that. I have to make the most of the hand I'm dealt."

"Life's not a game, sugar. What are you going to tell Arnie?"

Her father was right, of course. Her life *was* divided in half. Either half she chose would leave her just that...half a person.

"I don't know. I have two wonderful things going on in my life. How can I possibly choose one over the other?"

"You mean, how can you choose Arnie?" Her father's gray eyes pierced into her. "Figure out what means most to you. Then you'll make the right choice."

Tabitha bit her lip. "I'm *trying,* Dad."

"Good. Cause he's here."

A firm knock sounded at the door.

Daniel shuffled over to the table. "I'll give you two some privacy. Go on, angel." His gaze softened. "Just know that your mother and I want you to be happy."

"Thanks, Daddy." She gave him a quick hug and then grabbed up her crutches and made for the front door.

Her heart somersaulted when she saw Arnie. Under his unzipped navy coat he wore a soft, caramel flannel shirt that matched his eyes, and of course his usual jeans and boots. His hair looked freshly dried and spiked again, and she could not seem to get enough of looking at him.

"Tabitha." He smiled. "Going to let me in?"

"Of course!" Hastily, she moved backward and when he stepped inside, his large frame immediately made the room seem half its size. "Put your coat on the couch. Dad's in the kitchen, and Mom's at the store."

After disposing of his coat, the two stood awkwardly. Then she laughed. "Come sit down."

They sat together on the couch. Half of a couch cushion separated them.

Arnie cleared his throat. "My house seems pretty quiet without you."

"Is that a good or bad?" She smiled. "I know how much you value peace and quiet."

"It's lonely."

"When I go back to my apartment, it'll seem awfully lonely, too."

He nodded. His gaze rested on her, looking dark and thoughtful, as if he wanted to ask her a question. However, he remained silent.

Tabitha decided to direct their faltering conversation to lighter ground. "I just read an e-mail from my boss."

Slowly, he said, "More good news?"

"Yes. I get to start up a new mutual fund from scratch, partnered with one of the best fund managers on Wall Street."

Shock flickered across his features. "That's great."

"It's my dream. Everything I've ever wanted is happening right now." She wanted to reach over and touch his hand, but didn't. "How could I be such a lucky girl?"

"Is it what you want?"

Everything inside her screamed, *I don't know what I want! I love you, Arnie!* "It's the opportunity of a lifetime."

"So you'll go for it."

"I'll regret it if I don't at least try. But..."

Arnie rose, surprisingly fast, to his feet. "I need to go."

Her half-formed, impulsive plan to admit that she loved him died on her tongue. "Why? Where are you going? I thought we'd spend the afternoon together."

Pain flashed deep in his eyes. "I understand when I'm being given the brush off."

"No! I'm not brushing you off. This is killing me. I don't know what to do!" She grabbed her crutches and stood. "How could God put two such wonderful things in my life at the same time? You and my dream job. I don't know how to choose."

"Then I'll choose for you." He thrust his arms into his coat and headed for the door.

"Stop!"

He halted and looked back at her. Impossibly now, his brown eyes looked gentle. "I'll make it easy for you, Tabitha. Choose your job. I don't want you to give up something you love for me."

Tears filled her eyes. She swung closer. "You don't get to choose for me."

"Tabby." His hand brushed her cheek and lingered for a moment. "Be happy." He opened the door.

Tears ran down her cheeks. "We are not ending like this! I'm coming to see you tomorrow."

He gave her a long look, and then strode for his truck.

Frustrated and filled with pain, she slammed the door and fled as fast as possible for her room and burst into wretched tears.

It was over now. Forever.

How could she have fallen in love with the wrong man? She'd always believed the world had some sort of order and logic to it. That God had a good plan for her life. But what was his plan now? Her heart felt consumed by pain.

❊ ❊ ❊ ❊ ❊

With a hollow feeling in his gut, Arnie climbed into his truck and took off down the drive. Operating on autopilot, he checked for traffic and turned onto the main road.

Long minutes passed, during which time he couldn't think at all. He wouldn't let himself.

Only two miles passed before the pain boiled over, overwhelming him. He still tried not to think, or to feel, but he couldn't stop.

He was a fool. *A fool!* He took deep, heavy breaths, trying to calm himself down. How could he have thought, even for a minute, that he and Tabitha could have a future together?

The road blurred in front of him, and he blinked to clear his eyes. Agony seared through him, and his hands clenched tighter around the steering wheel.

Why had he let himself fall in love with her?

The road blurred again, and he pulled off to the side. He pressed a fist to the side of his head, trying to contain the pain, to suppress it. It didn't work.

He couldn't lose control of his emotions out here, on the side of the road.

Arnie struggled for logic, for reason—for anything to fight off the agony creeping in the corners of his mind.

Was he surprised by what Tabitha had just told him? No. She loved her job, just as Theresa had loved hers. Probably much more.

Tabitha had invested years in her career. Arnie had no place in her life. He never had, and he never would. Why had he allowed himself to hope?

Even if she did feel something for him, he would never ask her to leave New York. He loved her too much for that. He wanted her to be happy, and he would never ask her to give up her dream for him. He'd been selfish with Theresa. He wouldn't be with Tabby.

He couldn't have her. He couldn't have the one woman who had healed his heart and made him want to live again.

It had taken eleven years to piece his heart back together after Theresa. But Arnie didn't think he'd ever recover from Tabitha.

❀ ❀ ❀ ❀ ❀

Tabitha finally fell asleep on her bed, exhausted from tears and from the long, sleepless night the night before. When she awoke, it was growing dark outside. Groggily, she splashed water on her puffy eyes.

She'd lost Arnie. Now she'd be alone forever. Because she knew she'd never find another man who could hold a candle to him. And she'd never settle for second best.

But she had her brand new job.

That victory rang hollow.

Two lonely people would remain lonely. Unless, of course, Arnie tried to get out there and start dating, as she'd urged him to do. That idea brought fresh pain.

But Arnie didn't deserve to be alone. He deserved to be loved.

A tiny niggling of an idea teased her mind and Tabitha considered it. Then she smiled. Yes. Maybe she could give him one final gift before she left. Something that would keep his heart warm.

In the kitchen her mother served up pot roast. Both of her parents looked at her with worry in their eyes when she entered, but Tabitha asked for a phone number before they could ask how she was doing.

After placing the phone call, she felt a smidge better. She sat, waited for grace to be said, and began to eat.

"Honey, are you okay?"

"No, I'm not. Please, I don't want to talk about it."

Her father said gruffly, "We're here if you need us."

"I know, Daddy. Thank you."

She tried to keep up her end of the conversation during dinner, but it wasn't until afterward, when Daniel had finally gone to bed, admitting he felt exhausted, that Nancy turned her full attention on Tabitha. "You broke up with him."

"We were never dating. And he broke up with me. He told me to pursue the job."

"Did you tell him how you feel?"

"No. He took off too fast. Besides, what would be the point? Our lives won't fit together. We live and work at complete opposite ends of the spectrum!"

"Where there's a will, there's a way."

"Mom."

"Okay, Tabitha, but I still think you're going to regret this."

"I already do." Unable to help herself, she began to cry.

"Oh, sweetie." Her mother gathered her close. "Shhh. It'll all work out."

"I don't see how." She gulped on her tears. "I love him so much. I feel like I'm dying inside."

Her mother held her a long time, softly insisting that things would work out. Tabitha wished with all of her heart that she could believe her mother.

CHAPTER THIRTY-THREE

THE NEXT MORNING, Tabitha reluctantly said goodbye to her parents, and promised she'd visit again in two short weeks. Then she packed up, picked up all the components of her surprise for Arnie, and took off for his house.

Her surprise would not sit still. In fact, by the time Tabitha parked at Arnie's house, her present stood on her back legs, paws at the window.

"Come on, baby," she cooed. Lifting the soft bundle in her arms, along with the sack of food and dishes, she headed for Arnie's front porch. She felt nervous. What if she'd made a mistake? What if her impulsive gift wasn't wanted?

She set down the bag, knocked twice, and waited.

Long moments later, the door swung open. Arnie looked terrible. Stubble darkened his square jaw, his hair was mushed sideways, and blue smudges underscored his eyes.

"Are you okay?"

His gaze fell to the bundle in her arms. "What's that?"

"A gift for you." She thrust the soft white Labrador puppy into his arms. "Her name is Snowflake."

Something softened in his expression as Snowflake eagerly licked his hand and gazed up at him with adoring brown eyes. Slowly, he stroked the puppy.

"You can't live alone anymore. It's not good for you."

Quietly, he said, "You care about me, Tabitha?"

She loved him. But admitting that would only make things worse. "Of course I do. You know that. Besides," she tried to smile, "you saved me from frostbite. You have my eternal gratitude."

He nodded, and gathered the puppy closer in his arms. "Goodbye." The word sounded like a door closing.

She didn't like it. Panic clawed at her at the thought of severing their relationship now, forever. She couldn't handle it. She couldn't. "I'll be back in two weeks for Dad's birthday. I'll visit you then."

He said nothing. No encouragement lurked in his closed expression.

Tears blinded her eyes. "I'll visit whether you like it or not, you stubborn man." She rubbed Snowflake's ears. "Keep an eye on him," she whispered to the pup. "If he's grumpy, lick his face. He needs love to keep his heart warm." Then she turned and ran to her car.

❄ ❄ ❄ ❄ ❄

Arnie hugged the scrap of fur close to his heart and watched Tabitha drive away. She was right. He didn't want to be alone anymore. But he wanted Tabitha, not a puppy.

A line from one of the silly Christmas songs they'd listened to threaded through his mind. Elvis had sung, "Hear my plea...Santa bring my baby back to me!"

He shook his head, but knew the absurd song would stay. Pathetically, it spoke his heart. He longed to call Tabitha back right now.

But what did he have to offer her but his love? He wasn't naïve enough to think that would ever be enough. It hadn't been for Theresa. It wouldn't be for Tabitha.

Tears ached behind his eyes, but he didn't let them fall.

Arnie watched her car until it telescoped into a tiny dot on the horizon. Then it disappeared. Despair sliced through his soul like broken pieces of ice. He'd fallen in love again.

And yet he was still doomed to live the rest of his life alone.

CHAPTER THIRTY-FOUR

TABITHA FELT EMPTY inside when she went home every night in New York City. She enjoyed her new job. It was exciting. But she hated coming home to a dark, empty apartment. It was beautifully decorated and she loved it, but it was empty. And lonely.

She missed Arnie so much that it hurt. At odd times during the work day she'd remember his slow smile, and his warm brown eyes. And his compassion and his strength.

Other times she'd remember snippets of their conversations, or "discussions," and then bite her lip when tears blurred her eyes.

Tabitha remembered what it felt like to be held in his arms. The solid feel of him, and his steadiness. She wasn't weak, but it felt good to know that she could share her burdens with him, and that his strength doubled her own. With him she could be vulnerable, and yet secure. In his arms she felt peace, and a flame. A paradox.

She loved him. If she'd wondered if her feelings were only a product of being marooned with him for seven days, the last ten days told her otherwise. Her feelings had only grown deeper, and more rooted and sure. And painful, like an ache in her soul.

Her only comfort came from reading her Bible. At last she was returning to her relationship with God. Why did pain make her want to cling to him more tightly than ever before? She prayed more, too, and mostly for the impossible—for a future with Arnie. And for wisdom. She didn't know what to do.

Her mother called on the Wednesday before Tabitha's flight to Buffalo for her father's party. "How are you, honey?"

"Opening a new mutual fund is a lot more work than I anticipated. Definitely not just about picking companies."

"And Arnie? Have you spoken to him?"

Pain scorched through her, as it had over and over again during the last ten days. "No. He made it clear that he wants a clean break."

A pause. "Did you tell him you love him?"

"No."

Silence. "Why not?"

"What difference would it make? We can't be together."

"Do you want to be together?"

"*Yes!*" The truth burst out, unbidden. "Yes, I want to be with him!" she whispered.

"Listen to me, honey. I don't want to tell tales, but I'm concerned about Arnie, too. He came to church, but he didn't say 'boo' to anyone, and left right after. He looked miserable. I'm concerned about the both of you. Tell me the truth. Are you happy now, in New York?"

Tabitha fiddled with a pen on the countertop, unable to speak past the lump in her throat.

"Tabitha?"

"No, Mom," she said softly. "My life feels so empty. I like my job, but...it's not enough. Not anymore." She blinked back the hated tears. She was so tired of feeling sad and miserable.

"Tell Arnie you love him."

She said nothing.

"Tabitha, you still have a choice. Decide what means more to you—your job, or Arnie. I understand that your career means a great deal to you, but sometimes you can't have everything. Sometimes you have to sacrifice a little in order to keep what matters most."

"Arnie said that once. I didn't want to believe it."

"He's a smart man."

"I don't know how I could give up my career, Mom. I love it. It's so much a part of who I am."

Nancy was silent for a moment, and then she said suddenly, "What about a compromise?"

"How?"

"Could you telecommute? Didn't you do work for Robert while you were at Arnie's?"

Tabitha considered this tiny glimmer of hope...but only for a moment. "Maybe it could have worked with my old job. But even then I'd have to fly to New York a few times a month. That would be expensive. And that option is just not possible with my new job."

"Life is short, Tabitha. Think ahead twenty years. Where do you want to be? Think carefully. Then make your decision. But make sure that whatever you decide, you won't have any regrets."

Easier said than done. Tabitha lay awake that night, mulling over her mother's words. She imagined life twenty years from now through two different scenarios—one with her job, and one with Arnie.

With her job, in her wildest dreams she'd be a top mutual fund manager. Maybe with a reputation like Warren Buffet, if she wanted to reach for the stars. And she'd have garnered lots of respect and adulation from Wall Street. Not to mention money.

Was that what she truly wanted? Adulation? Money? Respect, certainly, but the first two... She had never been hung up on money. To her, the stock market was like a game she was determined to win, using facts as scalpels to separate the wheat from the chaff.

And adulation...well, she didn't want the limelight. She realized that she wanted to work on Wall Street as a mutual fund manager, and have the satisfaction of picking good stocks. She could pick stocks living anywhere in the world, since all of the information of the internet was at her fingertips, not to mention all of Brown's Brothers resources were only a downlink away.

And Arnie. If she married Arnie, she'd hopefully have a child, perhaps like the one she'd imagined him carrying on his shoulders that snowy day at the end of the blizzard. And she'd have twenty years of loving and being loved by the most wonderful man in the world.

It seemed pretty clear. She wanted Arnie. Life without him was meaningless.

Maybe her mother was right. Maybe some kind of a compromise could be made.

Tabitha had to tell him she loved him. Hopefully it wasn't too late. Would he want her enough to try to work through the compromises that would need to be made?

Did he love her? Maybe all of this angst was a tempest in a tea cup.

❉ ❉ ❉ ❉ ❉

Tabitha had been unable to get the Friday or the Monday off for her father's birthday weekend. She'd only be able to stay for Saturday and Sunday.

Her flight to Buffalo arrived on Saturday at one o'clock in the afternoon, and she barely made it home in time for her father's birthday celebration. She'd need to wait until Sunday to see Arnie, and it was hard.

The party was a small family affair, and her brothers came down for the weekend, too. To Tabitha's relief, her father looked better than the last time she'd saw him. He'd regained his normal color and he seemed happy, although he seemed quieter than normal. His leg was sore, but he didn't complain about it. Nancy didn't press Tabitha with questions about Arnie, and she was glad.

Late Sunday morning Tabitha packed up and drove eagerly for Arnie's house. Unfortunately, she couldn't stay for long. Next month she'd already secured a four day weekend and a ticket to Buffalo. Hopefully everything would go well with Arnie today, and when she came back she could spend more time with him.

She crunched onto his driveway, her heart beating hard with nerves. The house looked silent and still, but she saw his truck, so he must be there.

"Arnie!" she called out. A bark come from the direction of the barn. Eagerness and anticipation churned within her. He was in there with Snowflake.

She hurried into the barn. He stood by two sawhorses, which had a two by four laid across them. He looked larger than she remembered, and he wore a blue flannel shirt, which stretched across his broad shoulders.

Her heart beat faster. "Arnie."

When he looked at her, no surprise registered in his features. Had he heard her when she'd called out for him a moment ago? If so, why hadn't he come out?

Snowflake rushed up, happily yipping. Glad for the distraction, Tabitha swept the dog up in her arms and the puppy joyfully licked her nose. "What a sweetheart you are."

She pressed the pup to her cheek. Soon Snowflake wriggled to be free, and she set her down.

Arnie stood watching her, his tattered work gloves on, and a saw in his hand. It hadn't passed her notice that he still hadn't greeted her.

"Did you hear me drive up?" she asked, straightening.

"No."

"But you heard me call for you."

He didn't deny it.

Hurt blossomed. "Were you going to ignore me?"

"I was about to go outside."

She waited. He did not look happy to see her. She felt uncomfortable. It was true that he'd made it clear last time that he didn't want to see her again. Apparently he still felt the same way. Struggling to gather her thoughts, she said, "I got here late yesterday afternoon, but I couldn't stop by before now."

"It was for the best."

Still, he kept his distance, and pain and anger mixed within her. "You don't need to be so cold."

"I'm sorry. Why are you here?"

"I came here to talk to you."

"Let it go, Tabitha." He sounded grim. "We're done, so forget about me."

She felt sick. He truly had decided to cut her out of his life. Did he care for her so little? Anger spurted through her like hot fire.

"You want me to forget about you? Well, I can't. I won't!"

Arnie watched her for a long moment. "What do you expect from us, Tabitha?"

"To talk, like civilized people. I don't want you to write me out of your life!"

"It'll be best if we don't see each other again."

"Why?" she said fiercely. "So you can hide in your shell?"

"I've started to date again."

His words felt like a punch to her solar plexus. "What?"

"You told me I should get out and find someone, so I am. I don't want to be alone anymore."

She could not believe her ears. So fast? He'd *already* started dating? Had she meant nothing to him at all? And whom was he dating? Mitzy Mae?

"You're already dating?" She crossed her arms. This conversation was not going at all as she'd hoped.

"Yes."

"How many?"

He frowned.

"Tell me how many dates," she insisted. Maybe she was a glutton for punishment, but she had to know every last detail. And what if he was exaggerating the facts, just to push her away? It wouldn't be the first time he'd tried to erect a wall between them.

"One." He frowned even more fiercely.

She wouldn't ask if it was Mitzy Mae. "Why did you go out with her?"

His scowl blackened. "Because I want to forget about *you!*" he thundered. It was the first time he'd ever raised his voice to her.

Her throat ached. "Did it work?"

"No, Tabitha," he growled. "It didn't work. But I'll keep trying." He turned abruptly. "Just go."

She blinked harder and tried to firm the tremble from her lips. "I don't want us to end like this."

He turned back, and anguish was clear in the lines etched into his tanned face. "Then how do you want it to end?"

"I don't want it to end at all," she whispered.

"You want us to have a long distance relationship?"

"Yes. Anything!" she cried out. "I don't want to lose you."

"My life is here. Yours is in New York City. And you have a new, high powered job. I would never ask you to leave that for me. Theresa didn't want to come back here. I won't ask you to. I destroyed her life, but I won't destroy yours, too."

"That wasn't your fault, Arnie, for the last time. And I'm not Theresa. Don't confuse us. I make my own choices."

His shoulders twitched, as if impatiently dismissing her words. "I failed her, Tabitha, and that's the truth. I was a rotten husband. I cared only about myself. I won't do that again. Not to you. You deserve better, and I want you to go get it."

"There's no one better than you. Not for me."

"Go," he growled. "And don't come see me again."

"You don't mean that."

"I *do.*" With that final note in his voice, it sounded like he did.

"I *love* you, Arnie." The words choked out before she could stop them.

Hope flashed in his eyes, and then a tortured, tender look tightened his features. He closed the distance between them. "Stop it, Tabby. You'll find someone better. Someone who lives in your world."

Wordlessly, she shook her head.

"Yes." He kissed her, as if unable to help himself, and a surge of warmth and love rushed through her. She slipped her fingers to his muscular shoulders, and then around his strong neck. She loved him, helplessly, and forever. How could she live without him?

Arnie broke the kiss, His sandpapery cheek briefly brushed against hers. Closing her eyes, she leaned into the hard wall of his chest. He smelled of spicy shaving lotion. She loved the smell, and she loved him. She hugged him tightly, desperate for this moment to last forever.

All too soon, he pulled away. Pain darkened his eyes. "Go, Tabitha."

Reluctantly, she slid her hands from his shoulders. She tried to read his gaze. But she could only see that it looked steady and resolute.

Did he love her? If he did, it mustn't be enough, if he could send her away so easily.

Tears filled her eyes and she took a step backward. She wouldn't grovel, and she wouldn't beg. It hurt deeply that she needed this man to make her heart whole. And if he didn't want her... "Goodbye, Arnie."

"Goodbye, Tabby," he said huskily.

Suddenly, she couldn't leave quickly enough. She refused to break down in front of him. Tabitha hurried to her car, slammed the door, and as soon as the motor was running, she zoomed off. She couldn't look back. She wouldn't see Arnie ever again.

Her heart felt like it was shattering into a million sharp, painful pieces. She'd finally told him she loved him. It hadn't seemed to matter.

❄ ❄ ❄ ❄ ❄

Arnie watched Tabitha go, his heart pounding heavily in his chest. She loved him.

Agony tore through him.

Snowflake yipped reproachfully, and he knelt and ruffled her ears. He wanted to bury his face in her soft fur and cry. "I know, girl. I know," he whispered. "But she can't be in our life. It'll just have to be you and me, if that's all right with you."

Snowflake licked his nose. Tabitha had told Snowflake to lick his face to warm his heart. Little did she know that the ice had already melted long ago. Blistering pain tore through him again.

Chapter Thirty-Five

TABITHA COULDN'T CONCENTRATE when she returned to work. The numbers, the plans for the mutual fund—it all seemed meaningless. When Marty asked for her stock picks, she stared at him blankly, until she remembered that she'd saved a list on her computer.

Arnie didn't want her. Tabitha needed to accept this and move on. But she couldn't. She refused to cry anymore, but depression settled like a weight on her spirit. She prayed, but God seemed far away.

One day, her father called to tell her how much he enjoyed the sports magazine subscription she'd given him for his birthday.

"I'm glad you like it, Daddy." Tabitha struggled to maintain a light tone. The last thing her father needed was to worry about her. "How's your leg? Running any marathons yet?"

"Better, angel. Better. Your mother's making me take laps around the house. The woman's a drill sergeant."

Her breath caught at the military term, because it reminded her of Arnie and the tour of duty he'd done in the Army. "Great," she said brightly.

Silence came from the other end of the phone. "Tabitha. You trying to pull the wool over my eyes?"

She let out a sigh. "I'm going through a rough patch right now. Don't worry. I'll be fine."

"Is it your new job?"

"No."

"Man trouble, then. Don't you want to speak to your old dad about it?"

"Please don't worry. I just need a little time, and then everything will be okay." A little time? Eternity, perhaps. How long did it take to stop loving someone? How long would this horrible pain go on?

"Grab happiness while you can, angel. Life's too short."

She said nothing.

"Want to speak to your mother?" Daniel said gruffly.

"Maybe later." She didn't want to talk about her broken heart with her mother, either. "I love you guys. Remember, I'll be home in a couple of weeks."

Daniel muttered something unintelligible. Then, "Love you, sugar."

"I love you too, Daddy." For a moment, Tabitha wished that she was a little girl again, and her father's love could heal every childish hurt. Unfortunately, no one could help her now. No one except for Arnie. And God. She would pray again.

❀ ❀ ❀ ❀ ❀

On Monday, Daniel McCroy asked Arnie to come over and give him pointers on planting new alfalfa in the spring. Arnie wondered if the older man had an ulterior motive for the request. Before agreeing to come, he made sure Tabitha wouldn't be there. He couldn't handle seeing her. The last time had nearly destroyed him.

He entered the McCroy house at Daniel's "Come in!" holler.

Daniel sat in his recliner, his leg elevated on a stool.

"Good morning, sir."

"My girl's not happy," Daniel said with no preamble.

Pain gripped him. "She's not?"

"Nope. And I think it has something to do with you."

He shoved his thumbs into his pockets. "I wouldn't know how to fix that, sir."

"Don't you? Do you love her?"

He looked away.

Gruffly, Daniel reiterated, "Do you?"

Arnie took a harsh breath, and met the older man's eyes. "I have nothing to offer her."

"Never took you for a fool, Arnie."

His shoulders stiffened.

"I'm not trying to offend you, son. Way I see it, you're everything my daughter wants and needs."

"No, sir. She's a successful New York business woman. She'd be miserable on my farm."

"Didn't she do work for her job at your house?"

"Yes…"

"So what about a compromise? She can work here and fly into New York City a couple times a month."

Hope flared in him, but quickly died. "I don't see how that would work. Especially with her new job. I don't want her to give it up for me."

"I'm glad you care, son, but she won't have to give it up. Her boss needs her to make him look good. Remember how he got called up to be on that *Barron's* Roundtable meeting?"

He nodded.

"Well, that's prestige for those Wall Street types. Only way he got noticed was because of Tabitha's knack for the market. He knows which side his toast is buttered on. He'll give her anything she wants, just so long as she keeps giving him her picks on the Street."

Arnie felt another impossible flare of hope. He wanted to grab it with both hands and run. Could it be true? Would it work? But wouldn't it be selfish of him to ask Tabitha to leave Wall Street, just to be with him?

He loved her. Arnie had stopped trying to date after the one miserable attempt. He'd only been able to think of Tabitha the whole time, and he'd compared everything about the poor woman to her. She hadn't come anywhere close.

He desperately wanted Tabitha in his life. He loved her and needed her. And she'd said she loved him.

He cleared his throat. "You think I have a chance?"

Daniel smiled. "Ask her, son. Tabitha knows her own mind. She'll choose what matters most to her. And I wouldn't waste any time if I were you. Let's get this wrapped up before spring planting."

Arnie laughed, and it felt good. So did the bit of hope sprouting inside of him. If Tabitha loved him enough to try, maybe the long winter would finally end for him. Maybe spring could finally bud in his heart.

Daniel said, "Now, tell me all you know about alfalfa."

❈ ❈ ❈ ❈ ❈

"Who's the fox?" Tabitha's secretary hissed as Tabitha hurried back to her office after the four p.m. meeting with Marty and Robert.

"What?"

The woman fluttered her polished nails over her shoulder, ebony eyebrow arched.

But Tabitha's senses had already zoomed in on the tall man standing near her inner office door. He stood with his back to her, his shoulders impossibly broad in the well-cut dark suit. The breath caught in her throat. It couldn't possibly...

But her world tilted off its axis when he looked at her.

"*Arnie,*" Tabitha breathed. He was here!

"Tabitha," he said in his deep voice.

She greedily drank in the sight of him. And then belatedly, she ushered him into her office and shut the door. Confusion—and crazy hope—soared within her. "Why are you here?"

"I decided I need to diversify my investments." He moved closer, his steady brown eyes holding hers. "I hoped you would help me."

"Of course." She felt flustered, and wasn't sure whether to shake hands with him or kiss him. So she did nothing at all. "What...what are you looking for?" She smoothed trembling hands down her skirt.

He moved closer still. "A company with a solid foundation. One that's ready to expand and take on new ventures. I'm also interested in finding a few small companies that will grow up to be just like the first company."

Now he was right in front of her, and Tabitha stared up at him, not entirely sure that she was hearing him correctly. "Um." She cleared her throat. "Companies need a stable environment. And a healthy economy and lots of TLC. Do you know a place where these companies could grow?"

He nodded. "I know a company that will protect them. He'll take them under his wing and shelter them and provide for them. And cherish them for as long as he lives."

"Arnie," she whispered.

"I love you, Tabitha." She loved the gentle way he said her name. "I don't want to live without you anymore."

"I love you, too. My job..."

"Work from home. Tabby, please."

In these long weeks alone, without him, Tabitha had come to realize that her job didn't matter as much as it had before. Back then, it was all she wanted to eat, breathe, and sleep. Now she had something more to live for.

If she wanted to keep her job, she'd need to stay in New York until the mutual fund was up and running. After that, though, things would smooth out and she would probably be able to keep her position if she left the city. Robert wouldn't want to lose her. She felt certain of that. Somehow, someway, it would all work out. God's plan was now working everything together for the good. The impossible was becoming possible. The wonder of it all made her want to cry.

Arnie went down on one knee before her, and he wrapped his large, warm hands around hers. She stared down at him, amazed that any man—let alone Arnie, who had wanted to run her off the minute she'd first knocked on his door all those weeks ago—would humbly entreat her this way.

"Marry me," he said in a soft, low voice.

She smiled. "Yes, I'll marry you." Her voice trembled. "And I'll live with you on your farm forever."

"Our farm." He reached into his pocket and withdrew a ring. "It was my mother's. And my grandmother's, too. I hope you like it. If you don't, I'll buy you a new one." He looked up with a worried frown. It was a solitaire diamond, set in a spray of sapphires that resembled a wild flower.

"I love it," she whispered, and he slipped it on her ring finger. It fit her perfectly. Arnie kissed her knuckles and looked up at her. Never had she felt so cherished in her entire life.

"I'm glad you like it."

"Come up here," she said, tugging him to his feet. She kissed him with her whole heart, and with all of her love. He drew her close and kissed her until she felt breathless, and the world spun.

When they at last drew apart, joy made her heart feel light. Finally, she'd found the one thing she'd been looking for during all of these years on Wall Street. Who knew she'd find it in rural New York? The best investment ever...love.

Since it was priceless, it would yield incalculable dividends forever.

She twinkled up at him. "Everything's settled now, but I have a few small requests to make."

Laugh lines crinkled from his eyes. "Tell me. You know I'll do anything for you."

"And I will for you, too," she agreed. "But let's get one thing straight right now. Much as I love you, I don't want a son named Arnold Reginald Arnold IV."

He grinned. "I won't argue about that."

"And," she went on with a teasing smile, "I want us to buy a new hot water heater. I don't like cold showers."

"Done." His expression turned gentler, more serious. "I don't want you to be cold, either. After all, you melted the ice around my heart."

She smiled softly. "And you thawed the frostbite from my feet."

He laughed. "I think between us, we have enough fire to keep us warm forever."

"I know we do." Heart filled with love, Tabitha went up on her toes and kissed him again. And she offered a prayer of thanks to God for allowing her crash into Arnie's snow bank so many cold days ago. She would be forever grateful.

The End

Author's Note

I HOPE you enjoyed *Snowstorm*. I wrote it a number of years ago—about the same time I wrote *The Commander's Desire* and *Her Reluctant Bodyguard*. This story needed some extra love and attention, because I wanted so much for Tabitha and Arnie's love story to shine. The lessons Tabitha learned about working too hard, and choosing to focus on the things that matter the most in life are lessons I continue to learn. I hope one day I will get it right, too.

One final note. As a small press author, getting my books before readers is a real challenge. You can help! If you liked this book, please consider writing a short review on Amazon, B & N, or the retailer's website where you purchased the book. Each review encourages Amazon and other online retailers to promote the book to more readers. Each and every review counts, and means so much!

I love to hear from my readers. Please drop me a note at jennettegreen@jennettegreen.com.

Best wishes always,
Jennette